The HOLLOWAY GIRLS

SUSAN BISHOP CRISPELL

sourcebooks
fire

FIREreads
#getbooklit

Your hub for the hottest young adult books!

Visit us online and sign up for our
newsletter at FIREreads.com

 @sourcebooksfire

sourcebooksfire

firereads.tumblr.com

Published by Sourcebooks Fire, an imprint of Sourcebooks
P.O. Box 4410, Naperville, Illinois 60567-4410
(630) 961-3900
sourcebooks.com

Cataloging-in-Publication Data is on file with the Library of Congress.

Printed and bound in Canada.
MBP 10 9 8 7 6 5 4 3 2 1

*For my sister, Karen—I'm so lucky
to live life in "stereo" with you.*

The Book of Luck

As a Holloway girl, this book is your legacy. It holds your histories, your love stories, and your magic. By adding your name to its pages, you agree to follow the rules, binding all the names herein—both Holloway girls and those you choose to kiss—to the luck of the kissing season.

Your kissing season will begin with the summer solstice that follows your sixteenth birthday. For that year, everyone you kiss will be granted a stroke of good luck when it is most beneficial to them. It may manifest within a day, a week, or many years later. That is for the magic to decide. As long as their name is recorded in the book, the luck will find them.

In return for gifting good luck to others, your life will be charmed with true love and your own sprinkling of good luck for the rest of your days.

Rules for giving luck

- Your magic will affect the hearts of those around you who already feel affection for you.
- Both you and the person you kiss must do so willingly.
- Never kiss someone who's already in love with another.

part one

A QUICK TANGLE
OF LIPS AND
BREATHS

1

NOTHING HOLDS MORE POTENTIAL than a blank page. Especially a page from the Book of Luck. The leather-bound notebook is a family heirloom. It chronicles the name of every Holloway girl and a short account of the luck their magic has bestowed on the people they've kissed.

After being raised on stories of other Holloway girls, it's finally my turn to start writing my own. It's a rite of passage. But also, it's something I've looked forward to my whole life. And with a few quick strokes, I sign my name across the top of the paper, binding myself to the magic of the kissing season.

Remy Reed Holloway

My great-great-great-times-infinity grandmother was the first Holloway girl to experience the season. With just one little kiss, she gave some love-struck boy a gift of good luck. And just like that, all the women in my family were imbued with magic.

We became love goddesses.

Good-luck charms.

Before the ink's even dry, I can feel the magic claiming me for the coming year. It's a lightness in my chest, a buzzing in my blood. A promise that the charmed future I've always dreamed of—one with true love and a faint luster of luck clinging to my skin like glitter—is just one kiss away.

My season doesn't officially start for five and a half more hours. But there's no way I'd be able to sleep, despite it being almost midnight, if I didn't do this first. I do my best attempt at a happy dance with my sister, Maggie, squeezed onto my twin bed, hugging me from behind. It's basically off-kilter bouncing accompanied by jazz hands. But it serves its purpose.

"You're going to have so many boys lining up to kiss you that you won't be able to get their names on the page fast enough." She squeezes me tight, as if she doesn't mind that her season ends tomorrow when mine begins.

Which, to be fair, she probably doesn't. My sister's kissed more boys in the past year than I'll probably kiss in my lifetime.

Maggie subscribes to the kiss-any-boy-who-strikes-her-fancy philosophy. It's what all the boys hope for during the kissing season—equal opportunity and all that—but also

Maggie just really enjoys kissing. I, on the other hand, lean toward a different school of thought. When I kiss someone this year, I want to know it means something. For both of us.

"Let's not go wild, Mags." I nudge an elbow into her ribs, eliciting a laugh. "I'd be happy with just one who wants to be with me more than he wants the luck."

Holloway girls have zero control over who falls for us during the season. But if I could choose, that someone would be Isaac Fuller. I can't even think his name without a smile curving onto my lips. It's like a flashing neon sign that says *kiss me* every damn time I see him. If things go my way, I might get him to do just that.

Isaac and I aren't friends, exactly, but we're friendly thanks to a few mutual classes and a few more mutual friends. Our lockers are practically next to each other—just three people between us—and somehow last year we'd gotten into this ritual of Isaac knocking on my locker door as he passed every morning before first period and saying, *There she is,* and me replying *Here I am,* and him saying, *Now my day can begin.* He had a girlfriend then, so he didn't mean anything by it. But that hadn't stopped my heart from tripping all over itself every day. When he broke up with Hannah at the end of the school year, I'd finally let myself hope that maybe our morning ritual had started to mean something more to him too.

Reaching for the book, Maggie flips the cover closed. Then

she falls back onto the mattress, taking me down with her. She presses our foreheads together, her eyelashes whispering against mine, as if the contact will give her direct access to my thoughts. This close, the light smattering of freckles high on her cheeks makes an appearance, as opposed to mine, which are dark and abundant and cover both cheeks down to the curve of my jaw and up the bridge of my nose.

Tucking a hand under her jaw to protect my pillowcase from her raspberry-colored lip stain, aptly named *Girl About Town*, she says, "I get that the season makes it hard to know which feelings are real and which are fueled by a desire for the luck. Just remember that kissing people you have true feelings for trumps all."

It's a version of something Mom has said to us our whole lives. Like a Holloway motto. If we had a family crest it would be the cheesiest one around: *True love trumps all.*

I want to tell Maggie about Isaac. How I want to kiss him and no one else. But I know my sister—almost better than I know myself—and I'm not in the mood for a lecture about the rules and how I can't kiss Isaac if he's still in love with Hannah. So I just say, "That's the plan," and smile like I haven't already narrowed my choices down to one.

Nana always said kissing someone who's already given away their heart was one of the worst sins against the season, right up there with refusing to kiss anyone at all. But there's nothing in the Book of Luck about what happens if a Holloway girl breaks the rules. I can only remember hearing one or two stories about girls in my family who never found love. And even then, those were just whispers.

I push the worry away, refusing to let it spoil this milestone moment. As long as Isaac's pulled under the season's spell tomorrow, that means his feelings for me are real. And there's nothing to stop me from kissing him the first chance I get.

There's a piece of paper taped to my bedroom window when we wake, both still in my bed. Maggie—ever vigilant where I'm concerned—spots it before me and falls out of bed, her foot tangling in the sheets in her haste to see what it says. Pressing the back of one hand to my mouth to stifle my laughter, I extend the other to help her off the floor. She glares at me, but our fingers twine together as we examine the message facing us through the glass. The paper's been torn from a spiral notebook, the edges ripped and uneven. The words, written in a messy scrawl that slants down to the right despite the paper's faint blue lines, read: *Making you smile is the best part of my day.*

It's not exactly a love letter, but it's as close to one as I've ever gotten. Usually, Maggie's the one garnering all the attention—even before her kissing season started. Knowing that someone's choosing me over my sister for once is a serious hit of serotonin. I run my fingers over the glass, tracing the outline of the words one at a time.

"Who's it from?" Maggie leans closer, trying to locate a signature. "And how did he get it up here without us hearing him?"

"I don't know." But I do. I've seen hundreds of these types of love notes on Hannah's locker over the years. They were Isaac's way of letting her—and everyone who walked by— know that she had his heart. Maybe this is his way of saying that I do now.

"It's really sweet. And also accurate. Whoever he is, he should definitely be on your list."

"Why does there have to be a list? What if I like *him*?" I don't mean to ask it, but my heart refuses to comply.

She lifts our joined hands and taps on my chest like she can knock some sense into my heart. "It's called the kissing season for a reason, Rem. If we were supposed to kiss just one person, it wouldn't last all year. Or the magic would only work on one person."

"Yeah, but there's no rule that says we *have* to kiss more than one. Just that we can if we want to." Sliding the window open, I reach up to dislodge the tape. The paper flaps in the wind when I free it, almost ripping from my hold like it wants to blow away and spread its message all over town. I slip the note into the top drawer of my nightstand so Maggie doesn't sense how much it means to me.

"Oh, you'll want to," she insists. "Just give the season time to work its magic, and you'll see."

2

THERE'S A PARTY AT Firelight Falls tonight to usher in the start of summer—and a second kissing season.

People say they can tell the season is coming because the air smells sweeter, like it's been sprinkled with sugar. Or, on days when the humidity is so thick you can barely breathe, they claim it's like the air's been dipped in honey. Really, that's just their way of romanticizing the whole thing. The summer solstice is what triggers the magic in a Holloway girl's blood.

The magic's been building inside me all day. When it reaches full strength tonight, it's with a gust of hot air pushing in through the open car windows that tickles my skin and leaves the town smelling faintly of vanilla buttercream. But that could just be the dozens of whoopie pies in two of Mom's Wild Flour Bake Stop tote bags on the back seat. There's something about these small cake-and-frosting sandwiches specifically that all the boys in town love. Maybe it's just the name, which they usually say in low, suggestive tones, or maybe it's because they're easily portable and so fan-freakin'-tastic that you want a second one before the flavor of the first one has even left your mouth.

Either way, our mom's s'mores-flavored whoopie pie—fluffy marshmallow filling and a dollop of chocolate ganache layered between round puffs of graham cracker cake—is a staple at gatherings up at the falls. No matter how many we bring, we always run out.

The parking lot at the trail's entrance is overflowing with cars. They spill onto the street, blocking half of a lane and begging to have the cops called to raid the woods for underage drinking. Maggie parks at the Lookout Bed & Breakfast next to the trailhead. Mrs. Chastain has signs posted warning against doing exactly that, but since all her afternoon tea sweets are baked by my mom and me, she won't have us towed.

Maggie and I heft the tote bags from the car and follow the path from the lot as it gradually descends into the trees. The dense thicket of branches above us blocks most of the early-evening sun so only a little light filters down through the leaves. It also stifles the breeze. My dress clings to the sweat beading on my ribs and stomach. I pluck at the thin fabric so it won't be marred by dark, wet patches when we reach the falls—and Isaac. I want everything to be perfect if our first kiss happens tonight.

The whole way down the trail, Maggie keeps tossing smiles over her shoulder at me. Her eyes catch on mine for the briefest second, the glint of excitement setting the air between us on fire. And because I know my sister as well as she knows me, I'm certain she plans on kissing one last person tonight before the season's magic leaves her for good.

The past few weeks, she's been on her phone nonstop. Though she's barely contributed more than a passing comment or two in the group chat we have going with our best friend, Laurel. At first I thought her mystery crush was Theo, the hot barista from Pour House who's been writing flirty messages on Maggie's cup every time we go in. But she has no reason to hide that from me, and she's definitely been cagey about whoever's messages make her bite her lip to keep from smiling too hard. But since I haven't told Maggie about Isaac, I can't exactly be mad at her for keeping this from me.

So, I just smile back at my sister, hoping we both get the kisses we want tonight.

The woods give way to an expanse of sand and rocks and moss-covered logs bordering the pool at the bottom of the waterfall. I scan the faces, taking stock of who's here and who's not. I find Isaac without trying. Like I've been living in a real-life version of *Where's Waldo?* for the past few months and

I've trained my eyes to skip over everything that doesn't fit what I'm looking for.

He's knee-deep in the water, one hand shielding his eyes from the sun as he watches one of his friends leap from the top of the waterfall. His dirty-blond hair is slicked back with water, and his eyes, so murky green they're almost hazel, squint just a bit, causing a dimple in his left cheek. He splays his fingers to indicate a score of seven to the jumper. The two guys on his right, his best friends Ethan Wells and Seth Anders, give a seven and a nine respectively. They're all on the diving team at school, but Isaac almost always wins these impromptu competitions, so he's made himself a permanent judge so others can win too.

Isaac notices me a few seconds after Felix Vega splashes out of the shallows, already heading toward me. Last summer, I made out with Felix at Paige's midsummer party. That was before he'd realized kissing me wouldn't bring him even an inkling of luck since it wasn't my kissing season yet, but he'd just laughed when I broke it to him, then he'd kissed me again. He was a pretty good kisser. If I didn't already have my heart set on Isaac, I might have given him another shot.

Maggie slides the tote from my shoulder and whispers, "It doesn't have to happen tonight."

The magic in my blood surges in disagreement, and I turn to tell her I have no reason to wait, but she's already moving toward the cluster of people circling the firepit, whoopie pies lifted in offering. Paige and Audrey, who fill out the rest of our close friend group, wave to us from the far side of the fire, where they've already laid claim to a prime spot. They didn't save space for us to join them. Probably Hannah's doing. Since Hannah's dad married Paige's mom last year, Paige has been slowly going over to the dark side. Laurel immediately gives up her seat on one of the logs behind them to join my sister. Her smile rivals those of the guys' vying for Maggie's attention.

But before I can work through what that might mean, Isaac shouts, "There she is."

It's only been a few weeks since school let out, but hearing his greeting is like a favorite song randomly playing on the radio. "Here I am," I say.

All he has to do now is come and get me.

"Y'all are still doing that?" Felix asks, shaking his head to fling off excess water. He smiles at me, only a glimmer of disappointment lingering in his eyes.

I duck my head to keep my smile from giving away everything I feel for Isaac. "It's kind of our thing." My voice doesn't get the memo and comes out all moony and velvet soft.

Catching up, Isaac cuts between us and slings an arm over my shoulder. "Now my *night* can begin." His lips graze my ear just long enough to send a shiver racing across my skin.

We're basically the same height, so I know he had to tilt his head down just a fraction to make contact with my ear. The thought sends a wave of tingles coursing through my body. I can't look at him for a sign that he did it on purpose without positioning my mouth directly in kissing range. But judging from the huskiness of his voice, I'm guessing he did.

I step back, adding an inch of space between us to suppress the temptation to press my lips to his, and his arm falls away. He lifts the tote bag from my shoulder and hoists it above his head in victory, as if he'd been after the whoopie pies all along.

"Hey, now." I grab for the bag, but he dances it out of my reach.

Isaac gives me this shy, unguarded smile that's so much more intimate than every other smile I've seen on him it nearly stops my heart. "What? Were you hoping I was over here for something else?"

"Don't you know it's bad luck to mess with a Holloway girl's heart during the kissing season?" I tease and hold his gaze a few seconds longer, returning his smile and silently praying it has a similar effect on him as his does on me.

"Wait, is that true?"

The whole point of the Holloway magic is to send good luck out into the world. Make it a better place one kiss at a time. Follow the rules, good luck manifests. Don't follow the rules, there's no luck at all. Everyone in town has a basic understanding of the rules of the kissing season. But with Maggie's season just ending, anyone looking to get their share of the Holloway luck has already gotten the deep-dive explanation from her on how the magic works, even those she didn't kiss. So Isaac, like everyone else at the falls tonight, should know you can't take a kiss by force or kiss a Holloway girl if you're in love already.

Resting my hand on Isaac's forearm, I slide my fingers around his wrist where his pulse beats strong and fast and whisper, "Not even a little bit." I laugh when he curls his arm around me again, pulling me close.

I have all of two seconds to enjoy being tucked into his side before he tenses against me.

"Shit," he says. Then, "Hannah."

Stomach muscles tightening, I wait for the blow-off now that she's almost within reach.

And I wait.

And I wait.

And I realize he's not letting me go. He's not choosing her.

That alone keeps me from stepping aside when Hannah stops a few feet away, her glare incinerating the air between us.

"Your timing's a little convenient, Isaac, don't you think?" she says.

"Convenient, how?"

Arms crossed, her squared-off nails dig half-moons into her skin. "Just that you broke up with me right in time to fall

all over yourself for Remy's attention when one kiss from her will magically change your life."

"That's not what this is," Isaac says, turning to me, his breath warm on my cheek.

My heart urges me to believe him, but my traitorous brain warns that Hannah has a point. Can he really be over her this soon? They'd been together since eighth grade. On and off, anyway. Hannah was always the one to instigate the "off" times when someone else showed even the slightest bit of interest in her. Isaac always took her back. As if those days/weeks/months apart had shown her that she'd really loved him all along.

I look for Maggie to siphon some of her confidence. She's all cozy by the fire, sharing a towel-turned-blanket with Laurel as a handful of guys make one last play for her luck-filled kiss.

Shrugging out from under Isaac's hold, I say, "When I kiss someone, it'll be because I want to, not because he's looking to get lucky."

"Then I guess I'll just have to try harder to convince you that you want to kiss me." He says it like Hannah's not standing here. Like all our friends aren't hanging on our every word.

The grin Isaac turns on me says he knows he doesn't have to try very hard. But if he's telling the truth and wants more than just the Holloway luck, he'll have to prove it.

3

COME NIGHTFALL, ISAAC FINALLY makes his move. Or rather, he has Felix do it for him.

"Isaac's waiting for you." Felix points to a dark spot at the mouth of the trail that leads up to the falls. Slinging an arm around my shoulders, he dips his face closer to mine. To anyone watching, it'll seem like he and I are sneaking off together, Isaac all but forgotten. "He knows Hannah won't go up to the falls because she's scared of heights, so..."

So...this is probably my only chance to be alone with Isaac tonight.

To find out if everything he's said to me is true.

"I guess I shouldn't keep him waiting."

Most of our friends are settled onto the pebbly shore with blankets and towels and hammocks strung between tree trunks. Once the sun went down, they'd chosen the safety of nursing beers around the firepit over the possibility of mis-stepping right off the skinny path that snakes up the edge of the cliff. It wouldn't have been my first choice either. But for a little time alone with Isaac, it's worth it.

If Maggie was still here, she would try to talk me out of it, but she went to grab some bottled water half an hour ago and hasn't come back, so I have no reason not to say yes. If she's off following her heart, I should get to do the same. Maggie will just have to forgive me for being a tiny bit reckless.

More than a dozen pairs of eyes follow Felix and me as we make our way to the tree line through the shadows, the low beam from his flashlight guiding the way. There's no question where we're headed. Or what we'll do once we get up there. The sound of the falls whisks away their whispers, along with most of my guilt for using Felix this way. He's a good friend— both to Isaac and to me—for going along with this when he's hoping for a Holloway kiss of his own.

With my phone in Maggie's bag, I have no way of calling her to let her know what I'm up to. "If you see my sister," I say to Felix, "tell her I'm with Isaac so she doesn't need to worry."

"Are you sure you wouldn't rather go up there with me instead?" He says it with a laugh, but the way he looks at me, all puppy-dog eyes and hopeful smile, means he's serious.

Isaac snakes a hand out of the trees and tugs me a step closer, saving me from having to let Felix down. "Thanks for getting Remy over here for me. One scene from Hannah was enough for tonight."

"Yeah. Sure. Don't do anything I wouldn't do up there." Felix forces another laugh, then winds his way through the trees so no one sees him coming back out without me.

"Hey," Isaac says when we're alone.

There's so much packed into that one syllable. *Finally*, it says. *Now there's nothing keeping us apart.*

"Hey." My between-the-lines-message back: *I want this too. No more waiting.*

He holds out his hand, palm up, and I lace my fingers with his. The intermittent cloud cover only allows a trickle of moonlight through, and once we're a few steps into the trees, even that's obscured. The flashlight Felix loaned me flickers as if it's scared of the dark. I squeeze his hand, a silent plea not to let go until we're back in the light. The sweet scent of roasting marshmallows and coconut-lime suntan lotion from the campsite gives way to a wet, earthy smell. Next to baked goods, this one is my second-favorite scent. I want to capture it in a bottle so I can carry it around with me for the rest of the summer.

We pick our way over decaying logs and rocks slick with mist from the falls. My foot slips on a patch of leaves, and I fling my arm out to catch hold of a tree limb and regain my footing. The flashlight flies from my hand, the light swallowed up by the woods.

"Whoa. You okay?" Isaac releases my other hand and slides his arm around my waist to steady me, though his touch causes the opposite reaction.

Flecks of bark chip off underneath my fingernails and cling to my clammy skin. I wipe my fingers clean on my thigh. "Yeah. I'm good."

He pulls me closer, then pivots, scanning the ground for a wayward beam of light. It's too dark to distinguish anything that might be lurking down there, so after a couple minutes of searching for the flashlight, we give up and return to the trail empty-handed.

"Do you want to go back?" he asks.

Going back means staring/whispering/going our separate ways. It means denying us both what we want. "Definitely not," I say.

My desire to kiss him is strong enough to silence Hannah's voice in my head that says he's not over her and he's just doing this to make her jealous. His gaze drops to my mouth, and I know he's just as ready for us to kiss as I am.

It takes a little more effort, however, to dispel the worry about the consequences of kissing him if he's still in love with Hannah. What if it strips me of my Holloway magic the second our lips touch? That's the worst-case scenario I can think of anyway. Although in reality, if there is a consequence for breaking that particular rule, it probably wouldn't be as drastic as losing our magic. The Book of Luck would've made that warning loud and clear. I mentally crumple the thought and toss it into a dark corner in my mind, trusting the magic to keep me safe.

"I don't want to go back either." Isaac keeps hold of me all the way to the start of the cliff where the path narrows so we have to walk single file. I go slowly at first, checking every step before I take it because though I have the season's magic coursing through my veins now, I'm not sure the luck will extend to doing something my sister would deem reckless. He stretches his hand back to guide me through a particularly slippery part. My heart doesn't settle back into a normal rhythm until we reach the massive slabs of rock bordering the creek at the top.

"Finally, a little privacy," he says.

"We could've *started* this whole thing somewhere where it was just the two of us. You know, on a thing called 'a date.'"

"That probably would've been the smarter call. But I don't really know how this whole kissing season thing works and didn't want to assume you'd want to kiss me just because I want to kiss you. I know a bunch of the guys are into you, too, so it's not like I'm the only one in the running."

"You would know if I didn't want to kiss you." Not that it would stop him from hoping.

"Then I guess there's nothing stopping us, huh?"

For a second, I think he's going to kiss me right now. No

wooing, no fanfare. Just lips finding lips, and it'll all be over within seconds. I resist the urge to pull away, refusing to believe it's only about the luck for Isaac. That he wants me—and this kiss—as much as I want him. My faith in him pays off a moment later, when he dips his head and smiles, almost as if he's embarrassed he said those last words out loud.

Walking a few steps back from the edge of the cliff where the rocks give way to rushing water, he peels off his shirt and spreads it on the ground, offering a semi-clean place for me to sit before dropping down on the damp rocks himself. I kneel beside him and tuck my legs to the side, straightening my dress over my knees.

"It's so strange how you can't hear anyone down there over the sound of the falls. It really is like there's no one around but us," I say. The look he flashes me sends a rush of warmth tingling through my body. If he can do that without even touching me, will I combust when we finally kiss?

I tilt my head back, soaking in the perfection of this moment. The few seconds before I kiss the first boy of my kissing season and guarantee a lucky future for us both.

My whole life has been leading to this moment. Every neuron in my body vibrates faster and faster until I'm all fire and anticipation. I don't ever want this feeling to end. At the same time, if I don't kiss Isaac soon, I will have to hurl myself over the falls to cool off before I lose my mind.

This high up, the trees on the next peak over and the sky bleed together into a sea of ink, the shimmering dots of starlight the only distinction between the two. The crash and rush of the water spilling over the edge mimics the furious pounding of my heart.

"Do you feel it?" My voice drops to a whisper, so he has to press in closer to hear me.

"What?"

"The magic in the air. Like tiny sparks igniting against your skin."

Isaac's gaze skims down my neck and bare shoulders, then back up to my lips, and I have to keep myself from leaning forward and kissing him right then. "So what you're saying is that once I kiss you, there's no point in kissing anyone else because it won't be as...hot?"

I laugh. "Something like that."

His teasing smile vanishes. Sitting up, he hooks his elbows around his bent knees and stares over the edge of the falls, suddenly looking conflicted. "Remy, listen—" He stumbles over my name. Then he clears his throat and tries again.

But nothing good ever follows the word *listen*. And the fact that Isaac's gone from flirty to let-her-down-gently mode in the span of a breath makes absolutely no sense. Unless he's second-guessing what he wants.

Is the magic scaring him off? Or is it Hannah?

The thought sends my nerves into overdrive. I wish I could scoop them right out of my stomach and scatter them like the gritty pebbles coating the rocks. "It won't really ruin kissing anyone else. I promise," I assure him, heart still furiously pounding.

"I know. The guys who kissed Maggie this year would've said something if the magic permanently messed them up."

"I guess there's no 'don't kiss and tell policy' then, huh?"

"Not when there's Holloway luck involved."

"So why does it suddenly seem like you don't want to kiss me and get your share of that luck?" I ask. There's no point in delaying the obvious. Even if I really don't want to hear his answer.

He drops his head and braces it with one hand, his fingers curling into his hair. "I do. You're a really cool girl, Remy."

"But you're not over Hannah, are you?"

"Hannah is a master at manipulating people. I just let her get into my head for a minute, that's all." Isaac looks at me, the moonlight casting shadows across his face. "I'm good now. And I definitely want to kiss you." But there's a wobble of hesitation in his voice.

Here I am practically throwing myself at him, and he's thinking about the girl who regularly used his heart for target practice? Hannah's an ace shot; she hit her mark every time. She probably didn't even need the bull's-eye he'd drawn on his chest by always taking her back. But still Isaac's up here with me. On the verge of kissing me. So whatever he feels for Hannah can't really be love, right?

My heart plays out a steady beat of *pleasepleaseplease* when the doubt starts to creep in. Like my brain, it's not ready to concede defeat and miss out on the chance to kiss him. We've spent months in this dance, learning each other's rhythm and testing how close we can get without touching. Sitting here now with everything I've been wanting just a breath away, my lingering suspicions don't stand a chance, and I let his assurances that I'm the one he wants take their place.

It's just a kiss. A quick tangle of lips and of breaths. But hopefully it will turn into something more. Something worthy of a love song.

"I want to kiss you too," I say. *So. Damn. Much.* Somehow I manage to keep those last words from spilling out.

His grin is the last thing I see as my eyes close before his mouth's on mine, not tentative like most first kisses but hot and demanding and perfect. I press a hand to his bare chest, just over his heart, and sink into him, his hands framing my face, fingers buried deep in my hair. Giving myself over to the heat building between us, I am consumed by it.

Nothing else exists in this moment but the two of us.

When we finally break apart, it takes a good fifteen seconds for me to resolidify and an eternity after that to move.

When I do, Isaac says, "Maybe there's something to this magic after all."

"I wasn't lying when I said I could feel it in me. I just didn't know it could be that...intense."

"I feel sorry for every guy who doesn't get to feel this with you." He flicks his eyes toward where our friends still hang out too far below to have a clue what's going on up here. "Do you already know who else you're going to kiss?"

Who else? How could he think there would be anybody else after that kiss? "It's not like I have a list or anything."

"Yeah, I guess you want to keep your options open."

"It won't bother you if I kiss someone else?" I ask, giving him the chance to backtrack.

"Why would it? I mean, that's the whole point, right? It would be weird if you only kissed me. Plus a few of the guys might seriously riot if they thought they didn't have a shot at the Holloway luck."

His words detonate a bomb in my chest, turning my ribs into projectiles, the shards of bone piercing my insides in a thousand different places as I suck in a breath against the stabs of pain, but the air just bleeds right out of me.

"You're such an ass, Isaac."

"Because I'm okay with you kissing other guys?"

"Because I thought you liked me." My eyes burn with tears, but I blink them back. They'll be one more thing I'll have to regret about tonight if I lose it in front of him. "I thought this was more than just a kiss. More than you just wanting me for good luck."

At that, at least, Isaac has the decency to wince. "What do you want me to say? I do like you, Remy. And I wasn't lying when I said I wanted to kiss you. But after everything with Hannah, I'm not ready for something serious. One kiss isn't going to change that, even if it was literally magical."

"God, I should've known that after years of Hannah tearing your heart to shreds there'd be barely anything left."

"And yet you still want a piece of it," he says. It's not an accusation, just a statement of fact meted out in the same tone he would have told Seth about how he'd under-rotated on a dive and hit the water at an angle instead of going in vertically.

No, not a piece. If he offered me the whole thing right now, I'd take it. At least then we'd be even.

"That note you left on my window, why did you tell me that if all you wanted was a kiss? Why all that posturing earlier in front of Hannah when she was right?"

"You're making me out to be some kind of bad guy here. You're a Holloway girl. Kissing people is what you do. I waited until your kissing season started so I could kiss you, but Maggie might have been the better choice. She wouldn't have tried to turn this into anything more than a kiss."

My kissing season was supposed to be the one time in my

life I could shine all on my own. When Maggie's easy popularity didn't make me feel less than for being the quieter sister. Isaac may have waited to kiss me over Maggie, but a kiss was all he was after. Not me. Not my heart.

"You don't have to worry about that with me either," I say. "You got your kiss. Point made. Though feel free to go fall off a cliff for not being the guy I thought you were."

"Hell hath no fury," Isaac says. Then he turns and runs toward the edge of the falls, planning to dive off like he's done so many times before. But he jumps a second too late to execute the dive properly. Instead of arcing up and out, his body carries too far forward, and he simply falls.

I run to the edge, trying to separate the rushing water from a splash of his body plunging into the pool. But there's no splash—or not one big enough to draw attention over the roar of the falls—just a quiet smack and a crunch that nobody hears as Isaac lands half in and half out of the water, catching on the slick rocks below.

4

I'M THE ONLY ONE who sees Isaac fall. The only one who knows he's out there in the water, hurt and possibly dying. Seth and Ethan dive straight into the water to get to him when I stumble down the path screaming at them—at anyone—to help him. Someone else calls 911. Then everyone hurls questions at me that I don't have answers to or ones I refuse to share.

What happened up there?

Aren't Holloway girls supposed to be lucky?

How could Isaac of all people screw up a dive like that?

Is he going to be okay?

They carry Isaac from the water what seems like hours later, though it's only been minutes. Seth's arms are hooked around Isaac's chest, and Ethan has his legs. Isaac's breaths rattle out of him in quick, insufficient bursts as they lay him on the rocky shore. All I can think is *at least he's breathing*, even if it sounds all wrong.

Breathing means he's alive.

Kneeling in the mud next to him, Hannah strokes his hair and murmurs "You're okay, you're okay," as if she can will it to be true if she says it enough times. Isaac tilts his cheek into her palm, and the pain contorting his face softens a fraction. I'm so effing stupid for hoping he wasn't still in love with her. He might genuinely like me like he said, but it's nothing compared to what he obviously still feels for Hannah.

Nana's warning rings loud in my ears—the only thing worse than not kissing anyone at all during the season is kissing someone who's already given their heart away. Then the guilt replaces it.

Is his accident a consequence of breaking the season's rules? Is the Holloway magic punishing him for my mistake?

With no mention of what happens if a Holloway girl breaks the rules in the Book of Luck, I have no idea how to help Isaac. No way of making sure he'll be okay. The most I can do now is hope the magic will loosen its grip on him if I leave, taking the effects of the Holloway magic with me.

Zombie-walking around the camp area, I search faces in the glow of the firelight, looking for Maggie. With almost everyone crowded on the muddy bank, one thing's apparent. My sister is nowhere to be found. Leaving me to figure this out on my own.

Paige catches me by the arm and steers me toward the trail that leads up to the parking lot. "Let's go wait for the ambulance, okay?" Her copper-colored hair is falling out of a messy bun, and her eye makeup is a smudgy shadow as if she's been wiping her eyes dry though there's no trace of tears now. We've been friends since first grade, and though we've drifted apart in the last few months as she fell in with Hannah's clique, we're still close enough that I know that means she's scared and trying to hide it.

Audrey, on the other hand, lets her fear out in a flood of nonstop chatter as she follows, rubbing my back whenever I slow. I don't hear a word she says. Instead, I second-guess myself every other step. Maybe giving Isaac space is the wrong thing to do. Maybe the Holloway magic is the only thing that will save him. Maggie would know. My sister always knows how to fix things. But she's not here to talk through how the magic works or what it might be doing to him. I have no clue where she is, but I'm the one who feels lost. So I keep walking, hoping my first instinct is the right choice.

If tonight has proved anything, it's that my judgment cannot be trusted. And Isaac is the one paying the price.

Even after the twenty-minute hike back up, we still beat the ambulance there. When they finally arrive, the paramedics head down on foot, a stretcher suspended between two of them.

I'm not religious. I don't pray. But as the minutes tick by while we wait for them to bring Isaac up, I try. Even then, it's not so much a prayer as a plea to the universe: *Don't let him die. Please, don't let him die.*

Maggie comes home sometime close to midnight. She bursts into my room, breathless, like she's run the whole way down the mountain. Her damp hair clings to her neck and shoulders. She pries it away like it's choking her.

"Isaac's in the hospital." Her voice breaks, and she has to swallow before continuing. "They said he fell off the falls. He has a collapsed lung and a few fractured ribs. They said he's lucky to be alive."

The blackness in my chest spreads wider, tentacle-like fingers overtaking nerves and muscle to quell the feelings that try to spark back to life at her words. I don't tell her what Isaac and I were doing at the top of the falls.

Not about our kiss.

Not about how he was maybe/sort of/probably still in love with Hannah.

And definitely not about the way my insides feel like they are already rotting away, every drop of magic turning to ash in my blood.

How do I admit to her that my kissing season has barely

even started and it's already in tatters at my feet and that it's all my fault?

"Luck had nothing to do with it," I whisper.

She continues as if I haven't spoken. "And I didn't know where you were. Someone said you were with him when he fell and then you were just gone. Maybe in the woods or out in the water—I had no idea." Maggie presses the back of her hand to her mouth when her eyes well with tears, smearing what's left of her lipstick. Sinking to the bed, she leans her weight into me, testing that I'm real/solid/here.

"I came home."

"I can see that. I was losing my mind trying to figure out if you were safe or not. Why didn't you wait for me?"

Staying there with Isaac's friends after the ambulance took him away was not an option. Not after what I'd done. They didn't know yet that I'd kissed him, but they all knew I was to blame. "Because you weren't there, Mags. You couldn't find me only after I couldn't find you."

I'm being unfair. This isn't Maggie's fault. Not really. But if she hadn't disappeared who-knows-where, I would've been with her instead of sneaking off to kiss Isaac tonight. And everything would be okay.

He would be okay.

"You could've told someone you were all right and you had a ride home."

"If I'd had my phone I would've called you. But it's in your bag. You know, the one you took with you when you disappeared tonight without telling me where *you* were going or who you were with. You didn't seem too worried about me then."

A hint of the post-accident panic when I realized I couldn't call for help returns, and all the air in the room vanishes. My lungs burn with the effort to continue breathing. And suddenly I want Maggie as far away from me as possible. I uncurl and lie on my back, taking up as much of my bed as I can. She *oofs* out a breath as my knee knocks into her, but she doesn't get up.

"It was the first night of your kissing season. I didn't think you'd want me hanging around you all night," she says.

After a few shallow breaths, anger overtakes the panic. There are a lot of things tonight that are my fault. My sister leaving me alone isn't one of them. "It was also the last night of yours. I'm sure you were looking for one last kiss before your magic's gone. So don't pretend like you ran off with whoever you've been crushing on for my benefit."

Maggie twists to look at me over her shoulder. Her lipstick's all but gone, just a hint of red remaining. "Why are you so mad at me?"

"Because you're lying to me."

"No, I'm not."

"Pretty sure you just proved my point."

"Fine. What am I lying to you about, then?"

What *isn't* she lying about? We've never kept things from each other before, but suddenly there's a list piling up between us, pushing us apart when I need her most. "Well, for starters why you snuck off tonight. But also, *who* you snuck off with. Who you've been phone-flirting with for weeks now and think I don't know. I'm not stupid, Maggie. I know you've been seeing someone, and you're doing everything you can to keep me from finding out. What I don't understand is why."

"I just didn't want you to feel like we were leaving you out." Maggie's voice is soft, pleading, already asking for forgiveness before the full truth is even out. "You, Laurel, and I kind of have our thing. The three of us. And then she and I started having a side conversation a few weeks ago and things just kind of went from there."

"You and *Laurel*?" She can't be serious. How could she think dating one of our best friends was a good idea? Maggie's feelings shift as often as she changes lipstick colors—basically every other day—but if she's been keeping a relationship with Laurel a secret, it must be serious. Or she didn't want me to blame her when Laurel ditched me when things eventually went the way all of Maggie's relationships do. I sit up and flatten my back against the wall. Pulling my knees in, I loop my arms around them to keep from shaking. "Was she who you were with tonight? Have you kissed her?"

One look at her and I know she has. The ropes of her wet hair have dripped onto her shoulders. The fabric of her romper is only damp over her bra and underwear, so she hadn't worn it swimming. Of course, she hasn't admitted to swimming in her skivvies with Laurel either.

"Please don't be mad at me about this."

"Have you kissed her?" I ask again.

Pushing up from the bed, she hugs her arms around her middle and avoids my glare. "Yes."

"Why? Because of the season, or because you have feelings for her?"

Maggie might have been the better choice. Isaac's words are like a brand on my brain. My sister set the expectation that the kissing season was a free-for-all. Why would she treat Laurel any differently?

"Why did you kiss Isaac tonight?" she asks.

With the way she's evading my questions, Laurel must've been a momentary thing. One more name for Maggie's page in the Book of Luck and nothing more. Except Laurel's our friend. How could Maggie do that to her knowing that Laurel's feelings are real? So much for caring about who we kiss during the season, I guess. That's one more lie to add to the list. So I throw her words back at her. "True love is supposed to trump all, remember?"

"I just meant was it your choice or did he—"

"God, Maggie. No, he didn't force me. I wanted to kiss him."

Unlike my sister, I can't pretend that my selfish actions don't have consequences. Hurting the one boy I kissed during the kissing season is bad enough. But admitting that a part of me was worried I shouldn't kiss him? That's a ghost that will never go away if it gets out.

5

I DON'T KNOW WHO told my parents about Isaac's accident or my involvement in it. But they're in my room before the sun's even up, asking *first* if I'm all right and *then* what happened. I give them the condensed version. Enough details to get the gist of how things went down, but not the intimate details no one needs to know but me.

They never once say this is my fault. Though we all know that it is, even if they don't want to admit it.

Dad says things like, *It's a wonder more people haven't been seriously hurt jumping off the falls* and *No one should be allowed up there after dark, that's just asking for something bad to happen.* Mom's hands skim across my face, my hair, as if my physical form being unharmed is proof that I'm okay.

The truth is I'm far from okay. I was naive to believe in the Holloway magic so blindly. To trust that things with Isaac would work out the way I wanted because I had luck on my side.

Hospital visiting hours start at seven, and thanks to my parents I'm up and pacing. They both offered to stay home from work today if I needed them. I did not. What I need is to go see Isaac and own up to my mistakes. Tell him I'm sorry. I have to hope that he will take responsibility for his part in this too. Maybe when we do, the Holloway magic will call us even.

With my parents gone, my ride options are Maggie, which after last night is an automatic no, or one of my friends. Paige and Audrey didn't press me for details last night, but I think that was more due to shock than a desire to respect my privacy. There's no way either of them will take me to see Isaac without grilling me the whole way there and back. I wake Laurel when I text her, but she agrees to come get me without any questions. A little awkwardness with Laurel is preferable to not having to talk about what happened.

I slip out of the house to wait for her at the end of the driveway so Maggie can't invite herself along. I'm not in the mood to rehash our argument or have a front-row seat to whatever is going on between her and Laurel.

"What's Maggie doing today that's so important she couldn't take you?" Laurel asks when I'm settled in the passenger seat. The streaks of black running through the underside of her bleached-blond hair are on full display as she gathers her hair into a loose knot. My eyes catch on the trio of tiny braids left loose from her ponytail. Compliments of Maggie last night, I'm sure.

Okay, so maybe *preferable* was a tad misguided. I'm in this now so I'm going to have to suffer my way through it. "I don't think she's doing anything. I just didn't ask her."

"Oh. She told me she had something to do today but was kinda vague on the details. I figured she was taking a delivery for your mom or something. So she's *not* busy today?"

"She was still in her room when I left. If she has plans, I don't know about them." I rein in my frustration before it blows back on Laurel. She's not blameless in all this, but keeping her relationship with my sister a secret feels less like a betrayal coming from her than Maggie. "Hey, so I'm guessing she didn't tell you, but I know about y'all. That you kissed."

Laurel glances over at me, her smile tentative. "And you called me to take you on this ill-fated outing so you could give me the break-your-sister's-heart-and-you'll-break-my-face speech?"

Of the two, Laurel's is the heart I'm worried about. Her eyes have that hazy look of someone newly in love. Or at least serious like. I hate to blindside her with reality, but I know firsthand how everything can go to shit if you're not clear-eyed, clearheaded, and clear-hearted.

"The opposite actually. Be careful, okay? You've been friends with us long enough to know how Maggie is with relationships. It might not be as serious for her as you think."

"She's different with me, Remy. Now that you know about us, you'll see for yourself."

"I hope you're right," I say.

And I mean it. I'm still pissed Maggie kissed one of our best friends and hid it from me, but I don't want either of them to get hurt. I've done enough of that already.

When we reach the hospital ten minutes later, Paige and Audrey are sitting on the trunk of Audrey's car, which is parked under the shady canopy of an oak tree a few spaces down from Seth's Bronco. Laurel pulls in next to them.

Making sure Isaac is okay, putting an end to the bad luck we started with our kiss is infinitely more difficult with an audience. But I have to try. I owe us both that much.

As soon as I'm out of the car, Paige slides from the trunk, her flip-flops slapping the pavement, and practically shouts at me, "What are you doing here?"

"I came to see Isaac." I scan the hospital windows like I'll somehow sense which one is his. If I could just get to him, there has to be a way to make things right.

"That's not a good idea, Remy," Audrey says.

"Hannah's in there. Along with Seth and Felix." Paige's voice cuts a line in the sand. One I'm clearly not supposed to cross. "He told them you kissed him before he jumped. That you told him to fall off a cliff. They're all saying you cursed him."

Cursed. The word rips through me. "And you believe them?"

"I don't know, Remy. I mean, it's Isaac. When has he ever messed up a dive like that?"

Audrey grabs my arm to hold me in place. "And did you hear about his dad? While we were all up at the falls, his dad was packing up to leave. Like *leave.* He's already got a new place out in California or somewhere. I don't think he was even planning on saying goodbye, but then Isaac got hurt and he moved his flight back a day. A whole freaking day. Good riddance to that jerk."

"His dad's still leaving? Who the hell does that when their kid is in the effing hospital?"

"Apparently Isaac's dad does," Laurel says.

"How's Isaac handling it?" I ask, ignoring her brutal honesty.

Paige loops her arm through Audrey's and tugs her away from me. Like it's not safe to be this close to me. Like she thinks I'm capable of the things Isaac's friends have accused me of. We've been friends most our lives. How can she believe them over me?

I already know the answer. Hannah. Isaac was right when

he said she was good at manipulation. She's using that stepsister bond to pull rank with Paige.

"He doesn't know," Paige says. "His mom swore us all to secrecy before she let anyone in to see him. She's not telling him until he gets released."

"I'm pretty sure she plans to pretend like his dad never existed in the first place." Audrey lowers her voice as if there's a crowd listening in, and continues, "I wouldn't be surprised if she's already removed every trace of him from their house. She's scary-mad. Another reason you can't go in there, Remy. She'd probably kill you on sight for putting Isaac in the hospital."

She says it like I pushed Isaac. Like he didn't dive right off the falls of his own volition after crushing my heart. If Audrey thinks that and she's my friend, there's no way anyone will believe it's not my fault.

Apologizing now will be the same as admitting my guilt. Better to give Mrs. Fuller some space to calm down before I try to see Isaac again. It probably won't hurt to give Paige what she wants too. Let her see I'm not the bad guy here.

"Okay, I won't go see him, but I need to know how he is. Please?"

"How do you think he is, Remy? He fractured three ribs and punctured a lung. Breathing is *literally* painful. He might not get to dive this year if he's not fully healed in time."

Recoiling from the accusation in her voice, I back up until I run into Laurel's car.

Laurel walks to the driver's side and opens her door. "I think what Paige is saying is that he's been better."

"It's not funny, Laurel. He could have died," Audrey says.

"But he didn't," Laurel says.

"Last night you acted like you didn't know what happened. Why Isaac jumped. But you kissed him. And then you got mad when he said he still wanted to be with Hannah," Paige says, no hint of doubt that what she's been told is the truth.

"That's not what happened. Is that what he's saying?" I ask.

"That's what Hannah's saying." Audrey scans the parking lot to make sure her dissidence isn't overheard.

Paige sighs, and the tension in her face relaxes. "Is she wrong?"

Seizing on her uncertainty, I say, "Of course Hannah's saying I was jealous of her. She's mad that Isaac chose me over her when she confronted him last night." He chose the Holloway luck anyway.

"Is Isaac lying about kissing you?" Audrey asks.

"He said he was over Hannah. I wouldn't have kissed him if I knew he wasn't."

"So kissing you *is* why he's hurt?" Paige looks to me and Laurel in turn. "You both just need to go, okay? Before anyone comes out here and sees you. You don't want to make this worse do you?"

Worse? It's been less than twelve hours since our kiss, and already Isaac's life and family are in shambles. How much more can he take before the bad luck wears off? *If* it wears off.

The next day, I shut myself up in the glass-walled baking kitchen behind the house. It's the official kitchen for Wild Flour, Mom's bakery food truck, and the only place I can find any peace. With my music turned up to a deafening level, I lose myself in the anger and pain of Breaking Benjamin. Like the song, I know I'll end up suffering too.

I've strung up sheets and blankets over the windows to block the yard from view. I catch a few shadows outside every so often crossing the grass. But whatever they're doing out there, they don't involve me in it. Either the sheets are imbued with the power of invisibility and the kitchen, with me tucked inside it, has disappeared from view or everyone's finally clued in to the fact that I'd rather be alone.

Maggie's the only one who doesn't take the hint.

Her eyes sweep the room and linger on everything but me. "This is the mother of all blanket forts," she says once the volume is lowered.

I spare her a glance, a quick roll of my eyes, then go back

to ignoring her. We haven't had much to say to each other since I found out she was off in the woods kissing Laurel when Isaac got hurt. Or, rather, I haven't had much to say to her. Maggie's acting like nothing's happened.

"Still not talking to me?" she asks.

"What do you want me to say?"

"I don't know. Anything. Just stop shutting me out." Her voice is soft, pleading.

We've never had a fight last this long. But then Maggie's never lied to me before, either, so I guess there's a first time for everything. "It's been two days. I wouldn't really call that shutting you out. It's not like I've been keeping secrets from you for months now."

"It wasn't like that, Remy." She slides into the chair across the table from me and works her way down the line of whoopie pies, flipping over every other one for me to frost.

"Oh, so you didn't go behind my back with Laurel?"

"We didn't do it to hurt you. But you don't have to worry about that anymore." Her shoulders roll forward, the tension making her posture stiff. Maggie focuses on the cake mounds between us instead of meeting my stare. "I told Laurel I couldn't do this."

"What do you mean *this*?"

"A relationship. Be anything more than friends."

Isaac's words rush back to me, slashing the fresh wounds

open again. *I'm not ready for something serious. One kiss isn't going to change that.* Of course one kiss with Laurel wasn't going to change Maggie's mindset either.

"Wow. I think that's a record, Mags. That's what? Two days from claiming your feelings for her are real to breaking up with her."

"You're the one who didn't want me to be with Laurel. A point that you made abundantly clear."

"And you thought I'd be happier with you possibly breaking her heart?"

"Of course not. And it's not like I wanted to hurt her. But if my choices are hurting you or hurting someone else, I'm always going to choose the latter. No one means more to me than you," Maggie says.

That might have been true, back before the Holloway magic laid claim to each of us in turn. Now we keep secrets from each other. Now we don't stop and think before we hurt each other. "If you really believed that, you would have told me what was going on with Laurel instead of me finding out because I needed you and you weren't there."

She throws her hands up and swears. "I don't know what you want from me, Remy. First you're pissed that I liked her, and now you're mad that I'm not pursuing something with her. Which is it?"

I slam the piping bag onto the table hard enough to squirt

an inch of pink icing onto the table. "I was never mad that you liked Laurel. It was that you hid it from me. That you snuck around and lied about it. You were so determined to keep it from me when it was happening, but now that it's over, here you are, acting like some saint for coming clean."

"That's not what I'm doing."

"No, what then?"

"I'm trying to get you to forgive me." Maggie reaches for me. I jerk away, balling my hands on top of the table.

"Usually that involves an apology."

"I am sorry, okay? I wasn't purposely keeping you in the dark about Laurel." Her voice shakes with the admission. "It happened so fast, and I didn't really even know what— if anything—was happening with her. The season can tangle things up. At least it did for me."

I can still remember the desperate pull of my desire when I was close to Isaac. The way I'd leaned into the magic and used it to justify kissing him. But the choice was always mine. The magic didn't control me. Just like it wouldn't have made Maggie do any- thing she didn't want to do. For her to pretend otherwise is a slap in the face. "The season didn't make you act on those feelings, though. Or lie to me about it. You did that all on your own."

"You're right. I swear I won't lie to you ever again. I'll tell you the truth no matter what. All you have to do is ask." She draws an X over her heart.

I should take her apology and promises and let it go. But I can't. If she led Laurel on knowing how Laurel felt about her—knowing it wasn't going anywhere—then Maggie's no better than Isaac. The kissing season shouldn't be an excuse to get what you want at the expense of another person's heart. I can't say any of this to Isaac, but I can at least make my sister understand what she's done.

"If I hadn't said anything about you and Laurel, would you have broken things off with her this fast?"

"Probably not," she admits too quickly.

"Do you want to be with her?" I want her to say yes. To prove she's better than this. I could forgive her lying to me if what she feels for Laurel is not just superficial. "Am I the only reason you're not?"

Maggie studies me, like it's a trick question. Like she knows the wrong answer will wedge us further apart. "I like Laurel, obviously. It's easy with her. I don't have to hold back around her like with some of the guys I've dated, and it's been nice knowing that she likes me for me, you know? But am I going to regret pulling us back to being just friends instead of something more? No. As evidenced by the fact that I'm here trying to fix things with you and not locked in my room sobbing over a broken heart."

"Doesn't that bother you, though? That she means that little to you? Do you even care that you basically used her because she likes you and you like that she likes you?"

"I thought you weren't mad that I liked her?"

"But you don't actually like her! You go around kissing everyone who breathes in your direction without even caring if what you feel for them will last. You move from one person to the next like none of them matters. Did you even think about what ditching Laurel will do to her? You might not have been purposely leading her on like Isaac did with me, but the end result is the same. You made her think there was something more between you, made her hope you felt the same way she did, and then you walked away like her feelings meant nothing. Like *she* meant nothing. It's just so heartless."

It's a cheap shot. One she might not fully deserve. But I can no longer contain all the hurt and anger roiling inside me, and Maggie's within the blast radius.

"I'm sorry that Isaac made you feel like that, but that doesn't give you the right to put all of your shit on me." She shoves back from the table, her chair scraping on the concrete floor. She's halfway to the door when she stops and whirls around to lob her own razor-laced words back at me. "No, I wasn't there when you needed me. But I'm allowed to have a life apart from you. You're my sister, not my fucking shadow. At some point you're going to have to learn to save yourself. Or better yet, be smart enough not to put yourself in shitty situations to begin with. Me not being there has nothing to do with you kissing Isaac. You were going to kiss him no matter what, and he would have gotten hurt no matter what. Because *you* ignored the rules. So if you want to blame somebody, Remy, blame yourself."

My sister's right. Underneath all the hurt and anger, I know she is. But those words won't come. The ones that do are hell-bent on destroying this relationship right along with all the rest. Even knowing they'll push Maggie away, I can't stop them.

"You told me to make sure I kissed someone I cared about, but I guess you're just luckier than I am since the magic has never turned its back on you because you kissed the wrong person." What's left of my heart disintegrates with my next words. "I'm done. With the season. With Isaac. With you."

The damage is done. Now I have to live with the consequences.

6

Turns out, luck is a Bitch. Capital *B*.

In the week since Isaac's accident, not only has the Holloway luck wrecked his life but I'm convinced it's cursed me too. Every day, it feels like there's a swirling vortex in my chest, sucking in every spec of happiness before it can find a foothold.

I had thought losing my magic altogether was the worst that could happen if I broke one of the season's rules. But it would have been a blessing compared to this. I don't need to read the rules scripted on the first page of the Book of Luck to know what they say.

That the magic never touched Isaac's heart because he was already in love with someone else.

That I kissed him anyway.

That his bad luck manifested instantly because I ignored the rules.

And the book has no explanation of how to fix it. Not even a magical footnote.

I've tried every remedy I could find online to rid us both of our bad luck. I've waved a fun-sized hunk of amethyst over each page in the Book of Luck and buried algae-green moldavite crystals in Isaac's front yard to absorb all the blackness surrounding him. I followed a YouTube video to cleanse my chakra with a five-inch wand of selenite crystal and another to sweep my aura with salt-sprinkled lemons. And I burned so much sage in my room Mom asked if I was smoking pot.

None of it changed a damn thing.

Bad luck is still following him wherever he goes. The day he was discharged from the hospital, he received a letter from school that there'd been a mix-up with his final grades and he had in fact failed English and was due in summer school by the end of the week—medical excuses be damned—to avoid having to redo sophomore year.

I'm not giving up, though. I can't. I have to find a way to reverse the bad luck our kiss caused or I'll be the most worthless Holloway girl in history. And Isaac may be cursed forever.

I slide the Book of Luck from the stack of novels beside my bed. Usually it lives in the top right drawer of the china cabinet in the dining room. But since my season started, it's taken up residence in my room. Mom and Maggie haven't noticed its absence. Or if they have, they haven't asked me about it. They probably assume I want nothing to do with it.

That couldn't be further from the truth.

I open it so often I don't bother with tying the thin, leather straps that wrap around the book to keep it closed. When I lift it, the ties unravel, dangling from the butter-soft cover. Faint floral notes from various perfumes seep from the thick paper. I flip past dozens of pages topped with other Holloway girls' names without reading them until I find mine. Most pages boast more ink than mine, but they contain numerous names and lucky events, whereas mine is dedicated to one name, one bout of ongoing bad luck. That's the legacy I'm leaving.

At best, I'll be the cautionary tale used to make Holloway girls take the season seriously.

At worst, future generations won't even know I existed outside of the Book of Luck. But they need to know how badly things can go if they're not careful. Hence the meticulous chronicling of how Isaac's bad luck manifests.

Collapsed lung and fractured ribs from jumping off the top of Firelight Falls.

Unable to compete with the diving team, ruining his shot at a college scholarship.

Left behind when his dad moved across the country for a new job.

Still dating world's worst girlfriend.

That's just the bad luck I've heard about. Since almost everyone blames me for what happened to Isaac and only acknowledges my presence when they want to remind me this is all my fault, my social circle doesn't actually have enough people in it to qualify as a circle. Basically only Maggie and Laurel are still talking to me, even if they aren't talking to each other anymore.

A chance at real love. That's what I'd hoped for when I kissed Isaac. And here my sister is throwing it away, proving me right—and driving us further apart.

We had been raised on family fairy tales. Grand gestures of love. Epic first kisses. Homes filled with laughter and family. Maggie and I had memorized as many stories as we could and whispered the words right along with Mom as she'd tucked us in at night. Holloway girl after Holloway girl falling so far in love that she never came out.

One story goes that Annabeth Holloway kissed her true love on a whim during her season because the boy she'd pined for had been untouched by the magic and she'd hoped to spark his jealousy—or at least a passing interest—by kissing someone else in front of him. But instead, the kiss opened her eyes and heart to the quiet boy whose journal scribblings would one day be hailed as a classic novel.

Another, that June Holloway kissed all the eligible boys in town the first day of her season in hopes that one of them would replace the thoughts of her best friend Ruby's lips that kept her up at night. When that had backfired, she'd finally confessed her feelings to Ruby, and their kiss helped Ruby make a name for herself as the proprietor of one of the South's most infamous speakeasies, popping up in a new location every week to avoid detection.

And yet another page details how Cora Holloway had looked to get more than true love from the season and charged a hundred dollars per kiss. She'd used the money she'd saved up to buy a one-way ticket to France. There, she'd fallen in love with a man who grew roses that became the most coveted flowers in Europe for their pale-pink petals, which shimmered in the light like the inside of a seashell, and their sweet scent that lingered in a room for weeks after the flowers had died.

Not a single blemish on any legacy but mine.

I don't believe for a second I'm the only one in history who's screwed up, though. The others either didn't record their mistakes or...

I flip back page after page, stopping when I find where a page has been removed. Whatever this ancestor had done during her kissing season had been bad enough to get her scrubbed from the family history altogether. Sliding my finger between the remaining pages as a placeholder, I continue my search. In all, four girls have been removed/disowned/forgotten. I go through the book twice more to make sure.

The missing pages might not tell me how to fix things for me and Isaac, but at least now I know I'm not alone.

Since the book isn't giving up any answers about the missing Holloway girls, I have to hope my mom knows something. And that she's willing to tell me.

Mom hadn't believed me at first about Isaac's curse and had insisted his good luck would come later like everyone else's. Then I'd come clean. About Isaac most likely still being in love with Hannah and me kissing him anyway. And she'd conceded that while it *was* a possibility, she'd never heard of anything like it happening before.

Now she's stretched out on the living room sofa with a glass of wine and her favorite reality baking TV show. It's the one night a week she takes for herself, and here I am about to ruin it. I stop in the doorway, ready to backtrack, but she notices me, her eyes zeroing in on the book in my hands.

"Everything okay, lovey?" she asks.

"Sorry, I forgot what night it was."

"This can wait." She pauses the DVR and curls her legs, freeing up one of the cushions for me. "Plus, now I can fast-forward through the commercials."

I sit next to her with my back against the armrest and my knees pulled into my chest. "I've been going through the Book of Luck trying to find something that might help Isaac. And before you say his bad luck wasn't caused by Holloway magic, just hear me out, okay?"

"Okay. Show me what you found."

"It's more what I didn't find." I shove the book toward her, bending the covers back so the jagged remnant of one missing page sticks out. My nerves are creating their own mosh pit in my stomach. I need her to take this—take me—seriously. "Do you know what happened to these girls? The ones who were taken out of the book?"

Mom leans forward and brushes a finger over the torn paper. "I've never heard of anyone being removed from the book. Every Holloway who experienced a kissing season is in there. I'm sure this is just from someone messing up an entry and starting over with a new page."

With a finite number of pages in the book, do-overs would only happen if there were no other options. These pages must be something else. I have to make her see that. "Then why are there no other mentions of bad luck in the whole book?"

"Can I say it's because Holloway magic doesn't cause bad luck, or is that still off-limits?"

"I'm serious, Mom. What about the Holloway girls who didn't follow the rules? Where are they?"

"You say that like you think it's happened a lot." Her voice is the soft murmur of water flowing over rocks. "But it doesn't.

The kissing season isn't something any of us take lightly. I'm sure there have been mistakes along the way. Nobody's perfect. But you can't find things that never happened."

"How do you know they never happened? You're basing what you know off what's in the book. But what if the book isn't telling the whole story?"

"Listen to me. If those missing pages were important, we would know."

Not ready to let this go, I cling to any thread that might help unravel this mystery. "Could Aunt Jenna know something that you don't?"

Mom's younger sister was pregnant by the end of her kissing season, and when the baby's father used the season—and the other boys Jenna had kissed—as an excuse to shirk his parental responsibilities, she swore she'd never have anything to do with the Holloway magic again. If anyone knows the darker side of the Holloway magic, it's her.

"You know your aunt doesn't like talking about the season," Mom says.

I bend the book's spine so what's left of the torn page sticks up, impossible to ignore. "But she might talk to me if she knew how important this was. She might know why these pages are missing or maybe even what was on them. If there was another Holloway who gave someone bad luck, I have to find out." I have to know this isn't permanent for me or Isaac.

She sets her wine on the coffee table, then covers my hands with hers, easing the book closed. "Our family doesn't give bad luck. But if we did, I can promise you, no one would hide something that would help us fix it. As for Isaac's accidents, that's not Holloway luck. That's just ordinary bad luck. It's awful that he's having such a rough time lately, but he'll cycle out of it soon enough, and you'll see it has nothing to do with you."

I want to believe her, but I know the truth.

Any warning or instructions for cleaning up a magical mess they might have passed on are gone along with their names.

If I had known how kissing Isaac would backfire so savagely, maybe I would have made a different choice. Kissed someone else or no one at all.

Mom might be positive that Aunt Jenna doesn't know anything about the missing Holloway girl pages, but since she's one of the few Holloway girls who turned her back on the kissing season, I can no longer just take Mom's word for it. Her judgment is a little cloudy where her sister is concerned.

My cousin Shelby should have had her season three years ago, but when Mom sent the Book of Luck to her, Aunt Jenna returned it, refusing to let Shelby have any part of her birthright. According to Mom, Aunt Jenna hasn't spoken a word about the kissing season since.

I shut myself in my room where Mom and Maggie can't hear me and call my aunt. After the *Hellos* and *How are you?*s, I get straight to the point.

"I know you don't like talking about the season, but I was hoping you'd make an exception this one time. It's important, I swear."

Aunt Jenna sighs, and I can almost see the crease burrowing into her forehead like it does when Mom lectures her for bringing home a new rescue dog—she's up to seven now. "I don't like talking about it with your mom. She'll never get over my decision to keep this part of our family from Shelby. But I'm always happy to talk to you."

That's all it takes for the floodgates to open. I tell her everything. As I talk, I trace my fingertip over the embossed *H* on the Book of Luck's cover. Finally, I ask the question that prompted the call, "When everything happened with Shelby's dad during your season, did anything bad happen to him?"

"I like to think his Holloway luck is that your granddaddy didn't kill him. That's what I recorded in the book anyway." Her laugh is tight, like she would wish bad luck on him if she could. "But no, nothing bad happened to him as far as I'm aware. I haven't spoken to him since before Shelby was born, so if anything good or bad happened to him, I don't know for sure."

"Do you know why some pages were removed from the Book of Luck? Mom says they're probably just mistakes, but I don't buy that."

"You're looking for a way to fix your boy?"

"He's not my boy." Isaac never was. It still stings to admit that.

"And yet you still feel responsible for him," she says, no hint of a question.

"He's this way because of me. I just want us both to be able to move on. But nothing I've tried has worked." I'm tempted to remove the evidence of Isaac's curse from the book with one swift rip. Call it all a mistake and move on like I was never even here. But that won't do anyone any good. Instead, I swallow past the guilt and say, "Do you know anything about the missing pages, or did Nana ever tell you about a Holloway girl who was like me? I can't be the only one."

"Oh, sweet girl. Let me be clear, there is nothing wrong with you. I know it probably feels that way right now, but making mistakes is a normal part of life. Throw in some magic and it's almost impossible to not screw something up."

Generations of Holloway girls managed it just fine. If the Book of Luck is to be believed. I latch on to the hint of hope in her words, though. "Please tell me that means you know something that can help me."

"Not in the way you're hoping." Aunt Jenna's voice softens,

as if that will somehow lessen the blow. "My mother always told us that everything we needed to know about the magic could be found in the book. You just have to know how to use it."

"That's what I'm trying to do. And, not to be rude, but you and Mom haven't exactly been helpful on that front."

"There are hundreds of names in that book, Remy. Most of them are long gone, but I promise you, their stories aren't. Someone out there knows something that can help you. You're just going to have to keep looking until you find them."

I slap the useless book shut. "Why would they know something our own family doesn't?"

"Some people in our family place too much importance on the season and what's written on their page in the Book of Luck. And they refuse to believe there can be more to life than fulfilling our legacies as Holloway girls. They wouldn't allow anything to tarnish that. Not even the truth."

"I'm pretty sure Mom and Maggie are co-presidents of that club."

"That doesn't mean they don't love you too. Try to remember that."

"I'm trying," I say. "But it's hard when they don't believe me about Isaac's bad luck. I can't exactly talk to them about any of this, much less ask them to help me find a way to set things right." Not that I would ask Maggie for anything right now anyway.

"I wish I had some answers for you. All I can tell you is that the Holloway magic doesn't define you. You shouldn't kiss someone just because you feel like you have to. It should always be your choice, Holloway magic or not. And whatever you decide, make sure it's what you want. Even if that means walking away from the Holloway magic completely. I can't promise your life will be everything you want, but the magic can't promise that, either, no matter what all those stories in the Book of Luck make you believe."

But I already know that I won't turn my back on Isaac or my magic. Not until I've made things right.

7

My Maggie-free morning the next day ends halfway through breakfast when she tears down the stairs, her bare feet slapping the wood. She skids to a stop when she sees me with my bowl of cereal at the kitchen island. "I thought you were still out in the baking kitchen."

I side-eye her, the things we shouted at each other last week rushing to the surface like a fresh bruise. I hate that there's this space between us now. That I don't know my sister as well as I thought I did. But kissing Isaac broke something in me, and Maggie is not the only one I no longer recognize. "Sorry I interrupted your avoidance attempt."

"I wasn't trying to avoid you, Rem. I was just going to—" Her gaze whips across the room, as if she can see through the kitchen and dining room walls to the front door. Whatever it is that has Maggie sliding her eyes back to me with a nervous crinkle of her forehead, it involves something out front. Something she clearly doesn't want me to see.

"What?" I ask, her nerves transferring to me like we're psychically linked. I press a fingernail into my palm to give my brain something else to focus on. "Are they burning me in effigy in the front yard?" I'm only halfway joking, so the laugh that comes out cuts off as quickly as it started.

Maggie shakes her head. She looks in my direction but not *at* me. "It's nothing," she says with an air of confidence, her voice steady and lilting, the barest hint of a lie detectable only because I know her so well.

Shoving back from the table, I start for the hallway. Maggie sidesteps to block my path. She grips my right shoulder, spinning me away. Before she can stop me, I sprint for the door and run barefoot through the side yard. The grass is plush and cool under my feet. I reach the driveway, and the subject of Maggie's worry is impossible to miss.

Someone's constructed a wooden booth in our front yard. I'm guessing whoever set it up waited until they saw my parents leave the house before depositing it on our lawn. Maximum payoff. Minimum risk.

Even from a distance I can tell it's sturdy. That it was made to stick around for a while. The booth is wide enough for two people to sit behind side by side, though there are no chairs, and it has a small counter. Walking slowly around it, I stop right in front and face it. The wood is painted a dark graphite color to mimic the exterior of our two-story colonial house. Like it belongs there full-time. A board is nailed in place across the top, connecting the two side panels and making it structurally sound. But that's not its only purpose.

Splashed across the front of the board in red paint are the words: KISSES $1, CURSES FREE.

For a second, I have to give them credit for the ingenuity it took to think up and create the kissing booth from scratch. As far as taunting goes, this is pretty high up there. It would've had a bigger audience set up next to the food trucks or anywhere else in town where people would be able to stop and stare during Talus's July Fourth celebrations this week instead of here in the beginnings of suburbia. But here whoever put it up could be certain I'd see it. And that's the point. Hurting me. Never letting me forget that my kiss broke Isaac in more ways than one.

Now they've brought the fight right to my door. Literally.

Everything inside me screams to not let them win. My muscles aching and burning and willing me to finally fight back.

"Remy," my sister says, all pity and heartbreak. Her expression follows suit. First her lips curve into the perfect pout then her eyes go all big and doe-y. Her lashes work overtime to keep the tears from being more than a thought. We might be fighting, but she still takes her sisterly duties seriously.

"It's nothing." I throw her words back at her. But that's bull, and she knows it.

Maggie hands me a hammer she must have grabbed from the drawer in the kitchen on her way out. She keeps the long flat-head screwdriver for herself. Not that it'll do much good on the nails holding the booth together.

I swing first, leaving a half-moon divot in the wood. The force of the impact sends a jolt up my arm, and my body begs for more. For the first time since Isaac's accident, I'm in control. If only for a moment. Taking another shot, I leave a bigger indention. A few more, and a fissure cracks through the wood.

"I thought we could pry the boards off, take it apart piece by piece." Maggie shrugs. Then she smiles and whacks the sign with her screwdriver. This small act of solidarity from my sister does more to sway me than all of her heartfelt apologies and pleas for forgiveness combined. "But this works too."

Flecks of red paint and splinters rain down on us. We keep hitting until the words are unreadable and the booth crashes to the ground in a heap.

After working out another wave of fresh anger by baking a tray of strawberry whoopie pies with a patriotic blue-and-white swirled frosting as a surprise daily special for Wild Flour, I deliver it to Mom an hour and a half later.

Wild Flour Bake Stop is an old Airstream trailer Mom bought off Craigslist from some now-defunct bakery up in Asheville. There's no mistaking it's a food truck, with its silver-and-bright-aqua paint job and blood orange–colored metal counter jutting out beneath the service windows cut into one side. The food truck park where Wild Flour is permanently set up is home to four eateries on the left and four on the right, separated by a gravel lot and five picnic tables. The only people here this early are the other vendors and people in search of a sugar rush. But come lunchtime, it'll be standing room only.

Inside the trailer, there's a two-foot path cutting down the middle between the low row of coolers underneath prep counters, baking racks screwed into the walls and floor, and a few storage cabinets for to-go supplies and a stash of cleaning products. The limited space back here is part of reason we do all the baking and prep at home.

Mom takes one look at the Tupperware of unexpected sweets in my hands and says, "I take it you and your sister are still fighting?"

The fact that she thinks my bad mood is because of Maggie means she doesn't know about the kissing booth. Harassing her daughters is not something she would let go unacknowledged.

Pity all that hard work couldn't have been put into something worthwhile. Like curing cancer or making time travel possible so I could go back to the start of summer and dismiss

Isaac straight off. Then my kisses never would have caused bad luck instead of good.

I set the container on the counter and immediately wish I hadn't when my hands start to tremble. "I just needed to clear my head." It's not a total lie.

"Did it help?"

"A little."

"Want to talk about it?" Mom asks.

Even if I did, it wouldn't do any good. Since Mom doesn't believe Isaac's bad luck is my fault, she doesn't share my need to reverse it. And until I can do that, nothing will go back to normal. Even then, I don't know if Maggie and I will ever be the same. We might have shared a moment when destroying the kissing booth, but it didn't magically make the secrets/distrust/hurt between us disappear.

"I think I'm at least a dozen or two bakes away from being ready to talk." Hopefully by then, I'll have figured out a way to make this all go away.

"Well, I'm here whenever you need me." She smiles at me, but there's too much worry in it to be comforting. The deep wrinkles that burrowed into the skin around her eyes and mouth the day after Isaac's accident and refuse to smooth out no matter how much rejuvenating cream she lathers on every night are just another reminder that my mistakes are taking a toll on my whole family.

"I know." Retreating a step, I add, "Thanks."

Then I'm out the door before the weight of my guilt crushes me. Hurting Isaac. Fighting with Maggie. Worrying my parents. Throw in a heaping dose of not having a clue how to fix any of it, and it's too much.

Ugly crying in a food truck parking lot is dangerously close to rock bottom. So, I walk a few trailers over where Mom can't see me and count to ten, coordinating my exhales with the even numbers. I get to seven before a familiar voice snaps me back to reality.

"Hurry up," Paige says. "Or Isaac will be home from summer school before the recovery party arrives."

Isaac must be doing better if they're throwing him a party. I blow out a long, grateful breath. Maybe his luck is starting to change without my help. But why didn't Paige tell me? Even if she didn't want to respond to my other texts asking how he was, she could have at least told me that so I'd know he was going to be okay.

Before I can talk myself out of it, I cut between the Mexican street food and wood-fired pizza trucks to make her talk to me. Then I stop short.

Paige and Audrey are walking across the gravel lot, followed by Felix and Seth, each carrying a box of Jane Dough's signature doughnut holes. Isaac's traditional Friday-morning breakfast. Each week, he'd bring a box to school, sharing with anyone he passed. He'd always end up at our lockers with at least one extra left for me.

Audrey sees me first and tugs on the boys' arms, a futile attempt to get them to turn around without causing a scene. Paige notices me next. She spins around to block the boys' path and says something I can't quite hear. Instead of deterring them, whatever she said has them pushing past her and heading straight for me.

"Speak of the devil." Seth's voice carries across the picnic area, too loud, too full of spite. As Isaac's best friend, he must have appointed himself president of the We Hate Remy Fan Club.

I chance a glance at Wild Flour, but thankfully Mom hasn't noticed us. A few of the customers in line at Jane Dough's stop to watch, their hope for a spectacle evident in their eager eyes. But I won't give them one. I'll deal with Seth and co quickly so everyone walks away unscathed.

Turns out my version of handling it is pretending to be invisible.

Shockingly, it doesn't work.

"Gotta admit, I don't think I'd mind being punished for eternity by Remy." Felix drops his elbow to the side of food truck on my right. My kiss might have hurt his friend, but the lure of a Holloway girl in their midst is strong enough to override his fear. The others form a semicircle around him, blocking my escape, and glare at me. "What do you say, Remy? Wanna make me your love slave? Finish what we started a while back?"

"Sorry." I shrug like this is a joke and we're all in on it together. "You're going to have to sell your soul to someone else."

"I think it's too late on that front." Felix has that same sweet, dreamy look in his eyes that he did the night of the party. The one that says he genuinely likes me—and not just for the luck I could give him.

Not that it matters. I won't kiss him now. I won't kiss anyone else the whole kissing season if there's a chance I'll curse them with bad luck too.

Paige seems to be thinking the same thing. Gripping his arm, she twists Felix away from me. "How can you say that when one of your best friends got out of the hospital not two weeks ago after her kiss nearly killed him? You don't want to end up like that."

I want to tell her that Isaac isn't blameless in all this. That he'd courted bad luck by kissing me when he was still in love with Hannah, too caught up in what a Holloway kiss promised to follow the rules. But I don't say anything because without the Holloway magic, it would have been just another kiss. No luck—good or bad—left in its wake.

Pressing my back into the cold metal behind me, I let the edge of the trailer door handle grind against my spine. "You know what would help with that? Not purposely seeking me out."

"We just wanted to get Isaac some Jane Dough's to try and brighten his day when he gets home. We didn't come looking for you specifically." Paige almost sounds apologetic. Like my friend is still in there somewhere, buried beneath the caustic influence of Seth and Hannah.

"Speak for yourself," Felix says, his sense of self-preservation vanishing like fog in the warm sun. "I was definitely hoping Remy would be here helping her mom this morning."

"God, it's like you're not even trying." Paige lets out a strangled groan and tips her head back to stare at the sky as if she can't bear to look at him any longer. "I should've known when you asked me to help you stay away from Remy you wouldn't be willing to pull your weight once you were around her again."

So much for that moment of truce.

Seth's shoulders, thick from years of lettering on the diving team, roll back as he stiffens. "C'mon, man. Isaac might be out of the hospital, but he's nowhere near okay. This curse instantly wrecked his family, his future. Paige is right. That could be you if you don't get a grip."

Felix drops his chin so he doesn't have to look at anyone. "But I like her."

"No, you don't," Paige and I say at the same time. She's all exasperation and deafening sighs. I'm matter-of-fact.

I don't want to have to worry about Felix or his feelings. I have enough on my conscience as it is.

He backs away from both of us, rolling his eyes like we're the ones who are out of our minds, not him.

Seth grabs him by the shoulders right before Felix can walk into him. "You know acting like this undermines all our efforts, right?" It comes out as a raspy whisper, loud enough for me to still catch it.

So, they're coordinating their efforts to make my life hell. Probably building the booth in my yard, unless I have other enemies too. Well, this should be fun. I push away from the trailer and crowd in close to them. They take the hint and back up. "I guess I have you to thank for what's now a pile of wood for our next bonfire?"

"Damn. I thought we'd get at least a full day out of the booth. Maybe even make a few bucks that Isaac can put toward his college fund now that your curse got him kicked off the diving team." Seth catches my eye and lets his smile unfurl. "Guess we'll have to do better next time."

Any chance I might have had at containing the fallout from my kiss with Isaac vanishes. And I feel like rebuilding the booth just so I can tear it down again.

part two

SUGAR, HONEY, ICE & TEA

8

AFTER THE KISSING BOOTH incident a few days ago, Maggie's determined to win me back.

Forget the fact that the sister she's so desperate for no longer exists.

When she knocks on my bedroom door, toes a careful inch back from the threshold, and says, "Mom needs us to run to the store. Sugar emergency." I don't immediately shut her down. Running out of sugar *is* a legit emergency in the Holloway house.

She could go without me. Or pass off the keys to our shared five-year-old Kia and send me alone instead since, of the two of us, I'm the one who assists Mom with the baking for Wild Flour. But figuring out how to live with the shitshow that is my life is the only way I'm going to make it through the rest of my kissing season. And part of that is coexisting with my sister.

"Did Mom say what the sugar's for?" I ask as she reverses out of the driveway.

Maggie cuts a glance at me, then refocuses on the street as she pulls onto it. "Welcome gift. The new neighbors are finally moving in. She thought it would be nice if we made them something." Her too-bright voice is at odds with the guilty squint to her eyes.

I twist in the seat, as if whatever she's hiding might be scrawled in black paint across the robin's egg blue exterior of the soon-to-be-occupied house next door. "What aren't you telling me?"

After all her sneaking around with Laurel, she swore she'd never lie to me again. That won't necessarily stop Maggie from keeping things from me when she thinks knowing might hurt me. Now that I've asked, though, she has to tell the truth.

"She might have mentioned that the kids are our age. And since they don't know about the kissing season or what happened to Isaac, we have a chance to get to them first. Make a good impression so that you can—"

"No. Whatever you're about to say, just don't."

Don't tell me the next kiss will be different.

Don't pretend like the Holloway magic will make anything better.

Don't make me want things I can't have.

Because my heart's practically gone as it is. Another direct hit, and it's toast.

I lean my head against the window, the glass sun warmed and unyielding. Maggie's content to let the radio fill the silence on the rest of the drive into town. Her musical taste runs toward danceable pop while mine is all dark and moody, emotions pouring out with every note. We compromise on the local nineties station. It takes all of one and a half songs to get there, so it's not like she's missing much riveting conversation from me.

The grocery store is in the heart of downtown, and she finds a spot on the street a block away. Mom could've walked from the food truck park in less than the time it's taking us to run the errand for her. Maggie's out of the car and waiting for me on the sidewalk while I sit, still buckled in, recalibrating my mood by repeating my current mantra—compliments of a Bring Me The Horizon song: Turn the pain into gold.

After a few deep breaths, I get out and walk toward her. "I'll get the sugar, and I'll help you bake because I refuse to subject the new neighbors to your baking. But that's all this is." Then I leave Maggie outside along with all her hopes. I've already disappointed my family enough for a lifetime. There's no reason to pile on more when I can help it.

Not waiting to see if she follows, I navigate to the baking goods aisle and pluck a bag of sugar from the shelf. Then I head for the checkout when the aisle remains empty, no sign of my sister.

She reappears from the far side of the store a minute later, clutching something small in each fist.

"What's that?"

"A peace offering." Maggie presents the lip-stain tube to me like she's a game show model, the prize balanced on the palm of her unshakable hand. "A Fire Inside."

A Fire Inside. In addition to being the unabbreviated name of one of my favorite bands, it's also an apt description for how I've felt since my kiss with Isaac went so wrong. Burning, burning, burning from the inside out.

She untwists the wand and holds the tip close to my face to better assess how the color she's chosen for me works with my freckled skin. "I knew this would look good on you."

It's the exact shade of pinkish red I would've picked if I was still the girl who thought one perfect kiss could save the world. Bright/bold/fearless.

I miss that girl. Almost as much as I miss Maggie.

Standing here side by side, you'd think it would be easy to find our way back to who we used to be. MaggieAndRemy. So close that not even a breath separated our names. But her lies and my resentment are too big to move past. One of us is trying at least.

But that one of us isn't me because instead of accepting

her gift like a good sister would, I say, "You shouldn't have opened it. Now we have to buy it."

Which is exactly why she did it. We might not be MaggieAndRemy anymore, but I still know how her brain works. In my sister's mind, buying it means wearing it. Wearing it means kissing someone. And kissing someone means believing in love again.

But love doesn't exist during the kissing season. It can't. Not when people care more about the luck than the Holloway girl who's giving it.

Ignoring my comment, she holds up a second tube. A bright coral-pink shade that would make any lips the center of attention. "I found one for me too. They must be new because I've looked through that display a hundred times in the last few weeks, and none of them were right for us. Until today. I'm pretty sure it's a sign. Like the universe is happy we're here together. That it wants us to be friends again."

It might be a sign, but it has Maggie stamped all over it. She's all charm and charisma and a you-could-never-really-hate-me smile. She's right, I can't. I let out a long breath and almost smile. Not wanting to encourage her, I press a fist to my lips to keep the corners from turning up any more than they already have. "Mom didn't send us on an emergency sugar run, did she?"

Maggie pokes the one-pound bag of sugar still in my hand

as proof of her innocence. Her mouth, like mine, wants to smile when it shouldn't. But unlike me, she doesn't stop it. And the warmth of it wheedles its way into a crack in my chest where it wedges in deep, refusing to be sucked into the void like everything else.

"She always needs sugar, Rem. And we needed these."

Taking the lipstick from her I say, "You know I won't use this." Not when it's possible every guy I kiss will end up with bad luck whether I follow the rules or not because now the magic on my lips is anything but good.

"The next kiss will be different," she says. Just like I knew she would.

"I'm not like you. I can't just kiss anyone who walks by." I bite off the words, leaving them jagged and sharp.

She winces, and that stupid warm feeling from a few moments before *throb, throb, throbs* in my empty chest. The words "I'm sorry" flood my mouth. I swallow them back, washing them down with a fresh serving of anger.

"Don't be like that, Remy. I'm just trying to help."

If she really wants to help, she would back the eff off. But she won't. Letting things go isn't Maggie's style.

"It's a little late for that," I say.

I guess it's not really mine either.

She hands the lipstick tubes to the cashier, who's been silently observing our drama play out not two feet from her so she has gossip to share with the next customer who comes along. "I get that you're scared. And that Isaac's accident really messed you up. But I won't let you give up on your season or on finding love."

I guess she's forgotten what she said during our fight. I haven't.

I'm allowed to have a life apart from you... You're going to have to learn to save yourself.

Even with as horrible as I am to her, Maggie can't stop trying to take care of me.

And I can't find a way to say thank you.

9

EVEN IF I WANTED to let the new boy next door change my mind about the season, it would be impossible. And not just because it's further down on my priority list than learning to eat glass. As soon as the moving truck's backup beeping sounds that afternoon, Maggie's applying a fresh layer of lipstick and swaying her hips back and forth—in that way that mesmerizes all the boys within sight so they'd rather sell their souls to Beelzebub than rip their eyes off her—as she walks barefoot through the grass to meet him.

He's a goner, and he doesn't even know it yet.

Before Isaac's accident, I would've been right there with Maggie, hands linked, footsteps and breaths and identical laughs all synced up without even trying. My lips would've been just as stained as hers too. A promise of everything our kisses had to offer.

I fidget with the metal tube of lip stain Maggie slipped into my apron pocket after we got back from the store. I set up in the baking kitchen to make a batch of double chocolate whoopie pies. Letting it slip through my fingers to settle back into the depths of my pocket, I exhale the regret while it's nothing more than a pinch in my chest at the thought of passing up the chance to meet the neighbors before they've heard the rumors about me. I keep my face turned toward the table, but my eyes follow Maggie. She's smiling her bright, inviting smile, left hand raised in greeting. Our new neighbor flaunts the typical musician uniform: black graphic tee, fitted black jeans, and thick leather cuff on his left wrist. It's like the universe is taunting me. Putting a potential dream boy within reach.

Curiosity gets the better of me, and I'm up and through the door and halfway to them in seconds. I don't want to feel this pull toward him—toward anyone. Not while the Holloway magic is still in me. But I don't turn around. I don't take my eyes off him and my sister.

Maggie blocks his path, ratcheting her smile up to stun. He responds just the way any boy would when confronted with my sister—struck dumb as much by her beauty as by her natural effervescence. An appreciative smile lights up his face as he takes in all her curves and exposed skin.

But instead of lingering on her, he tips his head in my

direction and says something that has Maggie looking back over her shoulder at me too. Does he already know I'm the Holloway sister to stay away from? They continue their conversation without taking their eyes off me, and I suddenly—desperately—want to know what they're saying.

He hikes up the boxes he's holding, getting a better grip, and his shirt rides up with the movement, revealing a tan strip of taut stomach muscles. Something tells me he did it on purpose. That he knows he has my attention and he'll do whatever he can to keep it.

I'm grateful Maggie's too far away to see my reaction. It's bad enough that she knows I came outside to get a better look at him. If she thinks I'm interested, she'll be relentless in her quest to make me kiss someone else this season—and hopefully find my way back to being half of MaggieAndRemy.

That's when I notice the oven timer. It's been wailing for who-knows-how-long. Wrenching my gaze away from Hot Neighbor Boy, I rush back inside. Judging from the wisps of smoke leaking from the sides of the oven door it's been long enough that everything in the oven is well past charred. Not even a scrap of hope I might find some zombie-cakes able to be brought back from the dead by scraping off the outer layer of burn.

I yank open the door and the smoke tumbles out in a thick, never-ending rush, which I choke on, coughing and sputtering as it forces its way down my windpipe to wage war on my lungs. After expelling as much as I can, I hold my breath and turn back into it to give the two dozen pieces of quasi-coal a proper burial by dumping them right into the trash.

That's what I get for letting my guard down. For thinking the innocuous act of showing interest in a boy again wouldn't be the worst thing ever.

The metal worktable wobbles as I hop up on it, hoping to shoo the smoke away from the alarm overhead before it can reach. A screw in one of the legs is loose, making the metal grind and groan whenever I lean on it. The noise always makes Maggie's skin crawl, which comes in handy on the days she insists on hanging out with me while I'm working. Thankfully, she's still outside with Hot Neighbor Boy and doesn't know I just ruined a whole batch of whoopie pies.

I slap the towel at the air, but instead of fanning the smoke away from the detector, I seem to be directing more and more right into it. And right into my face. I squeeze my eyes shut, hoping the sting will abate, and switch directions. When the alarm blares to life, I swear my ears start to bleed. But I only have a second to care because Maggie's sprinting back toward the kitchen with Hot Neighbor Boy and an impossibly beautiful girl in tow.

With the way they're all moving you'd think the whole damn place was engulfed in flames. Maggie's voice shouting my name cuts through the air. If I wasn't so attuned to the sound of it, I probably wouldn't have heard her over the smoke alarm. My face burns as hot as the oven with the unwanted attention.

Maggie's dress whips around her legs, a whirl of deep purple dancing in the breeze. She shoves through the door I stupidly closed behind me, and the tainted air gets sucked outside.

Staring down at the three of them, rag still twirling through the air as if it's doing any good, I realize up close Hot Neighbor Boy is even more intriguing. With twin rings piercing his bottom lip and the black ink of some unseen tattoo reaching just above his collarbone. He doesn't take his eyes off me either. My heart gives a little shudder of attraction, but I shut it down before it has time to take hold. The last thing I need is to fall for someone new. No matter how much my heart craves it.

The girl must be his sister. They share the same eyes, the color caught somewhere between blue and gray with a ring of something even darker outlining the irises, and cheekbones that could make even an innocent smile seem seductive. She quirks a pale eyebrow at her brother. He mimics the motion and shrugs like they run to the aid of damsels in non-distress at least once a day.

"Are you okay?" Maggie wraps hot, sticky fingers around my ankle to hold me steady even though I'm perfectly capable of keeping myself upright all on my own.

"I didn't hear the timer." I wait for her to release me so I can climb down. Hot Neighbor Boy extends his hand to help me off the table when it shifts an inch or two toward him from my weight. The smart thing to do is avoid contact at all costs. Let him know from the start that I'm not interested/off-limits/cursed.

So why the hell do I take his hand, wrapping my fingers around his wrist like he's some sort of miraculous lifeline, and sink to the edge of the table so my feet dangle just a foot from the floor? And why do I hesitate before letting go?

"Thanks." The word comes out soft and breathy like I'm the type of girl who believes in love at first sight and happily ever after. Tensing my jaw, I force my lips to not betray me by smiling at him.

His hand drops away when I relax my grip, and we all move outside, away from the worst of the smoke where we can talk at a more reasonable volume. Maggie shoots me a look, her intense brown eyes widening in curiosity at my behavior. I don't have an answer for her. Not that I'd tell her even if I did. The thick grass tickles my bare feet as we cram close together to be heard over the noise of the alarm still going in the kitchen. Last summer, some boy hoping for one of Maggie's lucky kisses mowed it every week. I think Dad got used to not having to take care of it himself and has accidentally let it grow unwieldy this year.

Maggie says my name, and I assume she's introducing me to our new neighbors. Their names disappear into the air before I can catch them. The alarm shuts off a moment later, but my ears continue to ring.

"Well, that's one way to get my attention," Hot Neighbor Boy says. His smile is quick. Lethal.

"C'mon, Tobin," his sister says. "You and I both know this distraction was all for my benefit. My allure knows no bounds."

My ability to talk, along with all my thawing insides, trickle out of the gaping hole his smile has just carved in my chest. It takes a moment for her words to register. When they do, I glance at him—Tobin—and catch him rolling his eyes at her.

"We've only been in town a few hours and you've already called dibs on one girl. You can't have them all, Jet."

"Fine, you can have this one." She nods at me and laughs a laugh that's better than music, as if we're in this together.

It's been so long since anyone's treated me like I belong that I want to laugh too. But I bury the feeling because I'll only end up hurting them if I let them get too close to me, and say, "I hate to burst your bubble, but nobody's calling dibs on me."

"Fair enough," Tobin says.

"Sorry. That probably sounded super uncouth since we've only said like two sentences to you so far," his sister says.

She links her arm through her brother's, as if she's speaking for them both. "But we're actually decent people, I promise. We've just had a few close calls since I discovered I like girls too."

"Juliet and I agreed to set ground rules for each other when we meet new people so we don't end up fighting over anyone."

"Obviously if the person in question has other ideas about which one of us she wants, we will reevaluate. Come to a compromise that makes everyone happy. Or happy-ish anyway. Even if it means a lifetime of unrequited love on our part when she doesn't want either of us."

In an instant, I'm thrown back to the start of the summer when I thought I knew what—knew who—Isaac wanted. And how it all turned to shit.

There's no way I will put myself in that position again. No way I will hurt anyone else either. Not ever again.

When I try to move away from Tobin, my sister holds me still. She leans in, tucking her chin into place on my shoulder. Maggie's breath is hot on my neck as she whispers, "Give them a chance. They're not Isaac."

She's probably right, but that's not something I plan to find out firsthand. If I'm lucky, whatever pull I had as a Holloway girl is long gone. Buried somewhere way down deep with the girl I refuse to be anymore.

Maggie invites me to go next door and help Tobin and Juliet unpack after dinner, but I respond by locking myself in the baking kitchen to remake the whoopie pies I murdered this afternoon. In case she comes back with the twins as reinforcement, I throw on my apron that reads *I bake because punching people is frowned upon.* Dad bought it for me as a joke. Turns out, it's kind of my favorite thing to wear these days.

Then I crank my moodiest playlist on Spotify—affectionately dubbed Sugar, Honey, Ice & Tea—and lose myself in the dark lyrics and darker chocolate.

I don't hear Laurel knock on the door until I'm pulling the first tray of cakes—perfectly moist and fluffy—from the oven. When Maggie first ghosted her, Laurel turned to me for answers. The most I could offer was commiseration for our mutual broken hearts. Turns out that was enough to keep our friendship intact.

Though I suspect she comes by so often as much for Maggie as for me. Her lips, at the moment, carry the barest hint of a smile along with some shiny gloss that looks as out of place on Laurel, who has a strict no makeup policy, as Maggie would look on the climbing wall in Dad's outdoor equipment store. I twist the lock to let her into the kitchen.

She walks right past me to my phone and taps the screen, bumping down the volume on my music a few decibels. "I see the Maggie-repellent is working."

"I don't need repellent when there are new neighbors to win over."

Hopping up onto the table, Laurel's gaze shifts toward the Curcios' house, her dark eyes narrowing as if that will help her see through layers of brick and drywall. "Has she been over there for more than five minutes? If so, I'm pretty sure they—whoever they are—are half in love with her already." She swipes a thumb across her bottom lip and cleans off the residual gloss.

"They are Tobin and Juliet. Twins," I say. *Disarmingly charming* twins. A fact that I'm smart enough to keep to myself. No point in making Laurel feel worse about the lack of attention from my sister.

"And you didn't want to join in on the getting-to-know-you fun?" Laurel holds a straight face for all of three seconds before a laugh escapes.

"They already caused me to burn a batch of whoopie pies."

"How'd they manage that?"

By flashing their charming smiles in my direction. They're going to be trouble, I can tell. Tobin especially. I'm going to have to work overtime to keep my heart in line where he's concerned.

"They were just distracting me when they moved in. But now that Maggie has them occupied, I'm back on track." In more ways than one since I can't be tempted to kiss Tobin, let alone fall for him, as long as he's focused on Maggie.

"I'm surprised Hannah isn't over there already, warning them to stay away from you." Laurel swivels on the table, planting her feet on the empty chair beside me.

Almost losing Isaac was Hannah's wake-up call. She's been devoted to him ever since and is almost as evangelical as Seth when it comes to the kissing season—and reminding everyone what I did to Isaac. In my snarkier moments, I think Hannah finally giving Isaac the devotion he'd always wanted is another manifestation of his bad luck.

I open one of the plastic carriers Mom uses to transport baked goods to Wild Flour and set the whoopie pies inside, their edges a breath from touching. Without looking up I say, "What does she think? That people can just plug their ears with beeswax and ignore me like I'm a siren?"

"Honestly, I think she feels guilty that she didn't try harder to keep you from kissing Isaac. I mean, I know it wouldn't have made any difference, but in her mind, she failed him."

"And by that you mean she's worried I'll curse someone else if she doesn't stop me." I smash the next whoopie pie down so hard the icing squirts out the middle. There's no point in trying to save it, so I scoop it up and dump it into the trash. That's what I'll have to do with my life, too, if I can't find a way to save Isaac.

Laurel kicks her foot over to nudge my leg. "No one cares what Hannah thinks."

But we both know that's a lie.

"Maybe they wouldn't if what she's saying wasn't true."

"You can't possibly think you're responsible for Isaac's dog running away on July Fourth."

That was three days ago. How have I not heard about it yet? "Oh my God. Did they find it?"

"Not that I know of. Apparently the dog is terrified of thunder so it lost its mind over the fireworks. But the fact that you didn't hear about it is even more proof that it's not your fault."

"No, that just means they haven't blamed it on me yet." As long as Isaac is cursed, every bad thing that happens to him, even indirectly, is my fault.

10

MAYBE. CURRENTLY IT'S MY least favorite word.

Maybe Maggie's right.

Maybe my next kiss will be different.

Maybe I can salvage what's left of my kissing season.

It seeps into my veins, amping up the restlessness that's been plaguing me all week until I can no longer pretend that sleep is something I want tonight.

I need to get *maybe*—and all its infinite possibilities—out of my head before I do something I'll regret.

Sitting up in bed, I pretzel my legs beneath me and lean back against the pillow. I reach for my phone and accidentally knock the Book of Luck where it sits on the night stand. It topples to the floor with a sharp slap.

When I lean over to pick it up, it's open on the floor to my nana's page. Like it's trying to remind me what a disappointment I am. But the book is just as useless. There's nothing in there to help me break the curse. Only missing pages and reminders of how badly I screwed up.

I wait for the knock on the wall separating my bedroom from Maggie's that says she knows I'm awake and wants to make sure all is good. After a few breaths it doesn't come.

Some nights she forgets that we're no longer friends—or maybe she's hoping I've forgotten—and she knocks. Once: *Are you awake?* Twice: *Are you okay?* Three times: *Need me to come in there?* The replies to this decade-old communication system are much simpler. If the answer is yes, I knock however many times I want. If the answer is no, I do nothing at all. Though ignoring Maggie usually resulted in her climbing into bed with me within a few minutes of her first question.

I guess tonight she's giving me the space I constantly insist I want.

It's just as well. Maggie would probably rip my page out of the book if she saw the list of Isaac's luck I've been keeping. I flip ahead, resenting all the good luck inked on other pages. So many stories of financial windfalls, creative strokes of genius, chance encounters, and big breaks. Like Enzo Blythe, who, a few years after kissing Lizzy Holloway, picked up a painting at a yard sale for eight dollars and fifty cents that turned out to be an original Picasso worth upward of ten million. Right place. Right time. Thanks to the Holloway luck.

There's a smudge of ink on the corner of my page from my latest documentation of Isaac's bad luck. A black mark in the Book of Luck. That's what I've been reduced to. An effing black mark with no way to erase it.

I think in the back of my mind I'd known I'd be sneaking out to search for Isaac's dog again since I hadn't bothered to change into my pajamas when I'd gotten in bed. I've gone out every night, dog treats I made tucked into pockets, but so far, no luck. Or, more accurately, only bad luck in the form of the dog remaining MIA. Not a single sighting despite the missing flyers I've posted all over town.

Now, I throw on a hoodie over my Lacuna Coil concert tee and tiptoe to the door. The only one in the house who notices me slipping out the front door is Iggy, our smoosh-faced gray tabby, who opens his mouth to sound the alarm about me skipping out after curfew. I distract him with a few well-placed scratches under his chin. Then I'm out the door before he can stop purring.

Outside the air is sticky. Despite the summer heat, I pull the hood of my sweatshirt tighter around my face in case anyone happens by, even though it's well past midnight.

While the rest of Talus sleeps, I make my way toward the center of town, through the honeycomb of neighborhoods that grew up on the outskirts only to be enveloped by a vibrant downtown full of boutique shops and farm-to-table restaurants and microbreweries and mom-and-pop businesses that draw tourists from all over the tristate area. I continue past the artisan market where artists and hippie goat-cheese makers and winemakers and a whole mess of other types sell their wares out of stalls, like a year-round farmers' market, and then on farther down past the urban honey farm built on the rooftops of three adjoining buildings and the food truck park at the edge of Haight Plaza.

I skirt around the plaza, the sharp tang of grease and cooked meat from the closed-up trucks lingering in the air, and continue to the Talus Cemetery. All the plots have been filled for a hundred years. There's no one left alive who remembers anyone buried there to bring fresh flowers to the graves or to care that most of the headstones are crumbling into dust. Someone at least keeps the scant bits of grass in check every month or so, but that's about it. Most people just drive or walk right by without even noticing it anymore.

It's the perfect place for a scared dog to hide. The old, iron gate screams as I push it open as if I'm not welcome here. I itch to put in my earbuds and turn on my music, but I need to be able to hear any timid barks in response to my soft calls. Leaving a trail of dog biscuits between the gravestones, I walk every inch of the cemetery to no avail.

A warm breeze flutters the flyer I impaled on the cemetery gate a few days ago, sounding so much like a whisper that I almost turn around. Instead, I pull the hood farther over my face and run home.

As I slip through the dark yard between my house and the new neighbors', a sharp whistle cuts through the night air. Though my body freezes in place, my heart ramps into overdrive at the prospect of getting caught out past curfew. My parents have let a lot slide so far this summer—instigating fights with Maggie, refusing to talk about the rumors making their way around town that spread from eager mouths to even more eager ears about how I'd done much more than kiss Isaac, not to mention my listening to music so dark and brooding that Mom says it makes her want to cry for days—but disregarding curfew isn't one of them.

I immediately scan the tiny front porch of our house, which is thankfully devoid of pissed-off parents. Then I check the darkened windows of the house just to make sure I'm in the clear. Maggie's room faces the front yard, and I half expect to see her staring down at me all wide-eyed and worried because I wasn't in my bed. But her curtains are pulled tight. And though I'm relieved, I can't shake the flash of sadness that my sister didn't notice—that she never notices—that I sneak out every chance I get.

A soft chuckle carries from the neighbors' house. The

homes in my neighborhood are on the older side, not the cookie-cutter designs of the newer subdivisions, but they're still packed in close enough together that we have a front-row view of each other's business.

The window opposite mine on the second-floor dormer is cracked, the sheen of moonlight on the glass disappearing in the few inches between the sill and the bottom of the window. I flip my hood down and walk into the side yard that separates my house from the Curcios'. It's been as easy for me to avoid further interaction in the week since they moved in as it has been for Maggie to become instant BFFs with Juliet.

A shadow on the roof below the window unfolds from a crouch and stretches into the lanky body of Hot Neighbor Boy, aka Tobin. He's dressed in all dark clothes again, and I have to squint to see him. He motions to me, the blue light of his phone screen glowing in his hand. "Where do you go every night?"

I wave my hand to get him to keep his voice down before he gets us both in trouble. Then his words sink in. And I realize he must've seen me coming or going the past few nights. What if he was waiting for me tonight, hoping he'd have a chance to talk to me again? My cheeks warm at the thought, but I repress the instinct to tell him the truth or something close to it. There's no way I can explain about my nightly dog search without telling him I'm the one responsible for Isaac's bad luck in the first place.

"Out," I whisper-yell back.

"Yeah, I got that much." He tilts his head back, huffing out an exaggerated sigh. Looking back at me, he continues, "You know, if I were you I'd think twice about dating a guy who makes you walk home alone this late. I mean, I know Talus isn't exactly crime central, but he should still care enough to make sure you get home safe." His voice is still too loud for my liking.

I edge closer to his house and stop just before I'd have to tilt my head back to see him. The thought of me having a boyfriend is laughable. "Why do I need a boyfriend for that when clearly I have you here doing your own little stakeouts?"

"Hey, this isn't my fault. If you didn't time your sneaking around to coincide with my late-night stargazing, I would never see you."

The way he says it, it's almost like he knows I've been avoiding him. But the only way he'd know that is if Maggie told him that's what I'm doing. Which is definitely something she would do. And it would explain why she hasn't tried to stop me from sneaking out. But why does he care that I've been Little Miss Antisocial? "If by stargazing you mean hiding out on the roof so your mom doesn't catch you doing whatever it is you're doing out here."

Tobin leans over the side of the roof. The moonlight casts his upper body in a soft silvery light as he smiles. "I think this is one of those you-say-*tomAto*-I-say-*tomAHto* situations. I'm just out here enjoying the view."

Keeping my distance from a hot boy is a piece of cake. I've been doing that for almost a month now. Or they've been staying away from me. But a boy who's hot *and* flirting with me? This is so not good. I clamp my teeth together to keep from smiling back or saying something to encourage whatever he's trying to do here, between us.

"Not even a chuckle?" he says, when I don't respond.

"Nope. Sorry," I say.

"You couldn't even fake it to make a guy feel like he's got a shot?"

"I don't think I've ever heard a guy ask a girl to fake it before." The words are out before I can stop them.

Something about him calls to the girl deep inside me. The girl who flirts and laughs easily and daydreams about kissing boys and falls in love like it's the beginning of everything instead of a disease that eats you up from the inside out. And I can't figure out if it's him specifically that I'm reacting to or just that he's someone new, someone who wouldn't blame me for being that girl again.

A laugh bursts out of him, and he braces one hand against the wall to hold himself steady. He presses the back of his other hand to his mouth to stifle the sound. His phone screen lights up with the movement, flashing a Spotify playlist that's too small for me to make out any of the songs. And I do smile at him this time because, damn, it feels good.

"But seriously," he says after a moment, "the guy you're seeing's a dick if he doesn't even bring you home after."

"Maybe he offers and I refuse."

"Still doesn't make him any less of a dick. You deserve better."

I ignore the voice in my head that whispers *No, I really don't,* wanting to hold on to this pocket of happiness for a little bit longer. "That's awfully generous considering you don't even know me."

"I don't have to know you. Everyone deserves to be with someone who makes them feel like they matter."

"Speaking from experience?"

He sinks back into the shadows. I think he's going to evade the question, but eventually he says, "Let's just say relationships tend to work better when they're based on mutual attraction and, you know, actually caring about the other person and not just liking how dating them makes you look." He laughs, as if trying to take some of the weight from his words, but there's no mistaking the hurt that hardened his voice.

He's been screwed over by love too. A kindred spirit.

I want to ask about the girl that used him. How he got over it—over her. But it's safer to keep him overly confident and flirty. There's no danger of me getting too close to him that way. "In that case, would it make you feel any better to know there is no guy?"

"Not for the reason you're asking, but yeah. Much better. I mean, obviously it's good to know that you're not dating a total jackass who doesn't deserve you, but now that I know you're single that reason takes a back seat to this other one."

"The other one being?" I regret the question as soon as it's out. I regret the whole damn conversation because now there's a connection between us, a spark of feeling I'll have to extinguish to keep us both safe. But it's too late to take any of it back.

"That I haven't been able to stop thinking about you since the first time I saw you," he says. "That I've been hoping you'd come over with your sister so I could talk to you again."

My heart gives a little lurch, desperate for the attention. But I can't give in to it. Not when that could mean hurting someone else. So instead, I say, "That's the last thing you should want. You and every other guy in town who thinks they want to kiss me should quit while you're ahead." I force a laugh, but it comes out as a broken, jagged sound, slicing out in all directions, not caring who or what it cuts into.

He raises his eyebrows at me and just stares for a few seconds. The playfulness of his half smile giving way to confusion and then hurt when he realizes I'm not joking. He steps back, gripping the window casing and throwing himself into shadow again. "Wow. I did not peg you for the full-of-herself type."

"I'm not—"

"No? You just told me that it's pretty much expected for guys to want you. What else could you mean by that?"

Magic. The word screams in my head, but I don't let it out. Based on the few details I've gleaned about his ex tonight, she must've been a piece of work, and I don't want him to think I'm like that at all, but I'm sure he's heard by now what Holloway girls can do. And I need to keep him as far away from me as possible so I don't curse him too.

Burying my hands in the front pocket of my hoodie, I twist my fingers together to keep them from shaking. "Just forget it, okay?"

Tobin shoves the window up. "Yeah, sure." Then he disappears inside.

I stay there in the yard for another minute in case he looks back down, but he doesn't. And I have no one to blame for the stupid ache in my chest but myself.

11

As if I need a reminder to stay away from Tobin, the magic takes another swipe at Isaac later that week. This time in the form of lightning striking a tree, which crashes through the roof of his car while it's parked in his driveway. The car's a total loss.

And I'm still no closer to finding a way to break the curse.

I'm tempted to go back to Apothecary, the new age store where I bought the crystals and sage for my initial curse-removal attempts, and let Gideon, the store manager, do the tarot reading he'd said would provide some clarity on the situation. But I don't think I can handle if the cards predict a cursed future. It's better if I have a scrap of hope to cling to that I can still fix this.

I've been doing a decent job of avoiding any sort of prolonged interactions with people in the few days since my late-night run-in with Tobin. I let my guard down while baking today, though, and that was a mistake. Somewhere between removing two brown sugar cakes from the oven and whipping up a batch of salted caramel frosting, the baking kitchen's door swings open. Juliet and Tobin waltz right inside. No knock, no nothing, like they grew up next door and we haven't only had a handful of conversations.

But I guess I'm lucky it's them and not someone else.

Tobin hangs back, just a foot inside the door as if he realizes they've just invaded my sanctuary. Or more likely, he's determined to keep his distance after our last conversation. Juliet, on the other hand, practically skips across the room, eyes wide as she surveys the cakes I've stacked one on top of the other and glued in place with thick layers of icing. She jerks a thumb toward my house and looks at me expectantly. And I can only assume she's looking for my sister.

Wiping my fingers clean on a towel, I turn down the volume on my music. The room goes dead quiet once The Used is no longer blaring from the portable Bluetooth speaker I've connected to my phone and have sitting on the table. "Maggie's in the house."

"Oh, I know," she says.

I want to ask her why she's bothering me then, but I bite the comment off before it comes out. They're at least trying to be friendly. That's more than most of my actual so-called friends are doing. I roll my shoulders to release some of the pent-up tension and smile at her. At them. My heart gives a little shudder of hope. And I don't immediately shut it down again because it feels so damn good to not be dead inside. "What are y'all up to?"

"Your mom invited us and our mom over for dinner. You know, as a welcome-to-town slash let's-get-to-know-each-other-since-we're-going-to-be-neighbors-and-all kind of thing. Didn't Maggie tell you?" Juliet asks.

She might have. If she wasn't one of the people I've been avoiding. "We didn't really see much of each other today."

Tobin levels his gaze right on me, a hint of mischief sparking in his eyes. "Maybe she didn't want to give you a chance to sneak out before we got here."

I go to tell him to keep his damn trap shut, but Juliet slaps him across the chest with the back of her hand before the words leave my mouth. She doesn't even look over at him, just nails him with a practiced grace. I'm tempted to ask if she teaches lessons because something about the way her brother is looking at me—like he's cataloging which buttons result in which reactions—makes me think that's a skill I might need to become proficient in if we're both going to make it out of the season in one piece.

Juliet drops her forearms to the table, clasping her hands as if to keep them from sneaking a pinch of the layer cake I'm shaving into a near-perfect cylinder with the knife. She leans over the center of the table to inspect my work. "Please tell me that—whatever it is—is going to be our dessert tonight."

"It's a brown-sugar-and-salted-caramel cake. And it's all yours if you want it." I relax a fraction, despite how close she is to me. Her attraction seems to be solely focused on the cake, not getting a kiss from me.

"I can't just take your cake. You were making it for something. Or maybe someone? Something that labor intensive can't be a purposeless cake."

The knife slips in my sweaty palm. I set it down before I do any damage to me or the cake. "You don't see any dismembered body parts littering the yard, so it definitely served a purpose," I say, trying to dispel the dusty feeling in my throat.

Tobin cocks an eyebrow at me. "Passive-aggressive baking or mass-murder cover-up?"

My smile shouldn't come so easily. Not after the way my last conversation with him ended. And definitely not knowing how one kiss with Isaac is still wreaking havoc on his life. But there it is, settling on my face like it owns the goddamn place.

I meet Tobin's gray-eyed stare and say, "Salted caramel doesn't cover up the flavor of blood. For that you need red velvet. But thanks for letting me know you're *not* the person to call when I need help hiding the bodies."

He grins at me. And it's like a gun cocked and loaded,

finger on the trigger. One wrong move and this boy could blow my chest wide open.

I grab the bowl of caramel frosting I'd prepped while the cakes were cooling and stir it with the wide-blade icing knife to distract myself. Then I slap a large dollop of it in the middle of the cake and start spreading it clockwise over the mounded surface.

"You two are sick, with a capital S." Still draped on the table, Juliet looks over her shoulder at her brother. I catch a fistful of her hair as it swings toward my cake. The strands are about a hundred different shades of yellow and gold and white and caramel and give off a coconut scent. She turns back to me with a smile about as killer as her brother's, all full lips and flashing teeth. I release her hair a safe distance from the cake and glance at Tobin. He's twisting the leather cuff on his wrist, not looking at either of us.

"Maggie said you're a genius in the kitchen," she says, reclaiming my attention.

My breath catches and I replay the words in my head to make sure I heard them correctly. Even then I have to ask, "She did?"

Last summer, Maggie had begged me to leave the baking to Mom so we could have more time at the falls with the boys. She'd said I'd have my whole life after culinary school—which has been my post–high school plan for as long as I can remember—to bake, but I'd said me giving up baking was like her giving up lipstick, and she dropped it after that.

"Yeah. I kinda got the impression you're so busy baking you don't have time for anything else. Like making friends with your new neighbors. Hence, here we are."

Leave it to Maggie to use it as an excuse for why I'm not hanging out with her or Tobin and Juliet. Instead of admitting she's a hypocrite when it comes to finding love, she's blamed my schedule. I knife up more icing and concentrate on smoothing it over the sides without picking up flecks of cake. "I kinda need to concentrate when I'm working. So, you know, I don't set off any more smoke alarms."

Tobin's lips twitch into a smile again. And my heart makes a play for resuscitation.

Then a voice calls Juliet's name from outside, sharp and strangled. We all turn toward Mrs. Curcio, who is in the yard halfway between the baking kitchen and the back door of my house. She's a tiny woman—if she's broken even five feet I'd be surprised—but standing there with one hand in a fist on her hip and her face twisted into an expression that's part worry and part desperation, she looks pretty damn intimidating.

Juliet shoves back from the table, hands flying into the air as if she's ready to fight. "Oh my God. Am I not even allowed to talk to girls anymore?"

"And risk you getting within kissing distance?" Tobin

says, with a healthy dose of sarcasm. He slings an arm around her shoulders and pulls her in close so he can whisper, "Not on your life, Jet."

Shit. Did I read her wrong too?

I must have a freaked-out look because Juliet rushes to say, "Don't worry. I'm not looking to kiss you. Unless you're looking to kiss me back, then we should definitely talk—or not talk, as the case may be."

I shake my head, not entirely sure if she's serious. Tobin raises an eyebrow at me, which does nothing to help me figure out how to rejoin this conversation. And for some reason, I really want to keep talking to them. Not just right now but at dinner and tomorrow and next week and the one after that too. For the briefest moment, I allow myself to wonder what it would be like to have friends again.

"Could you at least wait to start your flirting until Mom's made it inside so she doesn't flip her shit? We don't really need to parade our family drama in front of the unsuspecting neighbors." Tobin lifts his sister's arm at the elbow and forces her to wave at their mom.

"Sorry," she says. Looking out the glass wall as her mom walks to our back door, she adds, "Our mom's a bit of a control freak. You'd think she'd be more worried about Tobin poking holes in his face and putting permanent ink on his body or, God forbid, knocking up some girl out of wedlock, but no. She catches me kissing one girl, and I can't be trusted to not try and hump every girl that walks by."

"To be fair," Tobin says, releasing her, "you and Chelsea were making out in the pool when Mom's book club arrived."

"Don't even pretend you wouldn't have done the same thing given the chance."

"Hell, given half the chance." Tobin sneaks a finger into my icing bowl and licks it clean. He keeps his eyes on me the entire time. "But that's not the point."

"Then what is it?" I ask before he can swipe another taste. And before I can analyze why listening to him talk about wanting to kiss another girl has my stomach going into free fall.

He raps his knuckles on the table twice. "Just that our mom needs a little time to adjust. She'll come around eventually."

"She's made it her mission to turn me straight, Tobin. Or did it slip your mind that that's why we're here now instead of back home?" Juliet's tone teeters between exasperation and tightly coiled anger, as if the slightest nudge could push her over the edge.

I know that feeling more intimately than any other at this point. And I know what might bring her back. "Well, then she's probably going to be very disappointed in the short term." I sprinkle coarse sea salt on top of the finished cake.

"Why's that?" Juliet asks.

"Because all the guys here are in love with Remy," Tobin

finishes, even though that hadn't been what I was planning to say. His lips curl into a smirk, and he crosses his arms over his chest, his biceps tense. A silent challenge to contradict him.

Which means just like that we're back to him thinking I'm a complete narcissist again. That's just effing great. Not that I want him to like me. But does everyone have to side against me in this? "I thought we—" I start.

"Well, yeah," Juliet says, cutting off my reply before I can finish. She gives me a hopeful smile, then rounds on her brother. "It's not her fault they all want to kiss her. I mean, kissing a Holloway girl will give them good luck, so of course, people want to get in on that action. But according to Maggie the magic only lasts for a year. Right, Remy?"

"Right," I say even though none of this should be news to Tobin. He's been in town long enough to hear the rumors. Or to have Isaac's friends tell him straight up what the kissing season is and what it can do. "What else did my sister tell you?"

"Just the basics, I guess. And that I shouldn't listen to what anyone in town says about you. She also said you might take a little time to warm up to us but that shouldn't dissuade us from trying to win you over. Lucky for you, my brother and I are patient.

"We also know what it's like to be the center of a rumor that bears little resemblance to the truth. So, we're not going to believe what anyone says about you and that Isaac guy unless you tell us to." Juliet ruffles Tobin's hair and dances out of his reach before he can retaliate, mischief slipping into her smile. "Maybe you, dear brother, just might be the one to restore her faith in the magic."

Tobin's smile comes back full force.

If they only knew all that the magic entails—that I don't know how to fix it once it goes wrong—they wouldn't be smiling at me like the kissing season is the answer to everyone's prayers. But for some reason, I can't bring myself to set her straight.

12

DINNER TURNS OUT TO be one of my favorites. Chicken salad over a bed of romaine in homemade tortilla shells. Not your typical comfort food, but to me that's what it is. And Maggie made it to ensure I wouldn't be a bitch about the Curcios coming over. I want to be annoyed at her for thinking I can't control myself around other people without being manipulated, but the kitchen smells so deliciously of fried dough and freshly cut pineapple that my mouth's too busy watering to frown at her.

There's a chorus of *Hey, Maggie* from behind me. I almost add mine to it, but then it's too late.

I join Dad at the island where he's throwing back handfuls of pecans Maggie hadn't yet cut up for the top of the salads. Tobin and Juliet file in beside me, leaning on the counter, as comfortable in my house as they are everywhere else. It must be amazing to have that kind of confidence. To be that sure of themselves and their surroundings. I don't even know what it feels like. As the extroverted and charismatic Holloway sister, Maggie has always been popular. And since I was practically her shadow, preferring to stand back and watch her shine, I was only popular by association. Now, thanks to my kiss with Isaac, I'm infamous.

"Hey there, you three," Dad says.

"We were about to send out a search party," Maggie says, a current of annoyance vibrating her voice. She adjusts the bowl tucked into the crook of her arm and lifts two more to take into the dining room. She does it all without even looking in our direction.

Even though I live in a constant state of not-ready-to-forgive where my sister is concerned, the idea of her being mad at me sends a hot burst of panic through me. And I need her to know I'm not trying to steal her new BFF. "I was finishing up a cake," I say. But she's already out of the room.

Juliet's eyes don't veer from the doorway where my sister disappeared. "And we were making sure she came in when she was done."

"No, you were waiting to see if Remy was going to cut into the cake right then," Tobin says.

"I know you were thinking the same thing. It is impossible to resist a cake that looks and smells as good as that one. It was like three layers of heaven iced in perfection."

Dad snakes an arm around my shoulder and squeezes me. "An irresistible three-layer cake, huh? Was your day that bad, kiddo?"

"Right now, every day is crap. You know that." But the cake—and Tobin and Juliet forcing their friendship on me—has dulled the worst of it. So at least I mean it when I add, "But I'm okay, Dad."

Maggie walks back into the kitchen and rejoins the conversation like she'd never left. "Dinner's ready as soon as the moms pick a wine."

That selection process takes another ten minutes, but when they're done we're all waiting for them in our seats at the dining room table. Dad and Tobin are at the ends, with Maggie, Juliet, and me crammed in on one side and the moms on the other. Maggie and Juliet put me next to Tobin in the least-sly move in history.

After we've all custom-built our salads from the half dozen toppings Maggie prepared, Tobin says, "Okay, I've gotta ask. How does cake equal a bad day?"

Dad answers before I can. "Oh, the girls' mom taught them from a young age to bake out their emotions. The more Remy needs to get out of her system, the more intense the recipe. And the better the end result."

He gets a serious case of dad-pride when he tells people about my baking skills. Usually it makes me want to stick my head in the oven—I mean when the scales are loaded with "bakes a mean cake" on one side and "curses boys" on the other, it's not hard to see which side wins out. But Tobin doesn't know all the bad that comes along with being me, so maybe the good can prevail for once.

I cross my fingers under the table, praying it will.

"It's pretty spectacular, really," Mom says.

"What about you, Maggie?" Juliet asks.

My sister shakes her head, a quiet laugh spilling out. "While Remy's able to channel her emotions into some really amazing eats, I tend to end up with catastrophe. I'm a decent baker normally—not anywhere close to Mom or Remy, but I can sell out a bake sale—but when my emotions are involved, it's like everything spews out of me onto a plate. It's not pretty."

"She's not kidding," I say. After the last mishap, Mom had banned her from the kitchen for a month and only let her back in when Maggie promised to never bake when she was upset ever again. "Remember that batch of brownies that exploded in the oven?"

Dad winks at me and says, "And the cupcakes that never cooked because you forgot the flour?"

Maggie grins. "Those have nothing on the caramel that hardened in the pan and I had to throw it away when I couldn't get it out. I thought Mom was going to disown me."

"I loved that pan. You're just lucky I love you more," Mom says.

"So, what you're saying is we should be grateful Remy's the one who had a rough day today?" Tobin asks.

"Yep," Maggie says. "Pretty much."

Juliet grabs my hand like she has something serious to say. "Well, if you ever need some place to dump off all your emotion-cakes, our doorstep is always available." She locks eyes with me and adds, "Not that I want you to have more crap days, but they kind of seem inevitable from everything I've heard. So, just sayin'."

"Don't you worry. There will be plenty of baking going on this year. You won't go hungry," I say. The one silver lining in all this is that by the time college applications come around, I'll have mastered every baking technique I could possibly need to know to wow culinary schools.

Mrs. Curcio eyes the three of us from across the table. She props her elbows on the wood, using her fork to gesture at Maggie and me. "I hear you two are quite popular with the boys. Do either of you have a serious boyfriend? Maybe one with a single friend for Juliet? She's good at developing friend-ships with girls, as you two have seen, but when it comes to boys—"

"Mom!" Juliet says. The word is both an admonishment and a plea to stop.

Tobin whispers, "C'mon, Mom. Not tonight."

"I just thought it might be nice for your sister to fit in here," she says.

"Oh, you have nothing to worry about. Juliet will fit in just fine," Mom says. "And I'm sure the girls would be more than happy to introduce her around."

Juliet's hands are curled in fists on the table. She takes deliberate breaths, slow and forceful through her nose.

Maggie shifts in her chair so her arm grazes Juliet's. Once they're touching, she doesn't move again. "Of course we will. And to answer your question, Mrs. Curcio, I'm not seeing anyone right now, so you never know who'll win my heart." She sneaks a side smile at Juliet. Then she adds, "And Remy's practically sworn off boys this year, so that expands the playing field considerably." The words slide out like honey, but there's something sharp hidden in between them.

Mrs. Curcio's wide eyes, the same intense gray blue as her kids', fly from me to Juliet and back again. It takes me a second to realize why she looks so worried. Then I replay Maggie's words in my mind and realize everything Juliet had said before dinner is written across her mother's face. But I don't contradict Maggie. In fact, I'm a little impressed with her boldness. I leave her implication out there to settle among the bowls of leftover chicken salad and pineapple chunks and chopped pecans.

"No boys, huh?" Juliet says. She leans over me and needles her index finger into Tobin's shoulder. He swats her hand away. But the tension from a few minutes before is gone, replaced with conspiratorial grins. "Looks like I'm going to have to fight you for her after all."

Mrs. Curcio chokes on her wine. Droplets of red dribble down her chin. Her napkin sits uselessly in her lap as she attempts to talk and coughs up more wine. Mom goes into instant hostess-mode, patting her on the back. I hand over my napkin to catch whatever hasn't already soaked into her shirt.

"You okay, Mom?" Tobin asks, taking the glass from his mom's shaky grip before the rest of the wine goes all over the table.

She coughs again but manages a croaky, "Yes."

Juliet shifts away from Maggie, "Sorry, Mom. I'll work on the timing of my jokes so they don't coincide with you taking a drink next time."

Mrs. Curcio dabs the napkin to the red splotches on her shirt hard enough to bruise. Then Mom leads her into the kitchen to get cleaned up. Dad stands to help, but Mom waves him back down.

Tobin and Juliet hold a silent conversation with each other through eyebrow raises, head tilts, and lip twitches.

Maggie's focus is still on Juliet. There's a slight hint of annoyance in the way her eyes squint. Like she doesn't want

Juliet to get the wrong idea about me. "Just so we're all clear, Remy's avoiding dating in general. She likes boys. She just doesn't *want* to like them right now."

No, I don't want to hurt them with my tainted magic. Big difference. "My love life is not up for discussion," I say, cutting in before Tobin gets any ideas.

Too late. He bites his lip rings to hold back a smile.

Holy hell. Just when I think I can keep him on the other side of the line I've drawn, he goes and pulls a move like that to make damn sure I'm thinking about nothing but his lips.

Cursed. Cursed. Cursed. The word cuts through my unproductive thoughts, reminding me that as long as Isaac is cursed, so am I. Everyone's safer if I forfeit the rest of the kissing season.

Juliet says, "I appreciate you waiting until my mom was out of earshot to make that announcement. She might not ever let me come over again after tonight, but thanks."

Tobin shakes his head, a smile teasing the corners of his mouth. "Temptation is everywhere, little sister. She's not going to let you leave the house."

Dad looks around the room, as if he can find where the conversation detoured into unfamiliar territory if he looks hard enough. My parents are progressive—all of Talus is, really—so Maggie dating a girl wouldn't faze him. But after a moment of silence from him, he gives up. And I'm a little disappointed he didn't offer some cool-parent advice to make Juliet feel better/welcomed/normal.

"Looks like we're about ready for dessert," he finally says, "so I'll go check on that and make sure everyone's okay in there."

We all nod, smile. Parents don't have a clue.

When he's gone, Maggie scoots closer to Juliet. Her face is pinched with nerves. "Is your mom really going to be pissed?"

"In her warped reality, I was attracted to a girl out of convenience, not because I looked at all the boys I'd grown up with and thought *meh*. And she thinks that moving us to a new place will fix that. Fix me. So, yeah, she's not going to be thrilled. But at some point, she's going to have to move into reality with the rest of us."

"You hope," Tobin says.

"Screw what she thinks," I say. I'm so done with people thinking they have any say in who someone loves. "If she locks you inside, Maggie and I'll come break you out."

We spend the next five minutes thinking up all the possible rescue scenarios we can—everything from positioning a trampoline under her window to cutting a hole in her bedroom floor to driving a car through the front window. Juliet enthusiastically approves of the ones that involve a little destruction. Then we come up with code words so Tobin can let us know she's in need of our assistance.

When our parents come back in, Mrs. Curcio with Rorschach-type splotches of wine on her shirt, we're in tears from laughing so hard over all of it.

Mom lists off the dessert options: my brown-sugar-caramel cake, strawberries and whipped cream, or salted-honey ice cream. Juliet raises her hand like she's in class and says she'd like a slice of cake and a scoop of ice cream. That's what everyone eats. Except Mrs. Curcio.

And for a moment, it feels like my luck just might change. All I have to do is open my heart to the possibility.

The music drifting from Tobin's open window a few hours later takes hold of me as soon as I step outside. The combination of the guitars and piano is haunting, broken, and perfect. There are no lyrics that I can hear, but I imagine they would fill the void in my chest so that, for a few minutes anyway, I would feel whole.

I tuck bars of this unknown song away to replay later when I'm not standing in the yard between our houses holding a cake box.

I should go to the door, ring the bell. I'm more likely to get Juliet not Tobin that way, but my mouth has a mind of its own. It calls his name. The music fades as the volume drops, and I half shout for him again, clenching my jaw to keep from smiling when he looks out the window and sees me. I shouldn't like his attention, but I can't make myself not care.

"What's that?" he asks.

"The rest of the cake. I forgot to send it with your sister when y'all left."

He checks over his shoulder at something in the room or farther inside the house. Then he climbs through the window and perches on the roof edge just long enough to steady himself. Then he jumps down to meet me. Of course he sticks the landing. "I'm sure you can be forgiven. Our family drama is a little distracting."

"Was Juliet serious earlier about your mom moving you here because of her?"

"That's her excuse this time."

"This time?"

"Since my dad died, we haven't stayed in one place for more than a year. It's like for a while Mom can convince herself that he's just on tour with his band and not actually gone. And then we settle into life without him, we start to move on, and she loses it. And then she comes up with some reason why we have to leave—the fact that Jet likes girls, or that my friend's brother is a tattoo artist and gave me one despite me being underage, or that she went to a psychic who said Dad's spirit was waiting for us in some obscure town where he'd played a show once—and moves us someplace new. And we go through it all over again."

"I'm sorry. I didn't know he was *gone*. I just thought he was—" There's no way to end this sentence without sticking my foot further in my mouth, so I don't. "What happened to him?" I cringe when I realize I've asked it out loud.

"He OD'd when we were fourteen," Tobin says after a few seconds. His voice comes out flat, no hint of how losing his dad—and in that way—must have shattered him three years before. "Apparently that was the thing to do for grunge rockers in the nineties. Dad might've been a few decades late, but you know, if you're following in somebody's footsteps, you've got to go all in."

"I shouldn't have asked. I'm sorry."

"No, it's not you. Most of the time, I think I've come to terms with it. With how and why he died. And then Mom slips off the sanity wagon or I think about all the things I don't get to share with him because he's not here, and I'm right back in the thick of losing him all over again." He flips open the box lid, breaks off a hunk of cake and icing with his fingers and pops it in his mouth, effectively putting an end to his unguarded sharing.

I've been so focused on my magic-induced problems, I'd forgotten there are other people out there who are struggling so much more than I am. To keep from triggering him further, I shift the conversation ever so slightly. "Is that why you were listening to a song that felt like having my heart ripped out when I first came over?"

Tobin's gaze snaps to mine, his eyes unreadable in the dark. "How long were you out there listening?"

"Just from the kitchen door to outside your window. Please tell me you're not one of those music snobs who only likes a band when no one else knows who they are."

"Did you miss the part earlier where my dad was in a band? I'm all for musicians finding success and having their work heard by as many people as possible."

"Good," I say. And then I bite the inside of my cheek in a last-ditch effort to condition myself to associate Tobin with pain. Because if I let this go anywhere, that's all I'll be left with when it's over.

13

TOBIN'S NOT THE ONLY boy I have to worry about. A few days later, Felix sets up camp in our side yard. Scanning the boxes and plastic tubs scattered around him, I shake my head. He has collected hundreds of seemingly random items and what looks to be a schematic of some type taped to the windows of the baking kitchen.

"What are you doing?" I demand when I walk outside, grateful it's Felix and not someone coming to take out their frustration from Isaac's latest run-in with bad luck on me.

Felix whips his head up to look at me, a grin cracking his face. He squints against the sunlight. "You weren't supposed to see this yet. Just pretend you didn't see me here, okay?"

"Can't do that because it looks like you're Rube Goldberg-ing my yard."

"I am. But it will all make sense when I'm done."

If it was any of Isaac's friends other than Felix, I'd worry the machine is designed to fling knives at me or something equally hazardous to my health. Being Felix, it's probably harmless. But I'm not taking any chances. "And why would I let you finish? It's going to take you hours."

"'Cause I'm doing it for you. I didn't just want to leave your gift on the doorstep. I wanted to do something over the top so you'd see that I'm for real and maybe reconsider kissing me this season."

Why would Felix even want to kiss me let alone go out of his way to get my attention knowing that Isaac's bad luck streak is still going strong?

"I like you, Felix." He pumps a fist in the air, grinning like I just told him he won the lottery. I rush to clarify, "Not like that. You're a sweet guy, and I don't want you to take this the wrong way, but us kissing is not going to happen. So you can pack it all up and go home. Save yourself some effort and disappointment."

He pulls out a skateboard and a bike wheel from one of the plastic tubs and lays them on the ground, taking stock, no intention of following my suggestion. "You don't have to be worried about me. Maggie said you just need to kiss someone else and everything will be cool. No more bad luck."

"Wait, Maggie told you to come try to what, woo me?" What the hell is she thinking? Telling people the bad luck will be lifted if I kiss someone else is beyond irresponsible. Even if she doesn't believe I'm cursed, she should know I'd never risk kissing anyone until I know Isaac is okay no matter how many guys throw themselves at me.

"Not this exactly," he says.

"But she told you to try and get me to kiss you?"

"Yeah. I mean, not me specifically. She was talking to a whole bunch of us at Haight Plaza a few days ago, but most of the guys didn't believe her. I figured I've got a pretty good shot. Especially after you see this when I'm done."

I grab the skateboard, a little tempted to know what role it plays in this whole machine, and drop it back into the container. "I don't need to see your contraption in action. Even if it is epic. I can't kiss you."

"*Can't* is different from *don't want to*."

"In this case, it's both, That goes for anyone who is desperate enough to listen to my sister. Will you make sure everyone knows that? Please."

His copper-brown eyes narrow as he studies me. "I don't get it, Remy. Don't you want to clear your name? Don't you want to help Isaac? Why won't you try?"

I want to fix this more than anything. But if I admit that now, he won't stop trying to kiss me until the season is over. "Why are you here building whatever this machine is if that's what you think of me?"

"Hey, I'm not judging you. Seriously," he adds when I roll

my eyes. "I'm just putting it out there that I'm willing to be your guinea pig if you have any theories you need to test out. Especially if it involves some tongue-on-tongue action." He waggles his eyebrows at me, eliciting a laugh.

"Duly noted." Felix digs a small box out of his pocket and hands it to me. "It would've been cooler if you'd let me finish and this came flying at you at the end, but here."

"You don't need to give me anything," I say.

"I want to. It's nothing really. Just saw it and thought of you."

Opening the box, I can't help but laugh. Inside is an enamel pin in the shape of a chocolate and vanilla whoopie pie that says "making whoopie!"

"It's perfect," I say, pinning it to my shirt.

"Now if you'll excuse me, I have theories to hypothesize."

Felix isn't wrong. I do need to try harder to find a way to break the curse. After my initial failed attempts, I've let myself get distracted. I just need one idea that works. Preferably something that doesn't involve kissing anyone.

My eyes drift toward the Curcios' house—to the bedroom window across from mine. There I go letting Tobin distract me again. I need to focus. Dragging the curtains shut, I vow to do better. But clearly I can't be trusted on my own. A task this vital requires supervision. I sit on my bed with the Book of Luck open on my lap and message Laurel an SOS.

Her reply is immediate: Is your sister home?

Me: No, it's safe.

Less than ten minutes later, she's settled onto my bed too, poring over good luck entries in the book.

"This is a little ridiculous," she says, her finger paused hallway down one Holloway girl's listing.

Ignoring the sting, I ask, "The fact that I'm supposedly the only Holloway girl to curse someone?"

"No, the luck in general. Have you read some of these?"

Everyone in Talus knows about the Holloway luck. But I guess knowing about it and reading actual accounts of the luck my ancestors have given out is a little more of a mind-fuck. "All of them. Too many times to count. Gun to my head, I could probably recite the whole book word for word."

She flips to a random page and tilts the book so I can't see. "Okay, then tell me what kind of luck Phillip Williamson received."

"You're supposed to be helping me investigate these lucky people, not grill me on them. Plus there's a distinct lack of a gun in this scenario," I say.

"You and I both know it's a metaphorical gun. So, Phillip."

I flop back on the bed and throw my arm over my eyes. "Fine. Phillip Williamson kissed Millie Holloway and years later returned home after six months missing at sea with a pocketful of gold coins and tales of a storm that swallowed him whole, then spit him back out on the shores of an island where he secured transportation back home in exchange for the location of the treasure he'd discovered. Happy now?"

"No. That one might have been too easy. Who forgets epic pirate treasure? What about perfectly nondescript John Smith?"

"John kissed Virginia Holloway and spent the last of his savings on un-farmable farmland on the top of a mountain in Tennessee. I imagine everyone laughed at him for that move, but the book doesn't say that. He built greenhouses on the land and transplanted a lone orchid plant from his family home back in England to turn his little nursery into the largest orchid grower in the South."

There are hundreds more stories like that. Assuming all of the stories of good luck manifesting are true.

"All the names in here, they're all people who kissed the Holloway girl whose page they're on?" Laurel asks. She's skipped ahead to Maggie's page. To her name listed below a dozen others waiting for their luck to be documented.

"Yeah, but it—"

"So, what exactly do you need help with?"

I roll with the subject change, taking the book from her and finding a less-triggering Holloway to start with. "We're fact-checking. Looking to see if any of the names in here had any bad luck before things turned around. If I can find one, maybe there's also a clue somewhere to how they did it."

"So, needle in a proverbial haystack?" she asks.

"More like the broken tip of a needle in a stack of needles."

"With optimism like that, how can we fail?"

Failing is not an option. "Let's start with lucky Phillip Williamson and see how he ended up in a shipwreck in the first place."

14

OUR SEARCH COMES UP empty. More than twenty names and good luck all around. By the end of the week, I'm ready to chuck the Book of Luck into the trash.

It, however, is much luckier than I am.

It's safe on the nightstand when, on Thursday, I get roped into running a delivery up the mountain for Mom because Maggie took off with Juliet this morning and she's not answering her phone.

"Oh, good, you're here," Mom says. Before I've even closed the trailer door behind me, she loads me down with two cake boxes and spins me around again. "Put them on the floorboards, please. Mrs. Chastain will have my head if they're smeared all over the sides of the box."

"I'll be careful."

"Thank you for doing this. I know you aren't keen on

taking deliveries right now, but I figured this one might not be so bad." The words *right now* practically burst with all the things unsaid. Mom's been good not to push me too hard about the season. After our initial talk about what happened with Isaac, she's given me space to decide what *I* want. Not that I've figure that out yet.

"I'm more than happy doing official Wild Flour deliveries. As long as I'm on my own." Plus, this one means I get drive up the mountain, which is always a thrill.

She follows me outside and runs a hand over my hair when I stop at Dad's Jeep. Maggie took our car when she snuck off this morning. "I know you are, lovey. But things haven't exactly been easy for you lately. I don't ever want you to think your dad and I aren't here for you. If you need to talk, come talk. If you need to bake, just tell me what ingredients you need and the kitchen's yours. Just try and find a way to be happy, okay?"

I nod because I don't have it in me to lie to her.

Mom nods back, and I can't help but wonder what she's not saying.

Driving up the mountain gives me this weird rush of happiness that shoots all the way into my bones. It won't last—happiness never does these days—but I revel in it just the same. There is absolutely nothing like zipping around the final curve where the steep climb up comes to an abrupt end and there's the town spread out below, haloed by a ring of wispy clouds. It's breathtaking. Every. Damn. Time.

The lanes are narrow, and in a few places I have to cut into the opposite lane to swing wide enough to make the turn. The first time I drove this road I was convinced I was going to run into the side of the mountain or straight off the plunging cliff side on one of those hairpin turns, but Maggie had sat in the back seat, one hand snaked between my seat and the driver's-side door, rubbing a calming hand on my shoulder while Dad had talked me through it. Now I drive it on reflex. A quick glance up to make sure the lane's free and then I'm off and around the bend and on to the next one. And up and up and up.

I pull onto the shoulder near the top where a highway sign encourages tourists to stop for a scenic photo op and soak it all in. Up here, it's peaceful, perfect. I can forget about the handful of wilted wildflowers twined with poison ivy that I found on my doorstep a few days ago compliments of a disgruntled luck seeker or one of Isaac's crew and the anonymous phone calls that are nothing more than someone recording the angry gush and rumble of the falls onto my voicemail. Turning my face into the cool wind blowing in through the open window, I close my eyes and whisper a prayer to the universe to let this feeling last forever.

Then a car roars by on the road, close enough to rock my car side to side, and it brings reality crashing back.

Moment of zen gone, I steer back onto the road, tires screaming when I hit the gas a little too hard. Luckily no one's around to cite me for careless and reckless driving. Or to see that my eyes are a little too wet for my liking.

Parked in the gravel lot at the trail entrance as I drive by is an old, navy Acura that makes me do a double take. It's Tobin's. And even with me actively trying to avoid him, I'm aware that it only starts half of the time, so the fact that it made it all the way up the mountain without crapping out on the side of the road is damn near a miracle. I also hadn't realized he'd befriended anyone to get invited out to the falls. But since he's here he must've made friends with someone.

Shoving the pang of jealousy that gives me to the side, I turn into the circular drive that runs in front of the B&B. I only check out his car in the rearview once.

The house-turned-inn is this old behemoth of a building with stone arches running along the bottom story and wooden beams and walls of windows up on top. It's the oldest building on the mountain, built back when this was a summer vacation spot for those who could afford it. Once, I'd thought I'd get married here, out on the back veranda overlooking the town. Now I just want to drop off the cakes before the romance of the place can get under my skin and start to tempt me to re-open my heart.

Mrs. Chastain greets me at the door. Her knobby fingers, curled with arthritis or too much knitting—I don't know which—reaches for the top box, but I turn just in time to save the cake from her iffy grip.

"Oh, I've got them," I say. "Do you want them back in the kitchen?"

"If you insist." Though her body looks like it's creeping closer to the final stages of giving up, her voice is still sharp, as are her eyes. She shuffles after me, the scuffing of her shoes' rubber soles ricocheting off the vaulted ceiling and exposed rafter beams, making the noise sound like dozens of invisible mice running rampant.

Mismatched teacups are laid out on the equally mis-matched tables in the dining room, which smells like lemon wood polish and freshly cut flowers. Something about it is so comforting and homey it makes me smile. Mrs. Chastain catches me and wrinkles a smile onto her mouth in return. Then she scoots past to get the swinging door that leads from the dining room into the kitchen. If it was anybody but her, I would probably scowl just to prove I wasn't enjoying myself, but she's already moved on like my smile was nothing, so I let that go too.

"How's your kissing season coming along?" she asks after

I've set the boxes down on one of the chipped and yellowing counters.

Seriously? Why does every freakin' person in this town think who I kiss—or don't kiss, for that matter—is any of their business? I briefly contemplate tracking down a T-shirt I saw on TV that said *Ask Me About My STDs*. Wearing that might make people think twice about talking to me. But knowing these people, probably not. In the end, I just say, "Just over one month down. Only ten-plus more to go."

"My boy, Gerald, spent quite a few months pining for your mother back when they were kids. He was shy and never quite sure of himself. I always hoped she'd see something in him that others missed and give him one good smackeroo so he'd get up the gumption to do something really spectacular with his life."

"Did she?"

"She never even batted an eye at him. But I haven't lost hope yet. My grandson's about your age. Maybe he'll have better luck with you."

Her grandson, Ed, is in my grade at school. He's a nice enough guy, with more friends than me. Though I guess that's not really saying much at this point. "Maybe," I say. I'm not in the business of crushing old ladies' dreams.

Her hope is so great it digs deep crevices into her face when she smiles at me. "You kiss who you want, dear. But if my Eddie's one of them, I wouldn't be upset."

It's impossible that she hasn't heard about Isaac's accident. Or my role in it. She's been around long enough to witness a few Holloway girls' kissing seasons. Maybe something she knows is the link I've been missing to finally break the curse.

"Do you remember if anything strange or bad has happened to anyone during the kissing season?"

"You mean like what happened to the Fuller boy who got hurt jumping from the falls a month back?"

I nod.

Mrs. Chastain pops the flap of the cake box open and inhales the coconutty scent. Reaching inside, she lifts the hummingbird cake by the cardboard base and motions for me to position a crystal stand where she can slide the cake into place on it. Once it's safely transferred, she lowers the glass lid over it. Then she looks at me as if just remembering I've asked her a question and says, "If memory serves, there were a couple young boys Gerald knew who talked about trying to trick your aunt into kissing them during her season."

Aunt Jenna never mentioned that. Did Mom ask her not to tell me so I wouldn't keep digging into our family's past? I brace a hand on the counter to keep from shaking the truth right out of her. "Really? What happened to them?"

"They didn't go through with it as far as I know. They were too scared of breaking the rules. They would have rather had no luck than risk getting hit with whatever breaking the rules would have done. I think you'll be hard pressed to find anyone who's been on the receiving end of one of your family's kisses who has anything negative to say."

I want to tell her Isaac would disagree, but that won't change the fact that she doesn't know anything that will help me. I'm beginning to think nothing will. "Right. Thanks anyway."

Turning toward the door, I move to leave before I ruin her good mood. She follows me out and pats my arm as if touching me might somehow give Ed an edge. Poor guy would be mortified if he knew his grandma was acting as wingman. I shrug out of her hold as politely as I can.

Heading for the Jeep, I can't shake the feeling that she might be right and no matter how hard I look, I'll never find the answers I need.

Mrs. Chastain's hope trails me across the parking lot. My hand slides around the Jeep door handle, two seconds from being in the clear, when someone calls out to me, freezing the motion cold.

The sound of my name on Isaac's tongue, spoken in his husky voice after all this time, jolts through my body. We haven't spoken since that night at the falls. His voice scrapes me raw. What could he possibly want from me now?

Isaac shouts my name again, louder, with a hint of desperation. Like I'm the one who's been avoiding him and he'll do anything for even a few seconds of my time.

That hurts more than it should. But I can't make myself open the car door. Can't make myself move one effing muscle or even begin to flee. I'm about as stupid as an ostrich when it comes to self-preservation.

Then he's walking toward me from the parking lot at the falls where he's double-parked behind one of his friends, picking his way slowly across the gravel to the pavement. And I'm still rooted to the spot, white-knuckling the door handle. What is he doing up here in his condition? Is he even well enough to be out of his house? It's been five weeks since he was hurt, and I can't imagine his fractured ribs have healed completely yet.

"Just wait, please," he says between labored breaths when he reaches me, one hand held out toward me. His fingers snake out farther and trail across the skin just above my wrist. Barely even a touch.

That's all it takes my brain to kick-start. I shake loose of his hold, guiding his hand to the side of the car for support. "What do you want, Isaac?"

His eyes lock on mine. "I just want to talk to you." The spaces between words are punctuated with deep breaths as his lungs struggle to keep up.

This would be so much easier if there was anything in his gaze besides the heat of blame staring back at me.

"No, you don't," I say, as much to remind myself as him. "You never did."

"That's not true. On either count. I just didn't know how to talk to you without it being weird."

Digging my fingernails into my arms, I let the sharp pain bite, but it refuses to obliterate what's building in my chest. Like I don't have enough guilt inside me already. "Then why are you trying to now?"

"Because I can't take it anymore. Getting hurt, having everything I love taken away from me. My dad. Hannah. When she realized the only luck I'd gotten was bad, she ended things for good. Guess you were right about her after all. Now I just want to move on. You're the only one who can give me my life back. So please just tell me what I need to do to make you fix this."

"Isaac, please don't—"

"No, listen, I already told my friends to leave you alone. At least about what happened to me. I don't know that they'll listen, but I want you to know that whatever they do, it's not coming from me. I shouldn't keep getting punished for what they do."

"*I'm* not punishing anyone," I say. Wrenching open my door, I nudge him back a step so I can get in. "I didn't mean for any of this to happen to you, and I'm sorry. I really am.

But don't you think if I knew how to fix you I would've done it by now?"

"There has to be something you can do," he says, his voice taking on a frantic edge.

How many times have I thought that exact thing over the past few weeks? Telling him I've tried and failed will take away what little hope he has left. "You would think that."

He stops the door from closing, holding it open wide enough to duck his head down and peer at me. The last time we were this close I'd given my heart over to the magic, trusting it to give me what I'd wanted in return. For a moment, I wonder if maybe Maggie got it partially right about needing to kiss someone again. But the person I need to kiss to set things right is Isaac. Kissing is what triggered the bad luck, so there's a possibility that's what might end it too.

It wouldn't take any effort at all to close the distance.

But what if another kiss makes things worse? That's not a risk I'm willing to take yet.

When I tug the door, Isaac releases it, and I lock it for good measure. He presses a hand to the window, the long curving lines on his palms mapping out a future I don't know how to read, then walks away, leaving me alone in the car. I squeeze my eyes tight, hating that part of me that wants to ask him to come back.

15

WHEN I GET TO Bold Rock Outfitters to drop off Dad's Jeep after the trip up the mountain, the shop is packed. Tourists and locals alike are making good use of the perfect late-July weather. I wind my way past the fifty-dollar T-shirts and three-hundred-dollar jackets and the kayaks and packs of dehydrated food to the climbing wall in the back corner of the room.

Dad's tethered to a customer, who's two-thirds of the way up the wall. "Hey, kiddo," he says, dropping his gaze to me just long enough to toss me a smile. My run-in with Isaac must show on my face because he adds, "Want to go up next?"

I can't remember the last time I strapped into a harness and spent time on the wall. Or did anything outdoorsy, for that matter. Rock climbing was the one area of my life where I'd spent more time with a friend than with Maggie since Paige had loved the thrill of climbing as much as I did. We'd race each other to the top and see if we could land a high five as we repelled back down. Meanwhile, my sister would sit on a blanket far below us, teaching herself how to execute intricate braids.

In the past few years, Maggie put her foot down about being dragged along, refusing to climb, hike, and camp—all the things we'd grown up doing. And since we'd done everything as a pair, I'd given it all up too. I think it broke Dad's heart a little.

"You're busy." Saying no is a reflex. One that suddenly feels wrong. Maybe I can't be the girl I was at the start of the summer, but she's not the only version of myself I've left behind.

"Only for the next few minutes. Then I'm all yours," he says.

Who knows if I even have a speck of talent left, but trying has to be better than doing nothing. "Okay. I'll give it a go."

His smile nearly breaks his face. "That's my girl."

My resolve lasts long enough for me to grab a scuffed pair of rental shoes and a harness from the storeroom. My palms are damp when I pull the harness over my hips and tighten the straps at my waist. What if I've forgotten everything he taught me? I don't want him to watch me fail at this, too, like I've failed at the season.

Dad nods his approval as he checks the security of my harness. "Doing okay, Rem?"

"Shouldn't you wait to ask that until I'm actually on the wall?" I force a laugh to expel some of my nerves along with it.

"I'm trying to gauge where you are before you go up. Make sure your head's clear."

Checking over his shoulder into the front of the store, I realize people are staring. My reputation for being the un-lucky Holloway girl has changed what people expect from me. Instead of watching to see who I'll kiss, they now look for signs of bad luck in my wake. "I'm good, Dad," I say because giving up now feels like letting them win.

"If it'll help, I can put up a sign on the front window," he says. "Something like, 'If you're not here to buy, take a hike!'"

"Punny and effective."

"I'm also serious."

He'd run off every customer before admitting I was the one who needed to go. He's good like that. Just wants Maggie and me to be happy and safe. Most likely in that order. "I'm okay. Really. You don't need to worry."

"A little bit of Dad Insider Info," he says, leaning close like he's going to whisper it. "I'm always worrying about you." He tugs on my hair, then holds my gaze to make sure I hear the truth of it beneath his teasing tone.

"You're wasting your time, then, because I am just fine."

Maybe one of these days he'll believe me. Maybe I will too.

He tightens his grip on the rope when I attempt to tug it from his hands and tie in. "I don't think you are, Rem."

"We really don't have to talk about this."

"Yes, we do. I know you're still hurting after what happened between you and Isaac." He doesn't look at me as he talks, as if he feels obligated to have this conversation but, like me, he'd rather be doing anything else. "First love inflicts a special kind of pain when it ends. One that never truly leaves you. But you can't close yourself off to the season or to whatever great love might be waiting out there for you because it didn't go the way you'd hoped the first time."

There will be no great love in my future, though. Not if I can't find a way to reverse Isaac's curse and restore my reputation as a Holloway girl. Because if I can't fix this, Mom may as well just strike my name right out of the Book of Luck and pretend like I was never even here.

"This isn't first love gone wrong." I spin the lock on a carabiner hooked on my harness at my hip, directing the next words at the floor. "I kissed Isaac, and it almost killed him."

Dad rubs the back of his neck, like my words are finally getting through. But instead of letting it go, he exhales a long breath that carries away any of his own words that might have agreed with me before they can make a sound. Then he says, "He got hurt because he was reckless with your heart and the magic."

"Please, Dad." It's just a whisper. A breath breaking into a thousand shards. "I know you're trying to help, but this isn't doing it. In fact, this is pretty much the opposite. I love you for trying to fix this—fix me—but you can't. No one can. And the sooner you all come to terms with that, the better. For all of us."

He stills my fidgeting with calloused fingers. "All right. I'll drop it for now. But, Remy, if you need to talk about any of it, I'm here. And I promise to listen—I mean really listen— to whatever you need to say about your mom or sister or the season. Even if you think I won't want to hear it or agree with you. No judgment."

The fight seeps out of me along with any retort I might have spit at him out of habit. "Thanks. I don't plan on needing it, but I appreciate the offer."

"Well, I'm here if you change your mind."

I nod, my throat too tight for words to escape. Dad's love is unconditional. I just wish I deserved it. Isaac may have faked his feelings for me, but I was so intent on kissing him I let my feelings for him blind me to the truth.

"Ready to go up?" he asks.

"I thought you'd never ask."

After tying into one end of the top rope, I step up to the wall. I tip my head back, sliding a breath through my lips as I scan the curved holds creating a maze of colors leading toward the ceiling. Then I climb. My first few moves are clumsy, my fingers fumbling on the holds and my feet hesitating before each step. Dad calls out encouragement and corrections to my form. I keep going. Higher and higher and higher. My muscles burn and shake and threaten to give up even as I grow more confident that I will reach the top. I shed my heartache like a second skin, letting it coil into a translucent pile on the floor below me.

And for a few minutes, I am free.

I'm on such a high from my climb that I almost miss her when I start my walk home. Hannah.

She's getting a piggyback ride from Trip Lancaster. With his hands busy holding her legs in place around his waist, Hannah presses against his back to offer him a taste of her chocolate ice cream that's melting down the cone and onto her hand. He licks the drips from her fingers instead. She retaliates by licking the side of his face, and her peal of laughter is like barbed wire slicing into my skin.

Why does she get to move on, to be practically dry humping Trip in the middle of town, and no one bats an eye? Hannah might not have magic in her veins, but she cursed Isaac long before I did.

Everyone makes my life hell now, I may as well share the hate.

I check to make sure Dad didn't follow me out and walk right into their path. Trip stops short and winds up with their half-eaten ice cream smooshed in his face when Hannah jerks backward. Trip and I stare at each other for all of a second before we both bust out laughing. Hannah scrambles out of his loosening grip, throwing the rest of the ice cream on the sidewalk.

Mission accomplished.

"What is wrong with you?" she asks.

"I could ask you the same thing. Did you actually wait for Isaac to get out of the hospital before deciding he was no longer interesting enough to even pretend to care about him?"

Hannah meets my accusation with a defiant smirk. "Says the girl who put him in the hospital."

"I didn't make him jump. Isaac did that all on his own."

"Are you seriously trying to blame this on Isaac?" She looks to Trip, securing a witness for the admission to come.

Holding on to the last shred of confidence from my climb, I set the truth free. "No. This is all your fault. You broke him first. Every time you left him for some other guy, then begged him to take you back when you got bored. Every time you realized he still loved you and would never tell you no. You've been hurting him for years, only it wasn't physical so no one called you on it. Not even Isaac. Do you even know the reason he kissed me that night?"

"Isaac wanted good luck," Hannah says, her voice acidic. She latches on to Trip's hand, laying claim to him as if my goal in life is to steal him away from her. "Just like every other guy in this town."

"He wanted good luck for *you*. He kissed me so you'd finally have a reason to stay with him. And you couldn't even do that when he actually needed you."

"Isaac's the one who broke up with *me*. And then while he was in the hospital, I was trying to be a good girlfriend again."

"Right. I can tell you're really heartbroken over him." I side-eye Trip, who has the good sense to look a tiny bit guilty.

"What? So, I'm supposed to stay with a guy who has no future, whose only claim to fame will be that he kissed a Holloway girl and got himself cursed? That's not a life I'd sign up for even if I did still love him."

"You've got a real keeper here, Trip."

He flashes me an unapologetic grin. I guess how she treated Isaac doesn't matter as long as she's done with him now.

Hannah steps over the puddle of chocolate ice cream to whisper, "You can blame me all you want, Remy. But we all know it was your magic that ruined him. There's nothing any of us can do to help him now."

16

HANNAH'S WORDS HAUNT ME the rest of the day. If I hadn't kissed Isaac the first chance I got, if I'd waited just a little bit longer to make certain he wasn't harboring feelings for Hannah, maybe then I'd have seen his charm for what it was instead of blindly handing him my heart.

Changing any one of those things might have made all the difference.

But since I can't go back and change the past, I don't have the luxury of being picky when it comes to possible fixes for Isaac's bad luck. Which means kissing him again can't be off the table just because I don't want to do it.

Now that I'm no longer clouded by my feelings for him and he's free of his feelings for Hannah, it just might work. So when Maggie and Juliet pass my room the next night on their way to Nightfall, the free, Friday-night cover band concerts at

Haight Plaza, I decide to put my new theory to the test. The band tonight is one Isaac likes, so I can bet on finding him there.

The plaza itself, with its micro-amphitheater and lush patches of grass arcing around, is a favorite hangout for kids from school. Especially during the school year when driving up the mountain and hiking down to Firelight Falls isn't feasible before the sun goes down. But even in the summer when they can't lounge on the two tiers of brick seating with their homework or an after-school snack from one of the adjacent food trucks, they're still there for the bands that play every week. This summer, I only come out here on days when the rain soaks through my clothes in seconds or on nights when it's late enough that most kids have been called home by their parents. But since Isaac will in all likelihood be here for the concert, I'll have to deal with the abundance of people tonight.

The opening band is already on stage, decked out in spandex pants and cheap wigs, cranking out some guitar-heavy classic rock song when I arrive at the plaza. For just a moment, I forget my mission and lose myself in the music/energy/normality. My head rocks to the beat, and a smile sneaks its way onto my face.

It's impossible to be dead to the world when there's music lighting it up. Lighting *me* up.

One song. Two max. I can allow myself to enjoy that much

at least. My mind drifts to Tobin, to his musician dad. Had his dad played at Nightfall in one of these no-name bands? Is that why his mom chose to move them to Talus? He's not here to ask. Not that I ever would. Tonight, I'm here for Isaac. And if I succeed, maybe then there's more I can do than just *think* about Tobin.

The sun's finally dropped behind the mountain, casting the center of downtown in a murky twilight. The lines for the food trucks run twenty people deep. The beer tent set up on the far side of the plaza is twice as busy. With Lumina Street closed off to traffic for the night, bodies spill into the road, dancing and knotting together to shout over the music pumping from speakers at the top of the small amphitheater.

I spot Juliet near the front of the line for grilled cheese sandwiches—Maggie's and my Nightfall dinner staple. Her hair's done up in this intricate fishtail braid, and her lips are glossy with a shade of pink that makes her skin all soft and rosy and glowing. Maggie's handiwork, no doubt. I'm being replaced one activity at a time.

And just like that, the emptiness in my chest expands, snuffing out the light that had worked its way in.

I turn away and shove through the wall of sweaty limbs pressing in on me. Anything to get to a place where I can breathe. Where the thought that I've finally pushed my sister too far away can't touch me.

And anyway, I'm not here for Maggie tonight. I'm here to kiss Isaac and put this whole craptastic start to my kissing season behind me. Turning away from them, I channel what's left of the old me. I just need to be like her long enough to convince Isaac this will work—okay, long enough to convince myself too.

"Boy problems?" Tobin asks, yanking me out of my internal pep talk. He looks at home in a crowd of concertgoers with his styled-to-look-messy hair and monochromatic clothes. His thumbs are hooked in his jeans pockets, and his fingers keep time with the music on his thigh.

I relax my face so I don't look like I was thinking about him a few minutes before and give him a nonanswer. "On a scale of one to burning the world down around me, I'm probably only at a six. So, there's a ways to go yet."

A whistle, long and sharp, slides out between his teeth. "Wow. I'd hate to see what necessitates total world destruction."

Isaac is the closest I've come. Since our kiss, I've hated everything enough to want it all to disappear. "Me too," I say and smile as if reaching my breaking point isn't even a possibility.

Tobin buys it. It's surprising how easy it is to pass off a lie as the truth when you really want to. I walk away before he can spot the difference.

Thankfully, he doesn't follow. The last thing I need is for Tobin to think this can go anywhere.

When I find Isaac, he's with Felix and Seth. They're the living embodiments of an angel and devil perched on his shoulders—one who would advise Isaac to at least listen to what I have to say and one who would rather see me burn.

They're sitting on one of the wooden barricades that block the streets surrounding Haight Plaza from traffic. A plastic cup—most likely Coke spiked with rum—is being passed back and forth between the three of them. At the edge of the plaza farthest from the stage, they'll be able to finish it off before anyone catches them drinking.

"Hey, Isaac," I call, still a few feet away. They all turn at the same time like a three-headed dog. Isaac shakes off Seth's arm that hooks around his shoulders to keep him from standing and closing the distance. "Can we talk?" I point down the street, away from his friends. Away from anyone who could see what I'm about to do.

Isaac takes the cup from Felix and downs half of what's left in one gulp before handing it back. Then he's extracting himself from them and climbing over the barricade, using his friends' shoulders as leverage to make it over without falling on his face. "Yeah. Sure."

"You can't be serious," Seth says.

"She just wants to talk," Isaac counters.

If only. But I can't tell him what I want to do with an audience. Especially not an audience that would rather stone me to death than let my lips anywhere near their friend again. I've lost count of the *I told you so*s and *None of this would've happened if*s Seth's thrown at me.

Felix's expression is equal parts longing and disappointment that I'm not here for him. When Seth smacks his arm, he mostly snaps out of it. For the moment at least. "Just make it back before the main band goes on," Felix says.

Isaac calls a half-hearted "Yeah, okay" over his shoulder and joins me where I stand.

I don't trust myself to talk until we're tucked away into an alley between two buildings out of view. The light from the plaza only makes it a few inches in, the noise of the crowd dulled by the bricks. "I'm not really here to talk."

"Okay. What do you want then?"

"I want to try and fix this."

He's close enough that I smell the alcohol on his breath. "Yesterday you said you didn't know how."

"I don't. Not for sure. But there's a chance that kissing again could reset the magic." My voice is steady, belying nothing of the way I'm shaking inside.

"What kind of odds are we talking? Ten percent? Twenty-five?" he asks.

"I don't know. But I'm willing to try if you are." It's not like I have any other options.

He peers around the corner of the building, as if his friends might overhear what we're talking about from twenty feet away. When he turns back to me, he says, "Like…right now?"

"I don't see a reason to wait. It's not like I expect you to take me to dinner first." The words are out before I can stop them, little daggers of *I don't give a damn* poised to rip this whole plan to shreds before it even gets started.

Isaac dips his head, avoiding eye contact. The dim light catches on a half-moon-shaped scar on his temple. If it's recent, it's not part of my list. "You really want to do this now? Here?"

"That was the plan. But if you don't want to, I can go." Calling his bluff is my best shot at making this happen. It's either kiss him again or give up before we've even tried. I'm going with the lesser of two evils.

"No, I do want to." He wets his lips. He's already made his decision, but if he tells Seth he caved without any sort of fight, he'll never hear the end of it. So, he says, "Does this mean you think it will work?"

"All I know is that if we do nothing, you might stay cursed forever." And I'll spend the rest of my life chasing after love but never being able to catch/hold/keep it. Everything with Isaac might have scared me off of love during the kissing season, but it's still something I want eventually. "I'm willing to try anything to make sure that doesn't happen. Are you?"

He catches my hand, trapping it between both of his. "Do you even have to ask that?"

"Apparently. You're the one stalling, not me."

"Forgive me for being a little gun-shy. The last time we kissed, it ruined my life."

Yeah, like mine's been a bucket of rainbows. I yank my hand free from his grasp and stumble back a step. I point at him to stay where he is. "The last time we didn't follow the rules. Tonight we will."

He's looking at me the way he did at the start of the summer. With hope and awe crinkling the edges of his eyes and the corners of his mouth ticked up in a hint of a smile. "That'll make it safe to kiss you now?"

"As long as you swear you're not still in love with Hannah or anyone else."

"I am one hundred percent done with Hannah. I swear. I might be a slow learner where she's concerned, but I finally understand she's never going to change, and being in love with her for so long was kind of a curse in itself. So, we're all good on that front."

This time I believe him. If I'm wrong, things could always get worse. But I have to risk it to free myself, so I lean closer to him before I lose my resolve. It's just a few millimeters of space different than we were, but it's enough to push me over my last holding-back threshold. He lifts his head, his lips parted just enough for air and secrets to slip through, and I reach out, letting my hand follow the curve of his jaw. The kiss is like a song with no lyrics. Strong beat, decent composition, but it's missing some vital ingredient to make me feel it all the way to my soul. There's no tingling, no electric current dancing up my skin.

And I know without a doubt, there's no magic in this kiss.

17

THE RUMOR MILL HAS been eerily silent in the week since I kissed Isaac. No new bad luck. And no new harassment from his friends. But as much as I want to believe the kiss did its job this time around, I can't shake the lingering hollowness that followed it.

Whatever feelings I had for Isaac that fueled the magic of our first kiss are long gone. And with them, I'm guessing, any chance our second kiss had of reversing the curse.

There are still a handful of boys tempted by the Holloway luck, though. The email I find waiting in my inbox this morning with a link to a private playlist in SoundCloud is proof enough that at least one of them is still intent on winning a kiss. I have no way of knowing who sent it. Because the playlist is marked private by this anonymous suitor, it's unsearchable, untraceable, un-everything-able. The sender's email address is just as useless: RemysMusicalEducation@gmail.com.

Not to mention it's also pretty damn presumptuous. Like there's something lacking in my taste in music.

There's no telling what's waiting for me on the other end of this link. It could be music. Love songs or some other sappy crap that's supposed to melt me into a puddle of teenage hormones. More likely, it's Seth or one of his friends recording messages about how much they hate me since I've blocked them on every app I have.

My thumb's still hovering between the link and the Trash icon when Dad comes through the kitchen door. I lock my phone screen and turn it upside down on the counter for good measure.

"Hey, kiddo." His breathing is still shallow from his morning run, his face a blotchy red from the exertion. He fills a cup with water and downs it in two long gulps. When he looks at me again, he frowns. "I know that face. What are you trying to stop yourself from doing?"

"Opening the anonymous gift I received this morning." Telling him the gift is potentially a playlist of songs tailored just for me will open things up to a zillion questions about what's happening with the season and how I'm handling it all, and it's too early for that. In another forty or fifty years, maybe, when this nightmare is barely even a memory, then I might feel like talking about it.

"You're not even a little bit curious what this no-name boy has to offer?"

That's the only reason I haven't deleted it yet. But to him, I say, "Nope."

He chuckles and leans in to kiss my head. "A nonconformist. That's my girl."

I wave him and his sweat-stink away. "Ugh. You need a shower."

"Love you too."

I wait until the shower upstairs starts up before giving in. Maybe listening to the songs will give me a clue as to who sent them so I can shut them down in person.

The first song straddles the line between pop and punk. Driving bass, a few tricky guitar riffs, and a singer lamenting how a girl makes breaking hearts look so easy. All in all it's a fun song. Laurel—emo at heart—would probably love it. Song number two, though? That one sends chills up my arms it's so effing good. It's dark and melodic, the lyrics practically bleeding with grief and loss. I play through the first fifteen seconds of the next few tracks, recognizing one as a cover of a Bring Me The Horizon song and another as a Breaking Benjamin song, before deciding the music—if not the guy who gave it to me—might be worth my time after all.

I spend the whole afternoon in the baking kitchen falling in love with the playlist. Any time it cycles back to song two, I listen to it multiple times in a row, letting the lyrics and the singer's honeyed voice replace every cell in my body until the only thing that's left of me is this song.

Eventually I move to my room to avoid being pulled into whatever my sister and Juliet have planned for the night. Out my window, I check to make sure the voices growing louder aren't Seth and his entourage wreaking havoc, but it's still just Maggie and Juliet—and also Tobin. Which almost makes it worse. At least if it was someone who didn't belong there, I could go out and run them off with one or two well-placed insults—and maybe a rolling pin if words weren't enough. But no such luck. The three of them are set up in chairs behind the Curcios' house, circled around the short, stone firepit with deep, orange flames licking at the air. The faintest hint of wood smoke sneaks in through my closed bedroom window.

They're shrouded in darkness, but for now their expressions are in full view thanks to the flickering firelight. Bright, excited eyes. Mouths that refuse to uncurl from their smiles. They're fifty feet away from me, but it might as well be a hundred miles.

I stuff my earbuds in and crank the volume on my playlist again. Song two is "All Who Remain" by Beware the Darkness. But the version I have is a remake. No band name attached. The same singer must have covered all the songs on the playlist since the voice doesn't change from song to song—and I was able to identify fifteen of the twenty songs with a Google lyric search. The longer I listen, the less I care about what the original versions sound like. This voice is the only one I want to hear. After the first few chords, the pull of the laughter coming from the yard dissolves in the bass line.

Each song is a story. A little piece of the anonymous boy who sent it to me. Whoever he is, he's as broken as me. And it's enough to make me feel not quite so alone.

Halfway through the playlist, my phone vibrates against my hip. I don't recognize the number and drop the phone facedown on my stomach without reading the text message. It buzzes again a few seconds later.

When I finally check it, it's the same message repeated. **Come outside?**

Unknown number. Invitation to leave the safety of locked doors. I've seen enough horror movies to know how this ends. Slipping my earbuds out so I'm not caught off guard, I type back: **I'm good in here.**

The reply is immediate. **You could be just as good out here.**

Then another. **You don't even have to talk to us if you don't want to.**

And another. **You could just come outside and sit here so I don't have to be the third wheel to our sisters all night.**

Their laughter presses against my window again, begging to be let in. It must be eardrum-bursting volume from Tobin's position next to them. I push up onto my elbows and prop myself on my pillow so I can peek out the window, surprised at how good it feels to hear Maggie's laugh again.

I type back: You could go inside.

I would. But I was promised some of your famous s'mores whoopie pies if I built the fire. Pause. New text. Can't leave until Maggie makes good on that.

Sounds like something you need to take up with her. I don't bother to set the phone down this time. Tobin is clearly in the mood to chat.

He responds: I can work two angles at the same time.

Then a few seconds later: So, are you coming?

Tenacious, that one. I hold off on replying right away, my fingers hovering over the dark phone screen. I want to be annoyed with him for pushing, for refusing to let me brush them all off tonight, but a smile sneaks up on me. Thank God he can't see it.

After another moment, I give in. You won't leave me alone until I come out there, will you?

I will if that's what you really want.

That's not what I want. It should be. But the pull toward Tobin is impossible to ignore.

I unplug my earbuds from my phone and tuck them under my pillow so I can find them in the middle of the night. Listening to music is my first line of defense against insomnia.

I pull a hoodie from the closet and check my hair in the mirror above my dresser. Then I muss it up again because looking cute for a boy is not on my to-do list.

There's no use in bothering with my shoes, so when I get outside the grass between our houses, freshly mowed, clings to my feet in clippings. The firepit is a ring of flat river rocks stacked three high, spanning about two feet. Smoke curls off the flames, disappearing into the dark sky, tiny flakes of ash drifting down to settle on hair/clothes/skin as I approach.

Tobin doesn't turn around, just says, "I knew you couldn't resist."

I drop into the chair next to him, the canvas giving a little beneath me. "I wasn't sure if I could actually trust you to stop texting me."

Juliet leans forward. "Oh, come on, that is a trustworthy face if I've ever seen one." She gives her brother a not-at-all-sly thumbs-up. He tips his head back and laughs.

"We're about to break out the snacks," Maggie adds, as if the lack of food is what's been keeping me inside this whole time.

"So I heard," I say.

We raid the baking kitchen. Maggie, Juliet, and Tobin go straight for my new stash of whoopie pies, each filling a paper bag with the different flavors they want. Tobin doubles up on everything. He holds the bag with both hands to keep the treats from spilling out the top as we make our way back to the fire.

"I can't tell what they are in the dark," he says. He plucks one from the top and passes it to me.

"And you think I can?" I ask. But one whiff and I know it's chocolate cake with coconut cream filling.

"Just sharing. I got extras in case you saw how much we were enjoying them and wanted to join in."

"You know what this shindig needs?" Juliet asks. She nudges her brother's leg with her foot. Even in the shadows dancing at the fire's edge, I can tell her toenails are painted the same shade of pink as Maggie's. "Music."

"Is that your way of asking me to go get the wireless speakers?" Tobin asks. But instead of getting up, he slumps deeper into his chair. A ghost of a smile crosses his face when he glances at me. Or maybe I just imagine it because a second later, he's tilting his head toward Juliet, the challenge clear.

Juliet pushes forward in her chair, meeting his eyes. "No, we need *live* music. I know it's totally cliché, but campfires really do go better with acoustic guitars. Go get yours?"

"You're right. That is cliché," he says. "Also, no."

"So you do play guitar," I say, without thinking. My interest on full display.

He turns back to me, one long-fingered hand splaying in the air between us while the other clutches the bag of sweets to his chest. "Whoa, you better be careful there, Remy. That almost sounded like you've been thinking about me when I'm not around."

I shake my head as if that will make it untrue. As if I can dilute the attraction simmering in my blood with a little lie. "I hate to shatter that illusion so quickly, but it's just that you look like someone who plays guitar. The hair, the clothes, the lip rings. Screams *guitarist*."

What I don't say is that it's a damn good look.

Really. Damn. Good.

Pinching the inside of my elbow to distract myself, I let the sharp burst of pain do the trick; whatever stupid emotions were trying to surface vanish.

Tobin taps one hand on the metal leg of his chair. "Well, I also play the bass, drums, and piano."

A hundred questions crowd my brain about what kind of music he likes and how long he's been playing and if he's heard of the bands I'm obsessed with. But then I think of what he told me about his dad. How he'd been a musician before he'd died. And I wonder if playing music is Tobin's way of feeling close to his dad now that his dad is gone. Instead of asking him and dredging up sad memories, I say, "Our very own Brendon Urie."

Maggie and Juliet swap I-told-you-so smiles across the fire from us.

Tobin shakes his head. "I prefer Trent Reznor, if you're going to throw comparisons around."

Juliet leans forward, licking icing from her fingers. "Tobin's basically a musical genius. Anything he picks up, he can play within five seconds. Our dad used to record him playing around with whatever instrument he was into that month, and then he'd send the videos off to his musician friends to pass on to their agents or record labels. And when he was on tour, he'd spend more time chatting people up about Tobin than his own band."

"He swore I was going to make it big like he never did." Tobin's shoulders tense as he polishes off the last of the whoopie pie he's eating. "Without the drugs and the wife and kids, he might've been great."

"That's not fair, Tobin," Juliet says. Her voice crackles like the fire.

"It's true, though. He made his choices, and we're all dealing with the consequences."

Maggie and Juliet whisper to each other. My sister calms while I distract. They're the same roles we took when our friends used to fight. Back when we had friends, but it's so ingrained we do it now without meaning to.

"What about you?" I ask Tobin, a feeble attempt at keeping them from arguing. "Are you as good as your sister says?"

"I have a band back in Richmond. We won a few Battles

of the Bands, so they let us open for some decently big-name groups at a club in town. I mean, we'd go on as the opening band to the opening band, so only a handful of people saw us each show, but, still, we were starting to make a name for ourselves."

"Did you have to quit when you moved here?"

"Officially, no. I'm still writing some music with my best friend Bas—Sebastian. But if my mom vetoes one more gig, I think they'll kick me out."

"I'm surprised she let you play shows in the first place."

"She didn't exactly know. I mean, she knew I was in a band, but she thought it was just this for-fun thing we did in Bas's garage. I slipped up once, though, and when she called me on it, I couldn't lie to her."

"Huh," I say. If I was still the type of girl to make a list of qualities I'd want in a guy, *honesty* would be at the top. *Musician* would be a bonus. But I'm not that girl, and I can't let myself be impressed into changing my mind. "Most people would've said whatever they had to in order to get what they want."

"I'm not most people."

"No, you're not." And the more time I spend with him, the more I realize that instead of being hardened and bitter from his dad's death and his mom's overprotective reaction to it, he's come out the other side with his sense of humor intact,

more charm than any teenage boy needs, and just enough cyn-
icism to show that it's all affected him more than he lets on.

My thoughts must show on my face because when I look
back at him he's a breath away. His cheek, warm from the fire,
grazes mine as he moves to close the gap between where we're
sitting. I swerve out of the way so fast I almost tip my chair
over sideways, throwing my hands up between us to block a
second attempt.

"Damn it, Tobin," I say, my heart thudding in my chest.
He almost ruined everything. "What are you doing? You can't
do shit like that."

"I'm sorry. I thought...I don't know." The words flounder
between us, less assured than I've ever heard Tobin before. He
stares at me, the red glow from the fire reflecting in his eyes.

"You can't kiss me right now. Have you not actually listened to anything we've said about the kissing season? What
other people in town have said?"

Maggie's and Juliet's quiet chatter stops. For a few seconds, the only sound is the crackling of the sticks in the fire as
they burn.

Tobin slouches back in his chair, but he's still close—too
close—as if hoping he can change my mind. "I told you we
know better than to believe rumors."

"And I'm telling you to believe *me*. Kissing me will only
bring you bad luck." Tobin needs to get on board with that

truth before he tries to kiss me again because I won't risk hurting him too. Until I have concrete proof my second kiss with Isaac worked, I have to assume we're both still cursed.

"Wow," he says. "Your friends really messed with your head. You know they're just jealous, right? You and Maggie, you have all the power, and that's hard for some people to accept."

"The magic might be in me, but I have no control over it. That doesn't make me powerful, it makes me dangerous. And they're not my friends. Maggie and I don't have any friends anymore." I grip the warm metal arms of the chair and hop it a few inches away from him.

"Hey, speak for yourself," Juliet pipes in. "I'm Maggie's friend. I'd be your friend, too, if you'd let me."

"As long as you don't try and kiss me, sure."

Maggie beans me in the head with a chunk of whoopie pie. It bounces to the ground, and Iggy pounces on it from the darkness. He bats it a few times, then clamps it in his teeth to cart off like a prize. When I catch Maggie's eyes over the firepit, her smile is tight—no teeth, lips pulled so thin her lipstick is barely visible. She gives the smallest shake of her head. "Rem, don't be a bitch."

Looks like I've hit a nerve. I smile at her. Not the heartless sneer I've perfected but a real, honest-to-goodness smile because as pissed as I am, part of me still wants her to be happy. One of us deserves that at least.

"It's okay, Maggie. I know she was joking," Juliet says. "Mostly." She rests her hand on my sister's arm, her bubbly laugh bringing Maggie's good mood back.

"What about me?" Tobin asks.

I turn to him, keeping my face as even as I can. "What about you?"

"Will you give me the same deal as my sister?"

"It wouldn't do you any good seeing as how you've already broken it."

He stands, not looking at me, and sets what's left of his whoopie pie haul on the edge of the firepit. "You shouldn't punish me for breaking the rules when we hadn't agreed to them yet." Then he turns and leaves me there wishing for just a second that I was someone different. Someone who wouldn't have pulled away.

"He's got a point," Juliet says, as their back door closes behind him.

I swallow my regret. Rules exist for a reason. And breaking them—at least where the season is concerned—is what got me into this mess in the first place. It's smarter to just walk away. Say *no thanks* and be done. With it. With him. That's the only guarantee neither of us will end up broken.

18

I WAKE UP THINKING of Tobin. The image of him leaning in to kiss me hijacks my brain before I've had time to secure my defenses. He was dazzled last night for sure, the season's magic pulling him toward me like I might be the answer to all his prayers. I close my eyes, letting the scene from last night linger. Instead of pulling away and acting like a freak, I inch forward to meet him. But our lips never touch, not even in this G-rated fantasy, because Tobin's sharp cheekbones and lip rings morph into Isaac's slender face and king-of-the-world grin and my body jerks, eyes flashing open so the sudden brightness forces both boys from my mind.

Kissing ruins everything.

I silence the voice in my head that says not kissing anyone else during the season might also ruin everything. A loveless future is easier to face than risking hurting anyone else.

I throw off the covers and stomp toward the bathroom to take a long, hot shower to burn the memories from my skin.

Maggie's waiting for me in the kitchen when I get downstairs. She's still in pajamas, her short hair spiking in all directions. I don't know what time she finally came inside last night, but I doubt she got much sleep. Studying me over the rim of her mug, she says, "You should have kissed Tobin last night. He really likes you, you know."

The look I shoot her says she's delusional. "You and I both know I can't do that." Though the more I'm around Tobin, the harder it is to convince myself I don't want to.

"Just because things went so wrong with Isaac doesn't mean the magic won't work right with someone else if you follow the rules."

If it was anyone but Tobin, I *might* be willing to risk it. And that's a big might. But it is Tobin, and I can feel the magic drawing us together like magnets, just like it did with Isaac, which makes staying away from him of paramount importance. He doesn't deserve any of the trouble being around me brings. Getting my sister to back me up on that is pointless, though.

"All right, fine," I say. "He can like me all he wants. I'm still not going to do anything about it."

Maggie sighs, most of the fight abandoning her. "Why not, Remy? Kissing Tobin could be what fixes things for you. Not to mention, it might actually make you happy." Her voice takes on a pleading tone to match the puppy-dogness of her eyes.

And for a second that hits me stronger than it should, knocking my better judgment on its ass because I really, really want it to be true. Then I come to my senses and shake off the lingering traces of hope. I don't know if kissing Isaac again did a damn thing. There's no reason to think kissing anyone else will either. "Short of time traveling back to the start of the summer and making different decisions, there is no putting things right. For either of us. And no amount of kissing—whether with Tobin or a dozen other guys—will change that. Just because you don't agree with the way I'm doing my season doesn't mean you get to come in all sneaky-like and take over mine. You had your season. You got to kiss whomever you wanted without me interfering. I deserve the same, whether you like it or not."

"That's not what I'm doing."

"Yes, it is," I say, my voice almost a scream. "It's what you always do. You think you know what's best for me, and you push me and manipulate me until I get in line with what you want. You've been doing it so long neither of us knows any different. It's practically the basis of our whole relationship. But that stops now. *You* stop now. No more telling boys they need to kiss me to prove I'm not bad luck. No more using my life like your second chance to get what you want. Go live your own life and stay out of mine."

"So you'd rather spend the rest of your life alone? Because that's what could happen if you don't hold up your end of giving out good luck during the season."

"Alone is better than having to pick up the pieces of the lives I ruin." And it's sure as hell better than willingly offering my heart up as a sacrifice. I know how that ends and have no desire to repeat it. Not even for Tobin. "You might be okay with the trail of heartache you leave behind when your relationships are over, but I don't have that luxury because instead of just broken hearts, I leave broken *people*. Laurel will get over you ending things with her. Isaac is literally scarred for life because of me."

Maggie sets her mug down but keeps her fingers wrapped around the ceramic. "God, get over yourself, Remy. You're not the only person in history to have a relationship end badly. Yes, yours involved magic, but that doesn't make other people's pain any less traumatic. Your real problem isn't that you hurt Isaac, it's that you're too damn scared to try again. One day you're going to regret it. And you'll have nobody to blame but yourself," she says.

"I might," I say. But right now, it's the only decision I know how to live with.

Without Laurel checking up on me every so often, I don't know how I would have survived the past six weeks. She doesn't suffocate me with friendship, just reminds me when I need it that I don't have to be alone.

And I don't want to be alone today.

I meet her at Haight Plaza to share a basket of bacon, parmesan, and truffle oil fries from one of the food trucks and purge all thoughts of Tobin from my system. We lie on top of one of the picnic tables facing each other with the fries between us and our feet resting on opposite benches.

"You're being awfully stingy with the details," she says when I've filled her in on the night before.

"There is nothing more to tell you. He tried to kiss me. I didn't let him. End of story."

"Oh, I think there's plenty more to talk about there, but Tobin is not the twin I want details on."

"You're interested in Juliet?" Not that I can blame her. Juliet's enough like Maggie—so full of charisma everyone else seems dull in comparison—to be just Laurel's type.

She lifts a hand and inspects her chipping metallic-blue fingernail polish. "Not exactly. I heard she's been hanging out with Maggie. Paige made sure to tell me. She claimed it was to keep me from getting my heart trampled by a Holloway, but you know Paige."

"Of course she did. Such a sweet friend, that girl." She used to be sweet. But the more time she spends with Hannah, the less she resembles the friend I've always known.

Laurel laughs, and I can't help feeling a little sorry for her. She genuinely likes Maggie. And I'm the reason my sister backed away from those feelings as quickly as she did.

"It would have been nice," she says, "to hear the truth from an actual friend. You know, like you for instance."

My chest constricts at her words. She's been there for me when no one else was. Even if I'd been hoping she was over my sister by now, I should have told her about Juliet. "Good point. I hate that I have to say this, but Paige is right. Maggie and Juliet are together pretty much all the time."

"Maybe she's just trying to make you jealous. You know, slip somebody new into the best friend slot in hopes that you'll notice and want things to go back to the way they used to be?" The hope in her voice makes me swallow my retort.

Instead, I say, "Maybe." Maggie already broke her heart. I don't want to cause any more damage.

Laurel tips her head to face me, her lips parted as if she can't decide how much more to say. After a minute, she asks, "Based on what you know about Juliet, do you think I have a shot still? Am I deluded for putting myself out there again when Maggie made it clear she didn't think we were going anywhere?"

"I don't know. Honestly. Maggie could have had real feelings for you, or she could have been caught up in the excitement of her season and your kiss was just that. A kiss from a Holloway girl during the kissing season."

"No sugarcoating with you, is there?"

"Being nice doesn't make the truth suck any less," I say.

Laurel shrugs and says, "Maybe not. But it doesn't make it any worse either."

19

WHILE MAGGIE DOESN'T AGREE with my decision to keep far away from Tobin—and everyone else—as long as Isaac is still cursed, at least she's respecting it. I can't say the same for Tobin and Juliet. And because there are two of them, they can coordinate their attacks. Twice the ammunition, double the effectiveness.

Tobin seems to have gotten over me refusing to kiss him. Within a day, he's back to trying to be my friend. All hurt feelings either forgotten or brushed aside.

He texts me in the mornings to see if I want to hang out or to ask if I have any "scratch and dent" whoopie pies he can take off my hands. He's not deterred by the one-sidedness of the conversations. Juliet calls to see if I want to go to one of the less populated waterfalls. Sometimes it's just her, but usually she has Maggie or Tobin lined up to go too. "Safety in numbers," she says. And I have to laugh. But I still don't agree to go. They both show up after dinners, finding me in the baking kitchen or letting themselves into the house and waving hello to my parents on their way up to my room where they barely knock on the door before pushing it open and inviting me out for end-of-summer shenanigans. Maggie goes with them every time. I lock the door behind them and then force myself to not watch out the window as they leave without me.

It's gone on this way for the past week, so I'm not surprised when Tobin and Juliet walk into Bold Rock Outfitters where I'm filling in for the day because one of Dad's employees called in sick—and I'm cheap labor. Maggie, this time, isn't with them, but it takes one look at their outfits to know why she's letting them do this without her. Juliet's in layered tank tops, a pair of hot-pink crop leggings, and running shoes. Tobin's as close to workout gear as he gets: a cotton shirt and khaki cargo shorts. And they're both wearing smug smiles as they walk toward where I stand at the base of the climbing wall.

"You know, you showing up like this after I've said I'm not available for lunch makes it damn near impossible to avoid you," I say.

Tobin grins. "You admit it, then?"

"That I'm avoiding you? I thought that was obvious."

Juliet pulls her braid over her shoulder and rubs the stubby end over her cheek. "But I thought we were all going to be friends?"

"I never agreed to that," I say.

Tobin wraps his fingers around the back of his neck, locking his eyes on mine as he says, "Oh, c'mon. We're not that bad."

"Don't take it personally. I don't want to be friends with anyone right now. Come back in ten or so months when everything's died down. You might be able to change my mind then." Even Laurel seems to have come to the same conclusion because since I told her about Maggie and Juliet she's gone quiet on me. Only returning my texts after a few hours have passed. I'm trying not to take it personally, but since she was the only one who'd kept contact with me it's making me wonder, how much was for me and how much was for Maggie?

"That's insane. You know that, right?" Juliet says. She throws her hands up, flinging her braid so hard it almost smacks her brother in the face. He uses it as an excuse to step closer to me. "You can't let one guy ruin it for everyone."

I stand my ground, refusing to let either of them know their tactics might be working. "You sound just like my sister."

"Well, that's because she's right."

Tobin tilts his head toward Juliet and mock whispers, "Maybe this whole winning-Remy-over thing would work better if we didn't keep reminding her of why she's trying to shut us out in the first place."

"Good point," Juliet says, turning back to me, her blinding smile covering any trace of her previous annoyance. "So, skipping ahead to why we're here. We think we might want to learn to rock climb." She looks at Tobin, her steely eyes urging him to agree.

"You know, when in Rome and all that," he says. "So we thought maybe you'd give us a lesson."

"It's my dad who teaches the classes," I say, refusing to play along as tempting as it is. If they really want to learn, he would be their first stop, not me. "He even has a camp coming up next week before school starts that you might be able to squeeze into if you're serious."

Juliet continues to smile, hardly looking at the wall. "We were actually thinking you could show us the ropes—pun a little bit intended—so we'd know if it's worth doing the full class."

I raise a challenging eyebrow at her. "Maggie doesn't climb," I say like that should matter.

She just holds up a hand as if to stop me from telling her any more truths she doesn't want to hear. "Oh, I know. When I mentioned wanting to try it, she cringed and then gave me a crash course in how my fingers will split open and how my inner thighs will chafe from the harness. But I figure it can't be quite that bad if so many people still do it. Thoughts?"

I play along. "Well, one session isn't going to hurt you. You might get a little torn up after a few times because your hands and feet aren't used to that kind of workout. But if you learn the techniques and do them right, you'll be fine."

"And you promise it'll be fun?" she asks.

"*I* think it's fun," I say. I've gone up a few times since that first night with Dad. My technique is shit, but some parts are coming back to me. Then I add, "But I don't know you well enough to make that decision for either of you."

Tobin hooks an arm around his sister's shoulder and pulls her face in so they're cheek to cheek, both looking at me. "Guess we'll have to change that, won't we, Jet?"

"Looks like," she says.

I shrug. Their minds are made up. Nothing I say will deter them at this point. The sooner we start, the sooner I can send them on their way before any of us gets attached. "Okay, let's get started. Top rope or bouldering?"

"Was that in English?" Tobin asks.

Juliet's mouth drops open, askance, and she raises a hand to cover it. "I think she was propositioning us."

Shutting my eyes, I just shake my head. There's no point in fighting it; I can't help but like them. "You two are going to make this impossible, aren't you?"

"Possibly," Tobin says.

"No," Juliet counters. She straightens, clasping her hands in front of her Catholic-girl style. "We'll cooperate. I promise."

Tobin jerks up a shoulder, a whisper of a smile on his lips. It's as close to agreement as we're going to get. "But you might need to pretend like we know nothing about climbing because we literally know nothing about climbing."

"Okay. That I can do," I say. "So do you want to do top rope climbing, where you're attached to a rope on the ceiling and you can climb higher up the wall? Or do you want to start out with bouldering, which is rope-less and sticks closer to the ground, at least for your first try?"

"The rope one for sure." Juliet cranes her neck to look up at the face of the wall. "I want to go all the way to the top." Of course she does.

"You probably won't make it there your first time up. Sorry," I say.

"Are you sure about that?" Tobin asks, tugging on Juliet's braid. She whips her head out of range. "My sister's as stubborn as they come."

I have to ignore the pang of jealousy that shoots through me at their easy camaraderie. The more time I spend around them, the more I miss the way things used to be between Maggie and me. I can't help but wonder where we'd be if I hadn't taken my anger out on her after Isaac's accident. But even if we were still *MaggieAndRemy*, Maggie wouldn't be here for a climbing lesson, so I put her out of my mind and focus on the task at hand.

"It's not about will," I say. "It's about how long your muscles will hold you up. You're about to put your legs through a serious workout. Your arms, too, but to a lesser extent. The point of the first climb is to get a feel for the wall and the holds and to trust that the belayer—who will be me—will keep you from falling. Actually making progress on the wall is just gravy."

"I'd rather it be icing," Juliet says. "Icing's so much better than gravy."

"Icing, then."

"Ooh, speaking of icing," Tobin says, "if one of us does make it to the top can we get whoopie pies as a reward?"

How those pies have such a hold over the guys in this town is beyond me, but as long as he's asking for sweets and not a date, I'm not going to complain. "I'll make it even easier. If you don't hurt yourself or me, you can have as many as you want."

He flashes me a grin. "You're on."

"Come with me, then."

Usually I would go to the storeroom to collect the gear for customers on my own, but I don't trust these two out here to not start scheming while I'm gone. Zach, Dad's second-in-command, gives me a confused look when they both say hi to him, then he turns back to whatever he's working on for my dad while I get them outfitted in harnesses and rental shoes. Juliet insists on clipping half a dozen quickdraws to the gear loops on her harness "to look authentic." Tobin mumbles that they both look ridiculous. I try not to notice how the harness hugs his ass, even in baggy cargo shorts.

I fail miserably.

Back at the wall, I run through the basics of belaying, even though neither of them will be doing it today. Then I move on to describing the different types of holds on the wall and demonstrate how to hook their fingers and position their feet to maximize balance and grip. Tobin's eyes glaze over at all the terminology as he bounces in the unfamiliar shoes, I guess preferring I set them loose on the wall to figure it all out for themselves. Juliet's almost as antsy, her thumb working the carabiner clip hanging at her thigh open and closed and open and closed. This is the point in training when Dad would show off by doing this cool upside-down maneuver where he's hanging by just his fingers from a jug, the technical name for the climbing holds on the wall, with his legs bent in opposite directions, but I'm severely out of practice—not to mention out of shape—so the best I can do is scramble a few feet up the wall like it's as easy as breathing.

"Who's going up first?" I ask when my feet are back on the floor; they both eye the wall like it's an enemy to be conquered.

Tobin looks to his sister, deferring to her.

"You can go," Juliet says.

"So I can make a fool of myself first? Gee, thanks, Jet."

"No, because it'll give me time to talk you up to Remy alone. Now get moving." She nudges his shoulder, and he stumbles a step closer to me.

I pick up the free end of the belay rope and shake it at both of them in turn. "Nope. This friend thing only works if you both abide by the rules. No talking anyone up. And no flirting." My eyes cut to Tobin and catch him chuckling. He sobers up in an instant.

Juliet sinks to the bench a few feet away, lying back with her arms pillowing her neck so she can still see us.

"Looks like you're up," I say to Tobin. "Come here so I can tie you in."

"I thought you said no flirting," Tobin counters.

"Oh, shut up." I have to turn away to hide my smile.

Once he's all hooked up and we've tested the rope/knots/carabiners to make sure it's all secure, I stand off to the side and throw my brake arm wide to signal he can start when he's ready.

Tobin steps up to the wall, squares his shoulders, and braces his toes on a low foothold. Reaching up, he curves his palm around a jug, then pauses. "What do I say here to get… going?"

"You mean climbing?"

"Right. Climbing." He uses a tone usually reserved for

going to the dentist or driving your grandmother to the beauty parlor.

"'Climb on,'" I say, trying to suppress a laugh.

He throws a sanity-stealing grin back over his shoulder and steps his other foot up to a higher hold. "There you go with the flirting again." Then his focus shifts back to the wall, and I snap my brain back into safety-first mode, all thoughts of how sculpted his calves look from behind banished from my mind. I all but swear it.

His movements are slow and calculated like picking out the best route up has his full attention. He'd told me when we'd first met that he likes a good challenge. He makes it about a third of the way up before he takes a real break. I brace my left foot and redouble my grip on the break rope to keep him steady. With his feet pressed into the wall, he sits back and hangs in the air, giving his arms a rest. His legs must be screaming out for relief, but he's not giving up.

Juliet rolls up from the bench, at my side in one fluid motion. She angles her head toward her brother and, determining he's a safe distance away, says in a low voice, "So, I hear my mom's been asking you about me and Maggie? She slipped that in between asking what my plans were for the day and 'suggesting' that I spend it with someone other than your sister. I hate to put you on the spot, but I kinda need to know what you told her because she's surprisingly good at getting my friends to rat me out."

That would make me laugh if I didn't think she was serious. But since their welcome dinner, Mrs. Curcio has cornered me half a dozen times to ask what Juliet and Maggie are up to most days. Her pointed little chats make it clear why Juliet thinks she has to hide so much of her life from her mother. "I just said she's showing you around town, helping you fit in. Also it sounds like maybe you need better friends."

She shrugs, her smile coming back full force. It's dazzling/blinding/infectious. No wonder Maggie spends so much time with her. "I think maybe I've found them." She says it with so much sincerity that I smile back, wanting to believe that I could have friends again. "Thanks for covering for me."

"Despite what a lot of people around here think, what other people do is not anyone else's business." I feed another foot or so of the belay rope to Tobin who's started climbing again. Then I spare a quick glance at Juliet.

"You know the proper response there would be to say 'you're welcome.'"

This time I do laugh, and the black hole in my chest shrinks a little more. "Damn. I never meant to give the impression I was proper. I've got to work on that."

"Oh man. I totally see why Tobin's falling for you. Cute and sarcastic. My brother is so toast." Juliet checks his progress, nodding her approval at his technique. "But back to my admiration for you. I owe you a thank-you coffee at the very least."

"You do know what it will do to your reputation if you're seen out in public with me, right?" I ask.

"I'm sorry. Did I give you the impression that I care about that kind of thing?"

Yep—it's official. Becoming friends with Juliet might be the only good thing to come out of the season so far. But that's more than I have a right to ask for, so I smile at her, letting this unexpected hope buoy me. "Not at all. I just thought you deserved fair warning."

20

MY MORNING WITH TOBIN and Juliet at Bold Rock two days ago was just enough to make me want more. To get my life back to normal. To be the old me.

As I'm packing up a special-order cake for Wild Flour to mourn the end of summer break, I hear voices outside the baking kitchen. The midafternoon sun reflects off the glass. I know from experience it's impossible to tell if there's anyone inside when the light's this glaring. I could stay put, keep quiet. They'd walk right by without stopping to try and convince me to join whatever they're up to.

The old Remy would throw open the door and race out to meet them with smile as bright as the sun.

I'm up and to the door before I can second-guess myself. Maggie and Tobin sit in chairs by the empty firepit, no Juliet in sight. They don't notice the door opening, and Maggie's voice stops me at the threshold.

"You like my sister, right?" she asks.

Tobin lets loose a sound that's part groan, part laugh. "I'm that obvious?"

"That's a good thing. Remy can't keep avoiding the kissing season and letting everyone think her magic's bad. She needs to get over it. Move on. She's lost over a month and a half already. The sooner she kisses someone new, the better."

So much for telling her to stay out of it. I should have known she wouldn't.

"Remy doesn't seem to want to kiss anyone. And as you saw that night when we were all hanging out, definitely not me," he says. The disappointment in his voice sends a twinge of guilt coursing through me. "Shouldn't you be on her side?"

"Remy *does* want to kiss someone. Fall in love with someone who loves her back. She's just scared. And she's letting what people are saying about her and Isaac get in her head. But you, Tobin, can help her. Just get her to kiss you. Remind her that not every guy out there is the enemy." Maggie shifts to grip both of his wrists, looking him dead in the eyes to convey how serious she is.

"I'm working on it." His smile is all confidence.

I hide farther behind the door, keeping it open just far enough to continue listening unnoticed.

"Well, work faster. I know how charming you Curcios can

be. Play it up a bit. Trust me, she won't be able to resist you. You're like Remy catnip in boy form."

Stiffening, Tobin pulls away from Maggie. The easy smile from a moment ago, only a memory. "So, I'm a drug that you're trying to get your sister hooked on?"

Does Maggie know how Tobin and Juliet's dad died? That if she was hoping to get Tobin on her side, she just said the exact wrong thing?

"No. I didn't mean it like that. You are a very cute boy who is exactly my sister's type. If that's not enough incentive, there's always the Holloway luck waiting on the other side of that kiss."

"Definitely can't forget about the luck," he says, the anger from a moment before vanishing at the prospect of a lucky future.

There it is. The truth about why he's so intent on winning me over. I curl my hand around the door handle to keep from storming out there and telling them both off.

"Does that mean you're in?" Maggie asks.

"I was in before you asked. Kissing Remy Holloway is basically the only thing on my summer bucket list."

"Summer's almost over, you know."

Whatever else they say, I don't hear it. By shutting the kitchen door, I effectively shut them out of my life too.

I knew Tobin was too good to be true. Maggie's right about

his charm. I'd been pulled into his orbit despite my efforts not to care only to find out I was right to be wary of his friendship.

Maggie's almost worse. Going behind my back to coerce guys to try and kiss me. First Felix, now Tobin. Who knows who else in between. All because she refused to believe my kiss with Isaac cursed us both.

But those missing pages from the Book of Luck aren't simply mistakes. They can't be. The only way to get Maggie and Tobin—and anyone else still stupid enough to want me to kiss them this season—to back off is to find something that proves I'm right.

Aunt Jenna said the Book of Luck had everything I needed already in it to break the curse. What I can easily see are names and major life events for everyone whose luck went right, but actually tracking down people who might have even a passing knowledge of the Holloway luck going bad is next to impossible. It's story after story after story of the luck working the way it's supposed to. Not a hint of it going wrong before me and Isaac.

Most everyone from the more recent kissing seasons have moved out of Talus, to give the luck a broader field to pull from. And the ones from before the 1930s are either dead or too old to remember anything of use.

The pages missing from the Book of Luck—those un-known Holloway girls with their unknown kissing seasons and the consequences they'd had—might be the key to ending Isaac's unlucky streak.

I take the Book of Luck to the Talus Cemetery, hoping to match up names in the book with gravestones. I just need one name to reveal something that will give me a lead. One name that proves I'm not the only Holloway girl who kissed the wrong person and gave bad luck instead of good.

But just because someone along the way decided they weren't worth keeping doesn't mean there aren't traces still left behind. They would have made an impression on the world— and on the book. I just have to uncover what's literally hiding beneath the surface of the remaining pages.

It's a last-ditch effort.

Everything I've tried so far has failed.

I can't stop until I find something that can help me.

I only find three names in the whole cemetery that align with entries in the Book of Luck. There's nothing on the grave-stones or my Google searches that even hint at anything but a charmed life that kissing a Holloway girl promised.

Just as I'm packing the Book of Luck back in my bag to leave, I notice a woman snapping a few photos of a grave-stone on her phone. She places a sheet of paper against the worn stone and rubs a stick of charcoal across it in methodical strokes. The names on the graves are all but lost. Just like the names on the ripped-out pages of the Book of Luck. But the impression revealed by the rubbing gives me an idea.

Turning to the first missing page, I slip a blank sheet of paper in its place, praying I can reveal the ghost of an imprint from the original page. Pinning it down with my fingers at the top and my thumb and the heel of my hand against the flattened spine, the binding crackles under the pressure but doesn't snap. Then, just like in the movies, I go all super-sleuth and rub a pencil across the paper, trying to get an impression. Mostly I end up with traces of the intact entry beneath. But there among the familiar words is one that doesn't belong:

wrong

I shade all the way to the bottom. No other words appear. The next two pages yield similar results: *hurt* and *broken* and *kiss*.

Not exactly helpful, but at least it supports my theory about why the pages were removed.

Something bad must have happened.

The fourth page, though, that's where I find it. A name.

Chastain

I'd all but given up on finding a way to fix Isaac, my hope nothing more than smoking embers. But this name is a fresh spark, and it flares back to life inside me. Maybe, just maybe, breaking the curse might be within reach.

21

I CAN'T GO UP to the Lookout Bed & Breakfast empty handed. Not if I want Mrs. Chastain to tell me what she might know about the name in the Book of Luck. So I spend the morning making lemon tea cookies from Mom's box of family recipes. They're always the first to disappear at the Christmas cookie exchange the elementary school puts on. No one can resist them.

The double hit of tart lemon and sugar in the melt-in-your-mouth cookies and the quarter-inch-thick icing is addictive. If you eat one, you're in for at least three more. Every damn time. And since Mom won't share the recipe outside of the family, offering up an entire batch is the closest anyone in town is going to get.

I box them up in one of Wild Flour's cake boxes, the stacks of pale-yellow discs visible through the cellophane window in the lid. As far as bribes go, this one's pretty solid. Let's hope Mrs. Chastain knows something—anything—about the name I found that might help.

Since she's not expecting me, I spend ten minutes wandering around the B&B grounds before I find her in the small vegetable garden in the side yard. Weeds run riot over the fenced-in area. Or maybe they're some herb that are too pitiful to be picked. I call out to her so I don't startle her and send her tumbling down the slope of the mountain. That would be just my luck. Her head whips around, the wide brim of her brown hat flopping over her eyes. Stretching out one arm for balance, she pushes up from her kneeling position and locks her eyes on me.

"Did I forget an order?" she asks.

"No, ma'am." I walk toward her and spot her as she bends over to lift a basket of tomatoes up. "I was hoping you'd have a few minutes to talk to me. I brought you some lemon cookies."

"Oh, well, aren't you sweet." She trades me the tomatoes for the cookies. Bribe accepted. Good. "I could use a break anyway. Let me get cleaned up, and we can have some tea with these. How about that?"

"Sounds good. Thanks."

Mrs. Chastain leads me in through the side door. The kitchen is dark and quiet. The dinner chef doesn't show up until early afternoon for prep, giving Mrs. Chastain most of the day to be in charge of the kitchen. She sets the cookie box on the counter and motions for me to do the same with the basket. Then she scrubs the dirt from her hands in the industrial sink.

My questions beg to be let out, common courtesies be damned. But I hold my tongue. There's too much riding on this to blow my chances by being rude. So, I wait.

First, it's the hand washing, then it's plating up the cookies, and finally it's teatime. Mrs. Chastain uses an electric kettle, which I'm sure spoils some of the rustic ambiance of the B&B for guests who picture this little old lady hovering over a vintage metal teakettle as it slowly boils on the stovetop. When the water's ready and poured, I carry the teapot out to one of the two-person tables in the dining room where Mrs. Chastain has set up cups and cookie plates.

I let her start on cookie number two before I bring up why I'm here. "I found the Chastain name in something pertaining to one of the kissing seasons. Maybe back when my nana was young. And the last time I was here, you mentioned that you had hoped my mom would kiss your son and give him good luck, so I thought you might know if there was anyone else in your family who did get a Holloway kiss? Someone from the Chastain side?" It's a long shot that she'd know all the sordid details of her in-laws' lives, but it's all I have.

She blows on her tea, a curl of steam rising from the cup. "I'm afraid not. My Johnny's older brother, Beau, was already married when your grandma and great-aunt were making their rounds."

"And you never—"

"Oh my, no. I knew from the time I was nine that I was going to marry Johnny. It took him a little longer to come around to that realization, but he never even looked at the Holloway sisters. Not even once."

Gripping the wooden claws carved into the end of the chair arms, I say, "No cousins or uncles or aunts or anyone you can remember hearing about who might have kissed someone in my family and gotten bad luck instead of good?"

"Nothing like that, dear." Mrs. Chastain sets the cup back in its saucer. The slight tremor in her hand rattles the china. With her fingers on the handle to still the sound, she adds, "But now that I'm thinking about it, Johnny's cousin, Lilly, came to stay with his family one summer when they were all young. I'd hoped we'd become friends because I was only a few years older than her, but she spent all her time following Ada and Edith Holloway around like they'd hung the moon."

"Did anything bad happen to her that summer?"

"Lilly got stung by a bee, if I remember correctly. Turned out she was allergic, and nobody knew until then. She spent a few days in the hospital, and then her daddy came and took her home. She never did come back for a visit after that."

"Did she—" What's the appropriate way to ask if someone died or not? If your family's curse was the cause of it? "Was she okay after that? Or did bad things keep happening to her?"

"She had a rough go of it for a while, but things turned around for her. I don't see much of her now that my Johnny's gone, but she sends a card every Christmas. Despite how close she came to dying, she has fond memories of Talus and her time here. Mentions it in every card, even after all these years."

Not exactly the reaction I'd expect from someone who was cursed, but I guess it's a start. There's only one way to find out for sure if it was Lilly Chastain's name in the book and why the page was removed.

"Would you mind giving me her contact info? I have some questions for her, you know, about my nana and Aunt Edith, and it's probably better if I do it directly so you don't have to be stuck in the middle."

"Of course. I have it back in my rooms. Give me just a few minutes and I'll find it for you." Mrs. Chastain scrapes her chair back, pushing herself up in the process, and shuffles across the dining room to the part of the main house where she lives.

While she's gone, I pick at my cookie until it's nothing but a pile of crumbs and clumps of icing. Such a waste. But with as twisted as my stomach is at the moment, anything more than the too-hot-to-taste tea would probably make a reappearance. No sense tempting fate.

I take the sheet of Lookout stationery paper with the address and phone number written out in precise cursive from Mrs. Chastain when she returns. Now, all I have to do is ask a total stranger if she got bad luck from kissing my grandmother or great-aunt.

And pray that she's willing to answer.

I make myself wait until I'm safely down the mountain before calling Lilly's number. I can't risk her saying something that will literally drive me over the edge.

Finding a parking spot on the street near Haight Plaza, I take a deep breath and dial the number Mrs. Chastain gave me. It rings and rings and rings. No voicemail. No old-school answering machine like my grandparents had. Just endless ringing.

If Lilly doesn't have the modern miracle of voicemail, I doubt she has caller ID either. I call five more times to the same disappointing result. She has to pick up some time, right? I'll keep calling until she does. Until then, I need a sanity check.

I send Laurel a message to see if she wants to meet me

at the food truck park, and unlike Lilly, I get a reply almost immediately.

Can't today. Working.

Okay, so it's barely a response—and definitely not the one I wanted—but it's better than silence.

After work? I'm baking.

Tempting. Early day tomorrow. Maybe this weekend?

Early? Laurel is a noon riser at best during the summer. A side effect of working at the movie theater when the last showing doesn't end till after midnight. Then there's cleanup and driving home and decompressing before sleep. A 2:00 a.m. text is standard with Laurel.

Before I can write back to ask what's getting her out at an ungodly hour, I spot her across the park, backpack slung over her very much not a work shirt. I toss my phone onto the passenger seat. If I don't call her out on it, she can't to lie to me again.

22

I HAVE TO SIDESTEP a headless mouse on my doorstep on the way out of the house the next morning. There's no ribbon tied around what's left of its neck, so I have to assume it's a token of love from Iggy and not one of Isaac's friends. Or worse, one of the misguided boys who still wants their shot at the Holloway luck. The cat's nowhere to be found, though, so I can't actually get confirmation. With the exception of the enamel whoopie-pie pin from Felix, the presents the guys in town have left for me this summer are decidedly less romantic than Maggie received last year. Like the half-empty bottle of perfume that smelled like a florist shop after the power's been out for a few days. Or the boy who shaved my name onto the back of his head along with a lopsided heart.

So a dead mouse isn't out of the question. *Lucky me.*

The air hums with the first strains of a sad melody played

on an acoustic guitar. I glance over at Tobin's open window as the song unfolds into one of the songs on my playlist. The lyrics bloom in my mind, and I can't help but wonder if Tobin's wanting to know the same thing. If we're both feeling the same attraction.

After our near-kiss at the firepit, I'd wondered if the playlist was from Tobin. But he would have no reason for wanting to keep his identity a secret. He's already put it out there that he wants to kiss me, so giving me a gift I can't even thank him for seems counterproductive.

Turning away, I nudge the limp mouse body over the side of the concrete with the toe of my shoe. It plops into the tangle of ivy creeping across the front flower bed. A smear of black-red blood stays behind on the doormat. I contemplate going upstairs for the perfume to mask the stench of decay, but that might be a worse scent clouding the front door.

I'm still thinking about that damn mouse when I get to Bold Rock to fill in again while Dad's leading his end-of-summer climbing camp. I've almost convinced myself it was just the cat. I mean, if one of the guys had left it, they would have included a note or stuck around to see my reaction in person. They would have wanted to get credit. Not from me but from their friends. To prove they're not tempted by the promise of luck.

Every night I've been saying a prayer that I'll magically find a way to end the curse.

But the universe enjoys making me suffer too much to let it all end that easily.

Goddamn universe.

Goddamn Remy, the universe replies. But the universe says it with much more flair. Namely by having Dad hijack my day as soon as I walk into the store.

"Grab some gear, kiddo. You're helping me with class this morning." He hooks a muscular arm around my neck, spinning me back toward the equipment room where we keep the rentals.

Nope. Not going to happen.

Trying to tug out of his grasp, I force a playful smile when I meet his stare. "Help as in load the Jeep and then hold down the fort here while you're gone, right?"

He shakes his head, not amused. "I want you to go with me. Do some belaying. Offer encouragement and maybe some pointers on technique to the students who are going up. It's a beginners' class and mostly kids your age. I think your presence will be a help to a couple of them."

He's lost his mind. That's the only explanation.

"That's exactly why I'll do better here. Away from people. That will be more helpful." After all, limited interaction is one thing; I can deflect any season-induced flirting and shoo the boys away before anything bad happens, but that's much harder to do when I'm literally attached to them by a rope. And then there's the fact that the curse isn't going to stop just because they're clinging to a rock face fifty feet up. Can we say liability?

But my dad doesn't seem to be thinking about all the problems my presence can cause. His forehead wrinkles as he frowns at me. "I'm not asking."

"I'm telling you, Dad, this is so not a good idea. Take Zach with you. I can manage the store by myself for a few hours. Please?"

He tugs on my ponytail, forcing me to meet his eyes, which I'd been doing a bang-up job of avoiding. "You can't hide from your friends forever, Remy."

It's sweet that he thinks I still have friends. Delusional, but sweet. Maggie's just like him in that respect. They can both completely overlook things they don't want to be true like it will cease to exist if they ignore it long enough. But if that really worked, half this town would have vanished by now with all the ignoring I've been doing.

"In case you haven't noticed, I'm more of a loner these days." I shrug. Smile. Pretend that it's not eating me up inside. "And anyway, I'm not hiding. The only people who want me around are you and Mom, and that's mostly so you can keep an eye on me." Though I can't help but think of Tobin and Juliet and their insistence that we can all be friends.

"You'll never be able to move past what happened if you

keep letting other people blame you, so this is me making you face the truth." Dad doesn't wait for an answer.

And even if he had, there's nothing I could say that would change his mind.

We don't talk on the drive up the mountain. Dad's back to ignoring reality, and I've got my hand on the door handle, ready to tuck and roll right out of this nightmare. Except my seat belt's still fastened. Not to mention if I actually jumped, Dad would probably freak out and swerve the Jeep to keep me inside, soaring us both off the side of the mountain by accident. So I keep my hand locked around the handle, my thumb thumping against the release button, and play out an elaborate escape in my head. In the scenario, we both survive my leap from a moving car, and I slip off into the woods where I live out the rest of the season sleeping in tree branches and learning to talk to birds.

Okay, so maybe I'm good at ignoring reality too.

With the windows rolled down, the canvas of the Wrangler's soft top snaps against the metal framing and roll bar as the wind careens inside. Mom's forever saying how it's not a practical family vehicle, but a sedan that could easily fit all four of us would take one look at the rock-ridden dirt road we have to take to get to up to Firelight Point and sputter to a stop before the tires even left the asphalt.

The road isn't really even a road. More like an extra-wide hiking path that people sometimes take their cars up. And once you turn onto it, you're committed. There's a wall of mountain on one side and a ravine on the other. No place to turn around if you change your mind.

We crawl over small boulders jutting up through the reddish-brown dirt and splash into mud puddles and inch-deep streams that wash across the road. The shocks on the Jeep are worthless, and we bounce in our seats. Dad sings an off-key *aaaahhhhh*, his voice vibrating and ricocheting around us. He takes his eyes off the road to smile at me, and I start in with an *aaaahhhhh* of my own. Satisfied, he turns his attention back to the view beyond the windshield. We keep the sounds going until our breaths give out. Mine first, then Dad's. We laugh at the same time, and the past twenty minutes of silence evaporates.

"There's nothing to be nervous about. You'll do great today. It's just like riding a bike." He grins at me as he pulls to a stop in the patch of gravel that serves as a parking lot.

"Sure. Minus the wheels and the ground," I say. There are so many ways this could go wrong, but I have to trust that my dad knows what he's doing. He wouldn't put anyone in danger on purpose. Especially not me.

The view from the top of the mountain is all lush treetops and blue, blue sky. A two-foot stone wall is all that separates the lot from the sheer drop-off that leads down to the climbing area a hundred feet below.

Half a dozen other SUVs and trucks are already here. At first glance, everyone milling around the dirt parking lot is male. All prime candidates to receive a kiss from me during the kissing season.

No effing way.

Dad did not seriously bring me along because the boy-to-Remy ratio is so high. There has to be another explanation.

"Please tell me I'm not here because of the season." I curl my fingers around the seat belt and yank it off. It jams. Dad looks over at me, worry pulling his face tight. I release the belt and try again but slower. A forced calm I don't feel.

"I'm sorry, kiddo, but you've been letting what happened with Isaac control your life for too long. School starts next week. I want you to find a way to move past it, and since you're not doing it on your own, I had to give you a fatherly push."

"This isn't a push. It's an ambush." My voice shakes without any provocation from me.

"Call it whatever you want. I'm not changing my mind." And with that, Dad leaves me sitting alone in the passenger seat, knowing I have to get out.

Next time I find a headless mouse on my doorstep, I'm going back to bed.

Since that's not an option now, I throw open the Jeep door and meet Dad at the trailer hooked up to the back. He tosses me the keys to unlock the heavy door, which I use as a shield, sorting the harnesses and ropes while Dad lets loose a shrill whistle that cuts through the chatter across the lot. Juliet and Laurel, surprisingly, stand among the students. They crane their necks to see me around the door. That's an interesting turn of events. Has Laurel been ghosting me because she's into Juliet and she's worried I'll mess it up like I did with her and Maggie?

I recognize a few of the others, including Ed, the grandson of Mrs. Chastain from the B&B, and Gideon, who works at Apothecary and sold me the crystals earlier in the summer, but I don't know anyone else well enough to know their names. Dad greets everyone, using the registration roster to match names with faces. He cranks up the cheerfulness to eleven when he says Juliet's name, like they go way back and haven't seen each other in ages.

I lean around the edge of the trailer door. All ten of the students know I'm here with Dad. A couple of the guys smile, their eyes glassy with wanting. Ed, despite his grandmother's hoping, is not interested in me. And I feel a twinge of regret that Mrs. Chastain is going to be disappointed by the kissing season yet again.

Taking a deep breath, I try to expel the nerves clotted in my chest.

It could be worse. I could have to help with a class that didn't include two of my only friends as students.

Juliet adjusts her sunglasses as the two of them walk toward me. Her hair is already pulling loose from the braid my sister most likely did for her over breakfast; she shoves the flyaways back into place. Laurel's traded in her habitual jeans and slouchy tee for black athletic pants and a formfitting tank. Her corpse-like complexion could definitely benefit from a little exposure to the sun. If she's in this class, though, it's not to foster her love of the outdoors, so that leaves checking out her competition for Maggie's affection.

Or maybe they've given up on Maggie and decided to date each other instead. Though I don't think Juliet would turn on my sister's friendship like that.

Juliet breaks away from Laurel when she slows to talk with a couple of the guys. I try not to be offended that Laurel seems to be blowing me off in person now too. "Please don't kill me for suggesting to your dad that he bring you with him today," Juliet says.

A coordinated attack makes much more sense than Dad deciding to throw me to the wolves on his own. "What are you even doing here?" I ask, barely even a whisper. "What is Laurel doing with you?"

"Funny story. My mom was losing her shit over how much time Maggie and I were spending together, so I kinda told her

I was taking this class. You know, one that's full of boys doing rugged boy things. It was just supposed to be a cover so she'd lay off me and Maggie and I could keep on keeping on. I didn't think my mom would actually check with your dad to make sure I was telling the truth. But she did. And here I am. But don't think I don't want to be here. It just wasn't part of the plan."

"What about Laurel?" I press.

"She heard me trying to convince Maggie to come do it with me and invited herself along. I half expected her to bail when Maggie told the two of us to have fun without her."

"She's hoping Maggie will see her as more than a friend."

Juliet checks over her shoulder to make sure Laurel is still out of hearing range. "No, she's hoping Maggie will kiss her. And then keep kissing her once she's started."

"And you're okay with that?" I ask.

"I can't be mad at her for being attracted to your sister. But at least if she's up here with me, she's not out somewhere with Maggie acting on her feelings."

"Good point." I guess I should be thankful that Isaac's friends aren't right here to raise hell about my presence. And that Tobin's not here with his sister. He's smart to keep his distance. Still, I can't help but say, "So you didn't rope Tobin into coming with you?"

"Oh, he picked up a part-time job at the used music store

down near your dad's shop. I'm surprised you haven't seen him over there."

"I haven't been looking," I say. Or more accurately, I've been purposely keeping face-to-face contact with him to a minimum to keep from liking him more than I already do.

"Well, maybe you should start."

"And maybe you should mind your own business," I say with a laugh and give her a little push back toward the rest of the class.

Dad whistles again and waves the stragglers over. I pretend they don't exist as I file in beside him.

"All right, everybody. Who's ready to get started?" Dad asks.

The group shouts a collective "Woo!"

Dad sends everyone down the trail to the base of the rock face they're about to climb with their gear while he and I check that the anchor bolt already in the rock is still secure. Normally he'd let the group watch—treat it as a learning opportunity—but apparently I look sufficiently nervous that he needs a moment alone with me.

He squeezes my shoulder and gives me the most obvious pity-smile. At least no one else is around it to see it but me. "You can do this," he says.

He's giving me a chance to prove it. To him. To myself. God, I hope I don't let either of us down.

23

DAD GOES UP FIRST to connect the top rope to the anchor bolt with a sling and a carabiner. Then it's my turn to do a demonstration climb. Something to show the class how it's done. I take a deep breath, keeping my eyes in front of me. After dusting my hands with chalk from the bag at my hip, I make my first move. I'm shaky and slow, but Dad turns my nerves into part of the lesson.

"This isn't a race. See how Remy's taking her time, looking for the right hold? That's what you'll want to do when it's your turn. And remember, if you slip, take a second to get your bearings and then get moving again. Remy and I will be belaying, so you won't be able to fall." He whistles up to me, and I sit back in the harness, letting him take on my weight through the rope. "How about you let go, kiddo?"

"Sure thing." Positioning my foot back on the small ledge,

I push up another foot and take a deep breath. Then I drop away from the rock, letting my arms and legs hang in the open air. Dad stops my descent almost immediately. Dropping my head back, I grin at the sky. It's a rush, letting go of the rope—and my fears—all in one go. He gives me ten seconds, then whistles again, and I find a jut of rock to give my right foot just enough leverage to start again.

Once the lesson is done, the students go up one at a time. I'm on belay duty, so my focus is tied to whoever's climbing and not the people still on the ground with me. Juliet and Laurel try to include me in their conversation, but since all my responses are limited to one or two words they give up after a few minutes and let me concentrate on the task at hand. I eff up a few times when we're switching climbers and need to work the kinks out of my neck from craning it up for such long stretches at a time. When I shift my focus, though, Gideon finds his way into my line of vision. And he moves another foot closer to me, pretending to look up.

He probably thinks he's being subtle, angling as if he's trying to get a better view of the climber up above's progress as my dad points out potential holds from the ground.

I know he's crossed into enemy territory when one of the other guys says, "Guess he didn't learn a damn thing from what she did to Isaac."

I don't look to see who's talking. Or to confirm Gideon's position.

"Hell, even Maggie did," another one says. "Have you noticed she hasn't kissed anyone since then either."

The first guy laughs, a rumbling uneven sound. "Well, would you go around kissing anyone if your sister cursed a guy the last time she kissed one? I mean, what if the curse rubbed off on Maggie too? You know she's got to be worried about that."

That right there is how rumors get started. It won't matter that it's not how the magic or the luck works. If I don't shut this down now, it'll be shared as fact by the time school starts next week. "I'm going to stop you right there since you seem to be confused on how this all works. Maggie's kissing season is over. If she's not kissing anyone it's because she doesn't want to, not because she's cursed too."

"Is that true, Remy? About Maggie not kissing anyone," Laurel asks, but before I can even decide how I want to respond—not that I have a clue what the right answer is— Juliet jumps in.

"Don't listen to them. They don't know what they're talking about."

Laurel's eyes find mine, then dart away, her cheeks pinking. "So Maggie *has* kissed someone else?"

My hands ache from being fisted so tightly around the

belay rope, but I can't release them until Ed, who's climbing above me, finishes his descent. I feed him the line, keeping my face turned toward him so they don't know I'm listening. Though there's no way I couldn't hear them. Dad and Ed are the only two not in on this conversation, and that's only because Dad is busy instructing Ed and Ed's too busy listening to him.

"No, she hasn't," Juliet says. "But that doesn't mean she won't."

Gideon is two feet away now. Impossible to ignore. He scuffs his heel in the dirt, kicking up dust. "Maggie says you just have to kiss someone else. That you're not really cursed and kissing someone else will prove it. So, why haven't you?" His voice is low so as not to draw attention to him or his question.

Without thinking, I turn toward him, my grip going loose. Ed lets out a high-pitched shriek as he drops too fast. Dad lurches toward me, but I get control of the rope and ease Ed the rest of the way down. He laughs, a deep gut-busting laugh, and Dad rubs a palm over his chest like I just shot him with a taser. The second Ed's feet touch the ground, I drop the rope and round on Gideon. "Because I don't *want* to kiss anyone."

"Not even if it'll shut them all up?"

Mentally, I replay my last kiss with Isaac, trying to call up any spark of magic I might have missed in the moment. But if his luck has changed, it's not because of me or anything I did. If he's still cursed, so am I. "That's not how it works."

"Have you tried? Because if you haven't kissed anyone since Isaac, how do you know you're right?"

I open my mouth, but no retort comes out. I can't be sure if Maggie's theory is right unless I test it. And better to kiss someone random like Gideon than risk kissing Tobin. Before I can second-guess myself, I lean into him and press my mouth to his.

"All right, everyone," Dad says, interrupting. He surveys the group to assess who's had a turn already. The only sign he notices the tension around is how his eyes linger on me a few seconds longer than they do on everyone else. "Who's up next?"

Gideon throws his hand in the air, pushing past me now that he's gotten what he wanted. "I'll go. I'm suddenly feeling lucky."

There's no way he's doing this. Not without knowing for sure I haven't just cursed him too. But when I look at him, he's taking the rope from Ed and clipping it to his harness like he's convinced the kiss did its job.

"What are you doing?" I say.

Someone else fakes an answer through coughs: "Trying to impress a girl."

They must not have seen me kiss him. My shoulders tense

at the dig anyway, but I don't respond. I say to Gideon, "You can't go up there. I'm pretty sure rock climbing falls under the category of an activity that very well might end with you getting hurt. And I don't want that on my conscience too."

Gideon, mouth open, hand clutching his shirt low on his belly, looks like I've sucker punched him. "Okay, then. I guess you'll just have to keep me from falling to my death."

Dad claps Gideon on the shoulder like they're old friends. "You've got nothing to worry about. You and Remy just need to trust each other."

Trust is not something that comes easily anymore, but I just nod and prep the belay device on my harness. I don't want to give Gideon any reason to doubt himself before he goes up. And since no one else seems concerned, I let it go. I don't need to add another thing onto their list of Reasons To Hate Remy. Tuning out their whispers, I take a deep breath to clear my mind.

After Dad checks that Gideon's harness is secure and the knots he'd tied will hold, they both inspect the rope per Dad's stringent climbing rules. Nobody goes up if they haven't personally inspected the gear first. They both give me a nod to signal it's all good, and Gideon steps up to the base of the wall, blowing out an audible breath before he starts to climb. He's nimbler than I'd expected. Before Dad even has a chance to point out a hold, Gideon is already reaching for it.

Maybe Maggie was right and Isaac's bad luck is contained to him. My Holloway magic could have reset the second I kissed Gideon and restored my faith in the kissing season again.

For the first time in months, I let myself think things might be okay.

"Way to go, Gideon!" I yell, adding my voice to the chorus of cheers around me.

Then Gideon pauses. And instead of sitting back in the harness and letting it support his weight, he leans into the rock. From below, it looks like he's struggling to catch his breath. Dad calls out to him, and he shoots us a thumbs-up. But then he drops his arm to his side and shakes it like it might be cramped. After another twenty seconds, he reaches for a hold above him, stretching up onto the toes of his left foot alone, his fingers latching on just as his right foot slips off the inch-wide ledge, dropping his leg. I yank down with my brake hand to ensure there's no slack in the line, but the slip is enough to steal his confidence. His fingers grapple with the rock, searching for purchase, and he kicks at the air and rock, sending out a shower of dirt.

"Sit back in the harness, Gideon," my dad calls. "You're not going anywhere. I promise." He walks a few feet to the side where Gideon can see him if he looks down. Then, just loud enough for me alone to hear, he asks me, "You good, kiddo?"

Dad might claim to not believe I'm cursed, but in this moment, I see the truth carving lines into on his face.

"I'm fine." The belay device is doing most of the work, but I clench my hands tighter on the rope to trick my brain into believing I'm the one in control. That Gideon can't get hurt like Isaac had as long as I'm doing everything I can to keep him safe.

"Tell him he's going to be okay. He'll listen to you, Remy."

Listening to me is what broke his concentration in the first place, but he's not responding to Dad. "I've got you, Gideon. Just do what my dad says, and you'll be fine."

Gideon looks down at me, calming enough to plant his feet on the rock face and sit back in the harness. He's weightless/fearless/invincible as he hangs in the air.

Another shower of dirt and rock rains down on us as something metallic clangs against the rock. "Dad, did you hear that?"

"It's just the carabiners on his harness as he's moving around. Nothing to worry about." But the muscles in Dad's face pull tight when he smiles.

Still, he's probably right. He does this for a living, so I should believe him without question. And I will. As soon as Gideon's safely on the ground. "Gideon, climb's over. You need to come down. Now," I say.

Gideon pushes out from the wall and twists to look down at me. "I'm okay. Give me a minute and I can keep going."

"Nope. Sorry. You told me I had to keep you from falling to your death. This is me doing that. Now get moving."

"Fine. Have it your way."

My hands sweat as I feed the rope back up, giving him some slack. Gideon shoves away from the wall and rappels a few feet. His feet barely touch the rock before he's pushing off again and again. When he's less than fifteen feet from the ground, another scattering of rocks breaks loose from somewhere above him.

Then the rope goes limp in my hand.

And Gideon falls.

His arms flail at his sides, the motion turning him just enough that he slams into the ground on his left side, not his head. The anchor sling and bolts that had ripped out of the rock land beside him in the dirt.

Not again. I'm frozen in place, my hands still clutching uselessly to the rope.

"Gideon?" His name slices my throat. *Are you okay?* and *I'm so sorry* prove too much and don't make their way out.

Dad rushes to his side while the rest of the group form a knot to my left, blocking Gideon from view. Their whispers are loud enough for me to catch snatches of what they're saying. *Hurt.* And *cursed.* And *dangerous.*

Gideon moans, and they all fall silent.

I release the length of rope, and my fingers throb from the

sudden freedom. My throat doesn't get the memo and stays clenched. I guess it doesn't matter since there's nothing I can say to fix this anyway.

"C'mon, everybody. Give us some room," Dad says.

The group disperses to collect the gear and their belongings. I move closer. I have to see for myself that Gideon's okay. He's on his back now, eyes pinched shut, cradling his left arm to his chest, which heaves with each labored breath.

Without the audience, Dad inspects Gideon's wrist—most likely broken—and tests his shoulders and neck for good measure—seemingly okay. I replay the moments before he dropped, trying to remember if I'd left too much slack in the rope or if it had been too tight and restricted his movements or pulled the anchor sling and bolts from the rock. Maybe Gideon wouldn't have gone up if he hadn't been trying to prove to me he could do it.

Any way I look at it, this is my fault.

My kiss definitely didn't work.

24

DAD DROPS ME OFF at home after the disastrous climbing class and heads straight to the doctor's office to talk with Gideon's mom. Damage control. Mea culpa. Whatever it takes to get her not to sue for her son's injury at my hands.

I lock myself in my room, wedge my earbuds in place, and listen to my go-to AFI song on repeat, loud enough to drown out everything but my thoughts. If I'd known how to make my brain shut the hell up, too, I would have. But at least the lyrics give me something else to focus on. A reminder that I trusted my heart to the wrong person and their cruelty killed my heart.

I imagine the song is exorcising every stubborn trace of hope I might still harbor for a happy ending. When it's done, there will be nothing left inside me to spark into anything resembling love.

I will be immune to everyone.

"To everyone," I whisper, thinking of Tobin as if saying the words out loud will make them stick and make me forget the part of me that wants to kiss him.

It could have been him. If I'd given in to Maggie's pushing sooner and kissed Tobin instead, he'd be the one hurt now. The most twisted part of my heart is grateful it was Gideon instead.

No wonder I'm cursed when my heart is that black and uncaring.

I don't answer any of the five times my parents knock on my door. They're decent about respecting my privacy and leave after a minute of silence from my end.

Maggie, not so much.

After I've pretended to go to sleep, my headphones in, she lets herself in by inserting a Q-tip into the hole in the door handle and popping the lock from the outside.

Light from the hall creeps inside, but I keep my eyes closed. That doesn't stop her either. She crosses to the bed and yanks the headphones from my ears, the music spilling haphazardly into the darkened room.

"Gideon's going to be okay." Maggie pulls back the covers and settles in beside me, not in her usual spot by the wall but on the outside edge of the bed. I don't have it in me to fight with her, so I inch over, giving us both as much room as my twin bed will allow. "Just a concussion and a fractured wrist. Some bruising from the impact. He's got to take it easy for a few days, but he should be fine."

"How is slamming into the ground from ten-plus feet up 'fine'?" It's so much like Isaac's jump from the falls that I have to force air in and out of my mouth, and it's still not enough to breathe properly.

"It could have been a lot worse. He got lucky, Remy. No need to torture yourself." Maggie smiles in the dark, slipping a hand between her cheek and the pillow to keep her lipstick from staining the fabric. Her hair smells like honeysuckle and fresh mountain water.

Except nobody really knows what it's like being that far off the ground with only a length of rope and some carabiners keeping you from falling until they're up there doing it. For me, the quick rush of fear lasts the span of a breath at most. Then I'm too caught up in the puzzle of it all, searching for a crack large enough for my fingertips to grip or a jut of rock I can use to push myself another foot higher. For others, though, the fear consumes them before they can make the first move.

I blink away the image of Gideon dangling from the ropes, eyes glassy with fear. "I shouldn't have been out there. Not with that group. Not while my magic is so messed up. And I definitely should not have let you get in my head and convince me that kissing someone else would end differently. It was asking for trouble, and that's exactly what we got."

"Well, yeah. That's what happens when you never expect anything good to happen."

My sister, always the optimist. Even when the facts don't support it. There was a time when I'd been the same, finding reasons to laugh when all I'd wanted to do was cry. Sometimes I even miss it. The ability to be happy without trying.

But I don't know how to do that anymore, so I say, "So I'm just supposed to forget about all the shit that's happened since my season started?"

"No. But we don't go through the season just for the heck of it. The whole point is to spread luck and find a little happiness of our own along the way."

"That might be what it was about for you, but for me, I just want to get through it with as little collateral damage as possible. Will you please just let me do that, Mags?"

She doesn't answer, but her eyes catch enough of the light coming in through the window to see that she's watching me. Debating whether to give in to me or keep pushing. I look away first.

Maggie reaches for a chunk of my hair that spills off the pillow. She runs her fingers through it, smoothing out the knots from my hours of lying here. She sections it into threes and begins a simple braid. One she could do in her sleep. The more intricate styles require time and attention, neither of which I give her anymore. But I stay still, taking comfort in the familiar movements.

"Can I ask one more thing?" she says.

I roll onto my back, elbowing her ribs to take back a little personal space. The braid tickles my neck as it unravels.

Maggie scoots to the edge of the mattress but stays curled on her side with her eyes laser-focused on me in the shadows. Whatever she's dancing around, she thinks it will get a reaction, and she doesn't want to miss it even without the light on. I stare at the ceiling as if the answer I've been looking for is written up there for me to decipher somehow. With Isaac a literal walking calamity and everyone, *everyone* hating me, the only thing I have a lock on is my own guilt.

"Why do you act like what's happening to Isaac is all your fault? It's not like he's some innocent bystander in all this." Maggie stares at me, her whole face pulled taut like she's trying to see all the secrets I have caged inside my head. But I won't crack that easily.

I doubt it's ever even occurred to her that I knew I might be breaking the rules when I kissed him. That, in the moment, I didn't care.

Instead of fessing up yet, I say, "Remember the bedtime

stories Mom used to tell us of the Holloway girls who'd gotten just as swept away as the boys who courted them?"

"Yeah, she used to say they'd 'had stars in their eyes and love on their lips.' I always loved that part."

"I think that was me with Isaac. I was so caught up in wanting to kiss him that I let myself believe it meant more to him than it really did."

"But he still kissed you. He let you believe it too. The magic didn't do that, Isaac did."

"And he's paying for it." I flatten my back against the wall. The coolness of the plaster cuts through my tank top, making me shiver. "My page in the Book of Luck is full of the luck I've given out."

"You're documenting Isaac's bad luck? Why?" Maggie asks.

"Because future generations need to know the luck can turn on them. And since the pages for Holloway girls who hurt someone with the magic have been torn out of the book, I'd had to make sure at least one entry remained."

Maggie shimmies closer. Her sigh is hot on my cheek. "It was one kiss, Rem. It doesn't define who you are as a Holloway."

The kissing season has turned into a *damned if I do, damned if I don't* situation. There are no good options as long as Isaac is still cursed. And I'm no closer to finding a cure.

All my calls to Lilly have gone unanswered. The weight of it threatens to crush me. "You of all people should know that one kiss can change you."

"What's that supposed to mean?"

"Just that you haven't kissed anyone since Laurel." It's my turn to try and read her thoughts. It used to be as easy as breathing, but now I'm coming up blank. "Some of the guys in Dad's camp today said that's because you're scared that I've corrupted the magic and you're now cursed too. Is that why?"

"No. Why would you even listen to something like that?" She cuts the last word off, ripping the one syllable to shreds in a way that scatters them over me like still-burning embers.

I scrub my hands over my arms, trying to brush her anger away. But it's already branded on me like tiny little burns that look suspiciously like hearts. "You know, if you want to kiss Juliet you should just do it." My voice is the ghost of a whisper. If I'm wrong about her feelings for Juliet—or what she possibly felt for Laurel—she can ignore my suggestion. Move on with the conversation as if I didn't even speak. And I'll let her get away with it. But she doesn't let it go, proving I'm right.

"Don't talk about me like you have any clue what's going on in my head. Or my heart." She turns her back, curling in on herself.

Even when she's pissed at me, she doesn't leave. I roll to my side, too, our backs pressed together for all of a second before we both shift apart.

25

MAGGIE'S GONE WHEN I wake up. Pressing my hand to the wall, I'm tempted to knock. To take the first step in making things right. I'm honest enough with myself to admit that Maggie is the reason last night was the first night since the season started that I've slept through the entire night. She didn't have to check up on me last night. She definitely didn't have to stay. Especially not after I'd dragged her friendship with Juliet into our fight.

But I don't know how to tell her I'm sorry. Or how to ask her forgiveness for the way I've treated her. I'm not even sure if I've fully forgiven her yet, either, so I let my hand slide back into the covers, my knuckles relaxing against the soft cotton sheets. Rolling over, I ignore the wall and everything else that now stands between my life and hers.

My plan to stay in bed until I die gets interrupted before

it really even starts. Dad's Jeep grumbles in the driveway. It's late enough that he should be long gone. If he's back home now it's because he forgot his wallet/cell phone/pants, but since he's the one we all go to when something's missing—and nine times out of ten he can direct us right to it—I can only assume he's here for me. Word travels fast in Talus. Someone's parents were probably waiting at the shop for him with a not-so-friendly little *Hey, could you keep your devil spawn away from our kids so she doesn't almost kill them too* kind of chat.

I don't make him wait.

He hasn't made it inside when I get downstairs, having been waylaid by Iggy, who's rolling around on his back on the concrete pad off the side door while Dad scratches his exposed belly. They both look up at me as I approach. Iggy stretches to bat at my toes. His claws snag on the straps of my flip-flop. Dad holds out his hand for me to help him up from his crouch. He's only in his mid-forties but his joints pop like he hasn't used his legs in years. That's what a lifetime of rock climbing will do to you, I guess.

"Hey, kiddo. Something happened over at Wild Flour this morning. Your mom needs you to get over there as soon as you can to help her."

I'd been expecting some form of lecture about needing to lie low until everyone calms down, so it takes a few seconds for his words to sink in. When they do, the wispy edges of relief scatter faster than kids playing hide-and-seek. "Help with what? What happened? Is Mom okay?"

"Your mom's fine. So's the Airstream." Dad squeezes my shoulder, then settles his hand at the back of my neck, his thumb worrying circles on my skin despite his assurances that everything is okay. "There was just some vandalism before she got in there to open things up this morning. I swung by when she called, and it's not as bad as it could have been. Nothing broken or stolen. I'm trying to get hold of your sister, too, but she and Juliet skipped out before sunrise again this morning, and she's not answering her phone."

After what happened with Gideon yesterday, I'd known the guys would do something to retaliate. Going after my mom's business is low, even for them. I won't let them get away with it. "What *exactly* did they do?"

"Just made a big mess."

I shrug out of his hold. His fingers leave a sheen of sweat on the back of my neck. "Don't worry about calling Maggie. They didn't do it because of her. No reason she should have to clean it up."

"We don't know why they did it," Dad says. His voice is steady enough that he almost sounds like he believes his words. But the tic in his right cheek says he's lying.

Plus, we both know I am the only reason anyone would go after either of my parents.

"Yes, we do," I say. "Isaac's friends will do whatever it takes to make sure I don't curse anyone else now that my kiss has hurt Gideon too. I guess they think their other efforts have been too subtle."

"What other efforts?"

I wince. "It's nothing, Dad. They just like to remind me what my kiss did to Isaac, that's all."

"That wasn't your fault, Remy. Neither is the mess at the bakery. I'm only asking you to help clean it up because it's got your mom a little frazzled and the more hands on deck the sooner it'll be done. It's not a punishment."

"Call Mom and tell her I'm on my way." Ducking back inside, I grab my bag. Then I stop to kiss him on the cheek on my way back out the door but don't linger because if I do, he might notice that I didn't agree with him.

The smell hits me first—spoiled eggs, burned sugar, syrupy-sweet chocolate. I follow a trail of flour-dusted footprints along the street and into the gravel where they disappear. Crime scene investigators wouldn't even have to bring their own equipment to get shoe impressions with the amount of evidence left right out in the open. But we all know who's behind this. No need for cops to be called in. Though I'm sure the cops have already seen it. I'd bet ninety percent of the town has seen the mess by now. It would be impossible to miss.

Eggshells crunch under my feet as I step up to the front of the Airstream and swipe a finger through the thick muck on the exterior. The glass is caked solid with a mixture of raw eggs, flour, and crystallized sugar that must have already been well on its way to becoming caramel before it was splattered Jackson Pollock–style on top of the rest. It looks like they'd tried to write a message in chocolate syrup, too, but it had bled down the face of the window instead, rendering the words indecipherable.

All except one—*Isaac*. That one is scrawled above the window like it was finger-painted on when their first writing efforts failed.

A river of brown goo runs along the counter and drips off the metal to pool on the gravel. Dozens of ants surround it, though a few who've gotten too close float lifelessly on the surface as a warning to the rest, which none seem to heed as they inch closer to the all-you-can-eat sugar buffet.

I wonder how many guys I'll have to hunt down and hurt before the rest get the message to leave me the hell alone. Because after this bullshit, I'm not above breaking their bones on purpose.

"One little, two little, three little idiots," I grumble-sing. Then I walk around, taking stock of the rest of the damage.

Every inch they could reach—and even some they'd had to jump for—is smeared in this mess. The trailer's a beast to clean on a normal day. It takes hauling it to our driveway where we have access to water and a combination of ladders and hoses and long-handled brushes. And at least four people. This confectionery disaster? I'll be here half the day.

Better me than Mom. She doesn't deserve to deal with this. Scuffing the soles of my shoes on the patch of grass at the base of the steps so I don't track anything in, I push inside.

There's barely enough room for two people to work back here, but without the natural light flooding in through the windows, it feels even tighter. Mom's at the small work sink in the back, filling the plastic mop bucket with water hot enough to send tendrils of steam into the air. Her dark curls twist erratically around her head, escaping from the elastic band that was supposed to hold them off her face.

When she looks up, her eyes are streaked with red. She musters up a smile that is one-part compulsory and two-parts pitying. "Are you okay?" she asks.

At least she's not going to pretend like this isn't my fault. Don't get me wrong, it's nice having a dad who's one hundred percent on my side, but I'm also a realist. There's no denying this wasn't retaliation for Gideon's accident. They're not even friends with him, but being cursed by a Holloway gives them a reason to care. "I could ask the same of you."

"I'll answer if you do."

"Honestly, I'm pissed." Really effing pissed, but cussing at my mom is not the smartest move when she's already worked up.

Mom shoves the tap handle off with the heel of her hand. "I'll see your pissed and raise you a heaping dose of guilt." She hefts the bucket out of the sink and sets it on the floor between us. "I know things have been tough for you lately, but I hoped that you'd find a boy who made you forget all about the heartache Isaac caused and the other boys would no longer have a reason to blame you. But I shouldn't have put that kind of pressure on you. I should have done everything I could to help you move past what happened instead of thinking it would go away on its own."

Everything in me wants to agree with her. To let her take the blame so that maybe—just for a minute—the maelstrom of guilt I've got inside me will stop sucking in every good thing around me. But it's not Mom's fault.

"There's nothing you could've done."

"I don't believe that."

"That's okay. Nobody believes me these days. I'm pretty used to it."

Mom steps around the bucket and folds herself around me in a hug. Her hair smells like vanilla/cake/home. It's almost enough to break my cracks wide open, to send me splintering in a million different pieces all over the floor in a way that can never be put back together.

I pull away before it's too late.

"If you want to go away until the season's over—" she starts.

"Leaving won't make Isaac's bad luck disappear. At this point, I'm not sure anything can," I say.

"I know, lovey. And I'm sorry about that. But maybe you'll feel differently just getting away from all the people you know. You could go stay with Aunt Jenna, or you and I hitch this place to the Jeep and find a quiet town somewhere where you wouldn't have to worry about anything that's happening here."

And prove to everyone here that they're right? That even my parents think I'm dangerous and need to be kept away from people? Not a chance. "I appreciate the offer, Mom, but I'm not leaving." And besides, at least here I know who I'm up against. The constant reminders of how quickly everything can go to shit will keep me from repeating the same mistakes.

"Are you sure?" she asks. "We could be on the road as early as tomorrow morning. I just want you to be safe. If you don't feel safe here, we'll go wherever you want."

"I told you, I'm pissed. I'm not scared of them. I can handle it if you can."

She cups my face, transferring water from her fingers to

my cheek. Holding my gaze until it becomes awkward, she wipes the errant wetness away with a sigh. "Okay."

My fingers itch to rub at the cool spot she left, but Mom already feels bad enough about how everything's played out. I smile at her like it's all good now. Though I'm counting the hours until I can confront the guys who did this. "So, any chance someone installed a spigot out there somewhere to make it easier to wash everything off?"

"Nope. Your dad double-checked when he was here. I've got this bucket and some sponges, though. As long as the sugar didn't harden directly onto the glass or metal it shouldn't be too hard to wipe up."

After filling a spray bottle with soap and more hot water, I lug it, the bucket of water Mom filled, a stepstool, and two sponges fresh from the pack out to the front. Tobin's surveying the damage when I get there. A trash bag hangs from a belt loop on his black jeans, and he's beating a roll of paper towels against his other palm as he glares at the windows.

The tugging in my belly is still there, drawing me to him like those stupid ants toward their sugary death. But at least with the other emotions rioting in my chest, I can keep myself in check. Mostly. The desire to be close enough to touch him sends a flush racing up my neck.

"What are you doing?" I ask. The weight of the full bucket

seems to multiply now that I'm standing still. I set it on the ground and stretch my swollen, red fingers.

Tobin tilts his head, studying me now. His bright eyes shine with amusement as if his being here was a foregone conclusion and I'm a bit dim for not realizing it. "Making a plan of attack."

"How did you even know about this?"

"I may have run into your dad after overhearing you two talk. Figured if it was as bad as it sounded, you could use some help." He rips off a handful of paper towels and wipes an arc across one window. It's more of an exchange than a cleaning, with some of the muck rubbing off on the paper and bits of paper snagging on the hardened sugar and ripping off.

I don't know if I should be grateful he wasn't one of the guys to do it or annoyed that he was spying on me. Yes, I know the promise of luck makes guys do stupid things when it comes to Holloway girls, but the lack of privacy is wearing thin these days. "Do you make a habit of lurking around my backyard?"

"*Habit* implies intent. My window was open, and your voices carry. I'm not a creeper."

"Says every creeper ever."

He puts a hand to his chest and gives me a wounded look, all batting eyelashes and pouty lips. Then just as quickly, he drops the act and says, "Hey, I get it. You've worked hard to perfect this 'doesn't need anyone' attitude to keep people from getting too close. But it's not going to work on me. So let's skip the part where we fight about it and go straight to the part where you let me help you."

I've spent too much time around Tobin already. I have to put a stop to it before one of us gets too attached. And by one of us, I very much mean me. "If I thought you were here because you wanted to be, I might agree. But you're not, so I'm going to have to ask you to leave."

"And I'm going to have to say no." Giving up on the paper towels, Tobin takes the brick-sized sponge from my hand and drowns it in the water. He doesn't bother wringing it out before smacking it on the side of the trailer. The metal reverberates with a low-pitched hum in return. Fat droplets of water and specs of flour fly off from the assault. "I know you think I'm only here because of this season or whatever, but that's not why I like you."

"Then why do you?" I ask, wiping some of the debris from my hair/shirt/heart.

He squats to rinse off the sponge and looks up at me over his shoulder. His lips quirk to one side, the silver rings pulling at the soft pink flesh. "Well, for one, you've got a seriously dark, borderline-badass sense of humor."

I shouldn't be flattered, but I am. Most guys during the season find generic reasons to declare their love. We're always sweet or sexy or smart. I'll take badass any day of the week over those.

"That's a recent development," I say, turning to spray the soapy solution onto the window. And to put a little distance between us.

"Either way, it's really damn attractive." There's a hint of longing in his voice, but otherwise he sounds like Tobin. Sure of himself. In control. Like the words are his own, not the season literally putting words in his mouth. Tobin's shoes scrape on the gravel as he stands. Then he's next to me, water dripping from the sponge onto my toes, and I force my eyes to stay trained on the swatch of glass I've revealed beneath the gunk. "And two, when I can manage to get a smile out of you, it's like I've won the damn lottery or discovered hobbits really do exist. You know, something so rare you don't ever expect to get it but you keep hoping anyway because you know if it ever happens, you'll carry that feeling of amazement around with you the rest of your life."

Did he just compare me to a hobbit? "Hyperbolic much?" I ask, so he doesn't see how close he is to winning me over.

"A little. But it worked."

I bite my lip to keep the smile from growing even bigger. Five minutes with Tobin and everything I should be focused on goes right out the window. How am I supposed to keep my heart in check when he's this cute/determined/unexpected?

If I'm not careful, he could ruin everything. And I could ruin him.

For a second, I think about running back inside and taking Mom up on her offer of skipping town. No packing. No good-byes. Just getting in the car and driving until it feels safe enough to stop. We could be long gone before anyone even noticed.

But then I look at the window, at Isaac's name, and know I'm not going anywhere.

The cozy little bubble Tobin created around us pops. I stomp out the feelings fluttering to life inside me until they are nothing more than a fine dust. One deep breath and they'll get blown away for good.

"You don't have to do this, you know," I say. I'm not even sure if I mean helping me clean or flirting with me. "I'm sure you have better things to do. Like sleeping or tagging along with Maggie and Juliet wherever they ran off to this morning or staying far away from the psycho girl who hurts boys for fun."

Tobin shakes his head. I wait for him to drop the sponge into the bucket and walk away, finally fed up with me, but instead he wrings it out and goes back to work on the section he's clearing.

After a moment, he looks over at me and says, "You must have a different definition of *fun* than I do."

There's nothing I can say that won't come off as me trying

to pass the blame on to the rest of the town. I don't even try to defend myself. If anyone's responsible for my reputation going up in flames, it's me. Others might have fanned the fire, but I struck the match.

Tobin continues, "I don't know what really happened between you and Isaac. I'm guessing the only ones who do are the two of you." He says it quietly, like he's approaching a cornered bear cub—as long as he stays calm and doesn't push too hard, he'll make it out of this in one piece. "So, whatever anyone here says, I'm not buying it. You wouldn't hurt anyone on purpose."

Maybe not deliberately, but I'd known I wasn't allowed to kiss someone who was already in love and I'd done it anyway. His faith in me is solid. Like it's been anchored into rock and will hold my weight if I just let go and trust it. Trust him. It's so damn tempting. "What makes you so sure?"

Tobin points to the top of the window with the sponge. "You haven't touched his name yet. Like you're leaving it there to punish yourself."

My gaze drops to the ground. Three more dead ants now float in the chocolate puddle.

"And that face you just made proves I'm right," he says, pulling my attention back.

Tobin's no different than the ants. So focused on what he wants he'd ignore the danger signs posted all over the place.

"Okay, what if you're right? I'm still not someone you want to be around. At least not during the kissing season. Maybe after it's over and the magic leaves me and we're both sure this is what we want. But right now, you really should listen to what they're all saying about me and stay far, far away."

"I like you, Remy. I don't care about the magic or the luck. I know you think that's all there is to you, but—"

"No, there is no 'but.' This friendship only works if you leave it alone. No saying you like me. No pushing for it to be something more."

No making me *want* it to be something more.

"You say we're friends, but I'm having trouble recalling what you've done for me to uphold your end of this deal."

I've done the only thing I can—kept my distance. "I haven't kissed you."

He shakes his head and laughs to himself. "Remy, not kissing me isn't really a selling point. In case you were wondering."

"I don't want to hurt you, Tobin. I don't want to hurt anyone. But that's what I do, apparently. That's what the season makes me do." First Isaac. Then Gideon. I refuse to add another name to that list. Especially Tobin's.

Making him think I believe this is the only way I know to get him to back off. Because the closer he gets, the harder it is to tell myself I don't care about him, and caring about him— falling for him—is the last thing I want right now.

26

When we're finished, I ask to borrow Mom's car. She assumes I just don't want to walk home after being out in the heat for hours already. I don't correct her. If she knew that I'd planned to go up to the falls and find out who the hell is responsible for trashing the trailer, she'd have never let me go.

Mom gives Tobin a bag of whoopie pies for his help. He says, "I can take Remy home." And then he practically rips the keys from my hand and passes them back to her.

Sure, he's the only reason the cleanup is already finished, but that doesn't mean I won't go into Automatic Bitch Mode on him if he doesn't back off. "You've already done enough."

Tobin slides his palm against mine and laces our fingers. "Just come on."

I wait until we're out of earshot of my mom to ask, "What are you doing?"

He doesn't respond immediately, just keeps walking through the park to his car, towing me a step behind him by our still-linked hands. I don't take the extra step to walk by his side. He can't know that I enjoy his attention. That I feel more like myself when he's around.

"Tobin," I say, pulling my hand free when we reach his car.

"I'm not letting you drive when you look this murdery."

"Yeah, but if you drive, then you'll be considered an accessory."

"There is that." Tobin opens the passenger door for me and folds his arm across the top, waiting for me to move. "But who would constantly put me in my place if you accidentally drove yourself off the side of the mountain and got yourself killed because you're too mad to see straight?"

I laugh despite myself and slide into the passenger seat like I belong there. And I can't stop the truth from slipping out. "You know there's something wrong with you, right?" I say when he gets in.

"What do you mean?"

"You should not be this nice to me when I'm basically awful to you most of the time. It's not right."

"You say 'awful'; I call it refreshingly honest."

"I'm serious, Tobin. I don't deserve it."

When he starts the engine, music blares to life. Turning the volume down so the local hard rock station is just a whisper of guitars, he puts the car in gear and pulls into the steady thrum of traffic. Just when I think he's going to let my confession go unacknowledged, he says, "Okay. Then how about I give you a chance to earn my niceness?"

"How?"

"You could be my friend. Like, for real, not just when I instigate it."

On the surface, his request seems harmless. But I don't think he knows how much he's asking of me. How allowing myself to get close to him is the last thing I should do. "I'm a little rusty when it comes to friendship."

"Well, you're in luck because we just happen to be stuck in a car together where you have nothing else to do but practice on me." Tobin glances my way, his hint of a smile softening his face.

"And what exactly does 'practice' entail?"

"Talking. Getting to know each other better. We can ask each other weird questions like would you rather eat pizza for every meal for a year or never eat chocolate again? I'd pick pizza, just so you know."

"That's good since it's the only logical answer."

"Okay, smartass. Here's one for you. Would you rather be able to bake from any recipe on earth but have everything always turn out just okay or only be able to bake one thing but have it turn out perfectly every time?"

Of course it's not a generic question. It's one tailored specifically for me. One that will bring him a little bit closer to understanding who I am. I can't not answer. Not when I'm trying to be the kind of friend he is. Still, I hesitate. Smacking his shoulder in a fairly good impression of Juliet, I say. "That's just mean."

"It is. But I still want to hear your answer."

"Fine. One thing perfectly. No one wants to buy from a baker who's just okay. What about you?"

"I'd rather you be able to bake one thing perfectly too." He grins at me like that's a fair answer, then says, "Now it's your turn to ask a question."

I let his response slide, pretending his charm has no effect. Though I'm fairly certain he knows it does. "Okay." I think for a moment, trying to come up with something that's both personal and seemingly casual. "Would you rather be forced to dance every time you heard music or be forced to sing along to any song you heard?"

Tobin does a little shimmy in the driver's seat. It's an adorable move meant to make me laugh. Which it does. Until the car veers to the right and hits the rumble strips that warn we're less than two feet from running off the road. He jerks the wheel back straight and says, "Sorry. Sing, absolutely. I pretty much do that already anyway. Even to the songs in my head that no one else can hear."

Of course he sings. If he's as talented a musician as Juliet says, I bet his voice is phenomenal too. It's probably a good thing I haven't heard more than a few seconds of him playing guitar through the window. Or resisting my growing attraction to him would be damn near impossible.

"You're the lead singer in your band, aren't you?" I ask.

"As a matter of fact, I am."

"Want to give me a free car concert?" The question comes out of its own accord, like my brain doesn't care that my heart's precariously balanced. One good shove and over the edge it goes, falling so hard for Tobin it might not recover.

He shakes his head. "You're going to have to work a little harder for that. But your questions are fun. Ask another."

Tobin has more sense than I do at the moment. And I don't give him the chance to change his mind. "Fine. Sticking with the music topic, would you rather only listen to songs by your favorite band for the rest of your life or listen to all other music but never hear your favorite band again?"

"Now who's being mean?"

"It is an impossible question, right?"

"It is. But I think I have a loophole. I'm going with all other music because one of those bands could turn into my new favorite band and then the old one could come back into the rotation."

His response jogs something loose in my chest; the blackness

I'd been keeping at bay creeps back inside me. I was the loophole for Isaac. A way for him to get the Holloway luck but keep his options open. I want to believe Tobin would never use me like that, but that doesn't mean he can't still hurt me. "That's not a loophole so much as using one band as a placeholder for the other. I'd stay loyal to the band I love. Next question from you."

He takes his eyes off the road long enough to look at me and I guess realize I wasn't joking. "Yeah...moving on. Would you rather reverse one small decision you make every day or go back in time and change a single important one?"

That's not even a question for me. If I could go back in time and not kiss Isaac, it would change everything. I would be me again, with my whole charmed future still ahead of me. I wouldn't have to keep Tobin at arm's length. I could fall in love with him like it was the easiest thing in the world.

But I'm not that girl. A fact no one will let me forget.

"Considering you spent your morning helping me clean up a mess that's a side effect of my biggest mistake, I'll let you answer that one yourself." I jam my hands between my legs and the seat underneath me, curling my nails into the soft skin at the back of my knees.

"Shit, Remy. I wasn't thinking." Tobin's hand jerks on the wheel like he wants to comfort me, but he keeps both hands suctioned to the leather as he turns into the first big curve heading up the mountain.

"It's fine," I say. But there are no more questions from either of us of the rest of the drive. And I can't help feeling like our tentative threads of friendship are already fraying.

When we get to the gravel lot at the Firelight Falls trail entrance, there are no open spaces. I tell Tobin to make his own spot behind Seth's Bronco. If we're blocking him in, he can't leave until I've found him.

Tobin's fingers stall on the keys, leaving the engine running instead. "Are you sure you want to do this?"

By way of response, I reach over and twist the ignition off. This ends now.

My breath catches in my throat as we get out and start down the trail. It's been almost two months since I've gone into these woods. At least this time, there's no one waiting at the end of the trail for a smile/kiss/promise of luck.

Thick vines of kudzu twist around tree trunks, creating curtains of impenetrable green. Squirrels chatter to one another from the branches above. They all go silent as we pass, though. The scent of damp leaves and underbrush is so thick I can taste it with every breath. I close my eyes for a moment and soak it in. My body wants to relax into the familiarity, and I almost do. But it's different now—I'm different now.

I slip twice on the hike. Tobin's hands find their way to

my hips to keep me from falling. Still, my ankle throbs from being wrenched the wrong way. I stop long enough to massage it a few times and confirm it's not sprained. When we start moving again, he slows the pace a bit. The downside to that is it gives me more time to stew—about the vandalism on the Airstream, about Isaac, about how not a single one of them deserves the Holloway luck. By the time we reach the bottom, my hands ache from being clenched into fists.

I hear them before we break through the last strand of trees. Their laughter and whooping yells and portable stereo playing generic pop music. There are less than a dozen of them, but their voices echo off the rocks like an amplifier. Most of them are cooling off in the water, but a few of the girls sunbathe on yoga mats stretched across the larger rocks that stairstep alongside the falls.

The firepit, a ring of rocks and rusting soup cans on the shore, still reeks of smoke from the fire they must have burned the night before. Charred sticks and glops of marshmallow litter the ground around it.

"Hey, assholes," I call. It's almost a song the way the words float out of my throat and mingle with the rush of the water. The harshness in my voice is smoothed over like the rocks at the base of the falls.

The boys all turn toward me. Despite the heat, no one's jumping off the falls today. Has anyone attempted that since

Isaac got hurt? I stomp through the squelching mud and pebbles leading to the edge of the water until I'm a few feet from the mouth of the pool. I glare at each of them in turn.

"Go after my parents or their businesses again and this will not end well for any of you." My voice is a growl, low and even. But I know they all understand me, even the ones too far away to hear the words.

"Is that a threat?" Seth asks. He's hip-deep in the water, black hair slicked backed from his sharp-angled face, arms tensed at his sides.

"Damn right, it is." I fist my hands, resisting the temptation to snatch up one of the slick rocks at my feet and hurl it at his head. They'd probably blame that on the curse, too, instead of their own jackassery.

"Oh, look. Remy's all riled up now. Better watch out," someone else says. The guys laugh too loud, too fast. Their nerves splinter through their bravado, and I smile at them. If I push hard enough, I might be able to break them.

"Remy, let's just go," Tobin says beside me. He slips his hand into mine, as if he can get me to leave as easily as he'd convinced me to let him drive me here. "You're not going to get them to apologize."

I step closer to the water, disentangling our fingers. "I'm not here for an apology."

"You know," Seth says, splashing a few feet closer through

the water to prove he's not backing down. "That threat would carry a lot more weight if any of us had any intention of kissing you. But seeing as how we're smart enough to stay the hell away, I guess you're out of luck on that front."

Seth might not want anything to do with me, but a few of his friends fight their smiles like they might not say no if I offered to kiss them. Despite what happened to Gideon yesterday.

Sweat trickles down my spine, right along the ridges, and beads in the back band of my bra. It's all I can do to not wick it away with my shirt. But any show of weakness right now is unacceptable.

"Believe me, Seth, I don't want to kiss y'all any more than you want to kiss me. That's the only reason you still have any control over how you feel about me. But the season's magic is tied to my emotions, so if I changed my mind about wanting you, you'd be falling all over yourselves to try and win my heart. And the things I could force you to do for me would make what happened to Isaac look like an effing cake walk."

That's not even remotely true, but I'm not above fighting dirty if they do. And I might even be tempted to follow through on my threat if I was certain my kisses wouldn't actually curse them.

Rocks crunch and slide behind me as if Tobin is putting

another few feet of space between us. I stamp out the regret before it fully forms.

"You hurt Isaac on purpose?" Paige asks. Her eyebrows draw together over the rims of her sunglasses as she studies me.

Unlike Seth and the rest, Paige should know me better than that. It kills me that she doesn't. "Of course not! Do you really think I did this to him on purpose? That I'm hurting him over and over again just for kicks? I might be heartless, but I'm not cruel, Paige," I say, my voice sharp enough to slice a rift in the atmosphere. Even if I'd known Isaac was only using me for the luck when we kissed, I wouldn't have wanted to hurt him. And I definitely don't want to hurt anyone else, but I have to make them see harassing my family is taking things too far.

"Right. Like we're supposed to believe that," Felix says as he exits the water a few feet from me.

I refuse to let the fact that Felix has finally joined the We Hate Remy Fan Club upset me. What he thinks about me—what any of them think—doesn't matter. "I don't care what you believe. You're free to think and say whatever you want about me. Just leave my family out of it."

Felix grabs a towel slung over one of the logs on the bank and tosses it over his head, drying his hair with a vigorous rub down. He mouths "sorry" and sneaks me a covert smile from underneath the green-and-yellow striped fabric.

I wish I knew if he was sorry for trashing my mom's business or for pretending to treat me the way his friends expect him to when it's clearly not how he really feels.

"Are you sure it was them?" Paige's resigned tone makes her voice waver. She knows they're guilty even as she defends them. But at least it means she wasn't a part of it.

"I'm positive."

"You can't prove we've done anything," Seth says.

A few of the other guys nod in agreement and throw their own *Yeah*s and *He's right*s into the mix.

"Real original defense. Did you steal that from *Law and Order*?" I ask.

Felix cough-laughs, keeping his back to the rest of the group. "Seth does have a point," he says, loud enough for everyone to hear.

"If you want us to stop, Remy, you could just kiss us," one of the others suggests, though there's nothing sweet or romantic in the words. He spreads his arms wide to encompass his friends. "Kiss us and give us a shot at the luck."

My heartbeat ticks up. So this is why some of them have been antagonizing me? Not because my kiss hurt Isaac but to punish me for *not* kissing anyone else like Maggie's been telling them all I should.

My surprise at that lasts all of two seconds. They're desperate, but they don't get to act like they're scared I'll curse them one day and then expect me to kiss them the next. "Not gonna happen."

"Why not?"

"Because I don't want to," I say.

Because they don't deserve to be let off the hook so easily. Because I don't deserve it either.

"And even if I did," I continue, "why would I kiss any of you after you've spent all summer telling anyone who'll listen that I cursed Isaac? You can't have it both ways. Either kissing me is bad luck or it's not. Make up your minds already." I weigh each option in my hands, and then spread my fingers wide to let them drop and shatter on the ground.

"C'mon, Remy. If Isaac's bad luck isn't a direct result of kissing you, what is it, then?" Seth rakes his arm across the surface of the water, shooting a spray of water toward the shore. It falls a few feet short of reaching me. "He can't dive anymore. Not like he used to. Too much damage to his lung, or some shit. Can't hold his breath right. Diving was his life. And you took that from him."

"He wanted to kiss me." I snap my mouth shut before the rest of the truth can slip out. That Isaac's just as much to blame as I am. To them, it will just sound like an excuse. Sometimes I wonder if that's all it is.

"He wouldn't have if he knew what it'd do to him," Seth says.

"Come off it, man. We all know what Isaac was like at the start of the summer." Felix picks up the shirt he'd draped over a rock and shrugs into it. "Getting the Holloway luck was all he talked about for weeks. No one was surprised that he dumped Hannah so he'd have a chance with Remy. Nothing was going to stop him. I'm not saying he deserved to get hurt, but he probably didn't deserve to get good luck either."

Seth and a few others protest, calling Felix a sellout and a liar and a whole host of other words that do nothing to change his mind.

"So, what, Felix? You think she should just go down the line kissing everyone here and see if we fare any better than Isaac did? Gideon tried that yesterday and broke his damn wrist within minutes," Seth says.

Felix glances at Paige, an apologetic smile dimpling his cheeks. Then he starts picking his way across the rocks and dirt to me. "All I'm saying is maybe it would work out right for someone else. Someone who *likes* Remy."

Having real feelings for a Holloway girl isn't a requirement for the magic to work. Some people truly fall in love with us, spurred by real attraction. Others fall in lust as their desire for future luck overtakes them. But most just pretend to be interested in us in hopes that we'll kiss them for their efforts.

"Is that what it would take to get you to leave me alone?

To kiss one of you that actually likes me and have nothing bad happen?" I ask.

Tobin steps around me, partially blocking Felix's path. "You don't need to kiss anyone to make your point," he says to me. "Especially not the guys who'll only use it against you."

A smear of flour mars the thigh of his black jeans. I stare at it, trying to determine if it looks more like South America or Africa because that's safer than looking at his face and the disappointment I know will be there waiting for me. Here I am, offering to kiss these boys I feel nothing for while Tobin's settling for friendship because that's all I'll give him. I do not deserve him. "I don't like it, either, but if it'll get them to back off I have to at least consider it."

"Not gonna happen," Seth says. The features in his face sharpen, as if the bones beneath are turning to stone. His voice is an arctic blast when he continues. "Forget the few guys like Felix who have no fucking sense around you. The only way we're going to let this go is if you promise not to kiss anyone else during the kissing season. Guarantee that no one else gets hurt because of you, and you won't hear a peep out of us."

He'll never admit that Isaac did anything wrong. He'll never apologize for all the things he's said and done to me this summer. But he'll stop making my life hell. All I have to do is keep denying my magic—and my heart.

Short of miraculously finding a way to fix Isaac, that's the best offer I'm going to get.

"Are those the only terms?" I ask.

"Yep, I'm making it easy on you."

"Does that mean you're agreeing?" Felix slaps a hand over his wounded heart and says, "You're gonna break my heart, Remy."

Tobin lets out a noise that's somewhere between a growl and a sigh. He looks back at the mouth of the trail, one leg bouncing like he can't wait to get us both the hell out of here. "You don't have to do this."

My heart makes a pathetic attempt at resurrection in the cavern of my chest, but it's not strong enough to restart on its own. As long as I keep focused on Seth, there's no risk of it getting the jolt it needs. I can't turn down this deal. Not even for Tobin. "Yes, I do." Turning to Seth and the rest of them still in the water, I say, "I promise no one else will get hurt this season because I kissed them." If that means I can't kiss anyone else the rest of the season so be it. But if I can fix Isaac—and my magic—my deliberate phrasing will give me an out.

"I wish I could say it's a pleasure doing business with you, but well—" The words cut off in a sharp laugh.

"Remember that whole friendship balance we were talking about on the way up here?" Tobin asks, stuffing his hands in his pockets. Judging by his pinched lips and clenched jaw, he's gone straight past frustrated to pissed. Because this deal ensures he stays cemented in the friend zone, no chance of a kiss that might only intensify my feelings for him. "This kind of feels like the opposite of that."

"Me agreeing to this has nothing to do with us." As soon as the words are out, I realize it sounds like I think we are a *we*. An *us*. And I rush to clarify. "With us being friends. This is a Holloway-girl thing, not a Remy thing."

Felix's forehead crinkles as he looks between Tobin and me. "How is that not the same?"

The fact that he doesn't get the difference is exactly why I can agree to not kiss him without any regret. Tobin, on the other hand, must understand that the girl I am around him is not who I am with most people because he's looking back at me like I've just put his heart in a blender.

I wish I could tell him I'm sorry. That he makes me want to believe in love again even as every cell in my body rebels against the thought. But I have to keep him firmly on *that* side of the friend line until I'm free of the season's magic. Until I'm me again.

27

THE NEXT MORNING, MY head is too full of everything I want and can't have to even think straight. I need to empty it out. Gut it. Bleed it dry of the excess emotions for Tobin before I do something I'll regret.

I leave the house before Maggie can lay into me again for the deal I struck with Seth and end up at the cemetery. There's zero chance of anyone bothering me here.

Closing my eyes. I crank up the volume on my phone to stop my heart from attempting to change my mind.

A shadow settles over me a few songs later, and my eyes startle open. For a fraction of a second I hope Isaac's dog has decided to show its face. No such luck. Juliet squats next to me in the early-morning sun, one hand braced on the head-stone to keep her from tipping. She snags one of my earbuds, and the Starset song from my anonymous playlist pours out into the air before I can hit Pause. The singer's inability to feel anything mirroring my own.

The eyebrow she raises at me says it all, as does the way her lips tug down in pity.

I refuse to take the bait. "Shouldn't you be meeting my sister for whatever y'all are sneaking off to do today?"

"Change of plans." The earbud dangles from her fingers as she offers it back to me. "I'm totally capable of being friends with both of you, even if you insist on not being friends with each other. And since you look like you could use a friend right about now, you and I are going to get a coffee instead and show everybody that they can't scare you off so easily."

"They haven't scared me off."

"Says the girl sitting alone in a cemetery."

Okay. She might have a point there. Plus, I can still count my friends on one hand with several digits to spare. "So what if I *am* scared? Wouldn't you be if you'd hurt everyone who'd gotten close to you?"

"You haven't hurt me. Or Tobin."

It's like she's trying to tempt the universe into turning on them. Without Lilly Chastain's help, I'm out of luck. Literally. "No, not yet. And I'd like to keep it that way. So I need you to stop trying to be my friend. This is as far as it goes."

"Now you're just being ridiculous."

"Am I, though?"

"Yes. And if you don't come out with me, I'll tell Tobin that you're lying about not wanting to kiss him, and we'll see how long you're able to resist him." So much for Juliet taking the high road on that.

"Do you really want a friendship built on blackmail?" I ask.

"I'll take it any way I can get it, Remy." She pulls me to my feet and links her arm through mine, leading me around the crumbling headstones, careful not to walk over the graves.

We don't say much on the way to Pour House. No talking is necessary as far as I can tell. But once we've settled at a table with our iced coffees, she stops holding back.

"You don't have to hide from the world. You know that, right?"

"I'm not hiding." I gesture to the crowded room.

"What I mean is that you can come out with your sister and me any time. We usually avoid public places, so you can still have a life without being right in the middle of all the crap you're avoiding. Best of both worlds."

"And what would playing third-wheel entail?"

"Well, sometimes we go up to the mountain and find a quiet place in the woods with no one else around. And some-times we sneak up to the roof of the urban bee place and lie on our backs, listening to the buzzing all around and watch them zip back and forth. Sometimes we just drive and drive to no place in particular. Windows down, radio up."

"Is all of that just to keep off your mom's radar?"

"You've had the pleasure of chatting with my mom. Can you imagine how much worse she'd be if she saw me hanging out with Maggie in full view of everyone?" Juliet lifts her spoon and mimes carving her heart right from her chest. "Plus, it's easier to talk when there's no one else around."

"Talk?" I've seen the way they look at each other. If all they're doing is talking, I'd be shocked.

She plucks a packet of sugar from the container in the center of the table and lobs it at me, nailing me in the chest. It drops down the front of my shirt, and I have to dig it out while she laughs ten times harder than the situation calls for. When I look up, she says, "Yes, talk. About things we love and things we hate. What we want to do with our lives. You. A lot of her stories involve you. Maggie really misses you, you know?"

"Maggie misses how easy things used to be." I mash the small bag of sugar between my fingers and thumb. The granules bite back through the paper.

"Can you blame her? You were her best friend—*are* her best friend. But now you two barely talk. That's gotta be so lonely."

"Lucky for her, she has you now. Problem solved."

Juliet sets her iced mocha down without taking a sip. She twirls the straw around the inside rim of the glass, mixing in the traces of coffee leaking from the melting coffee ice cubes.

When she looks up, she gives me a half smile. "As amazing as I am, I am a poor substitute for you. She says you know how to reach over and steady the wheel when she has to sneeze while driving. And you know what songs are banned from being played in the car. And you know the names of all her lipsticks, so when she asks which one would go better with the dress she plans to wear the next day you don't have to ask to see the colors first like I do. When I say she misses you, I mean she misses you. A lot."

I shake my head. Clearly, Juliet is grasping at reasons here. "Those are all things you can learn to do. She doesn't need *me* for any of them."

"Okay, fine." Juliet huffs and sags back into her chair, annoyed. "How about the fact that you're apparently the only person on the planet who makes her laugh so hard she hiccups and can't stop?"

That one is true. Maggie's always been someone who laughs easily—and often—but sometimes when she and I are goofing around, her diaphragm can't take it, and her laughing sends it into spasms. Then I start laughing, too, and she really can't stop. Vicious cycle and all that.

"Once she starts," I say, "it lasts, like, twenty minutes be-cause neither of us can stop laughing long enough to get her breathing under control."

Juliet sweeps her hair off her shoulders and into a messy

knot on top of her head. Then she smiles, triumphant. "You miss her too." It's not a question.

"Don't," I say.

"Don't what?"

I rub the sugar packet way too hard, and the crystals dribble out onto the table from two or three holes I've just ripped in the paper. "This is not something you want to get in the middle of, Juliet. My relationship with my sister isn't something you can fix." Brushing the spilled sugar over the table's edge, I ignore how much this conversation makes me want to fix it.

"I have to at least try," she says.

"Why is it so important to you that Maggie and I become friends again?"

Juliet reaches out and covers my hand with hers. Her slender fingers are cool from the condensation on her glass. "I care about her, Remy. And if I know there's something that will make her happy, I want to give it to her. Don't get me wrong, I would like to be the reason for said happiness, but until y'all have made up, there's always going to be a part of her heart that's broken. Or cracked, at the very least. So whatever happiness she feels will eventually seep right back out again."

"It will probably be easier to buy her some duct tape."

"You have a snarky comeback for everything, don't you?"

"It's what I'm good at these days." I smile to ease some of

the tension. She's trying. The least I can do is meet her half-way. "I know you mean well. And, yes, sometimes I think forgiving Maggie might make things better. But too much has happened for things to go back to normal."

Perching on the edge of her chair, Juliet rests her elbows on the table and leans forward. "What did she do to you that needs forgiving?"

Lying to me about Laurel was such a betrayal. Like she didn't trust me with the secrets of her heart. And maybe she was right to not trust me because clearly I don't have a clue when it comes to love. All I'd wanted was to find something real and failed right out of the gate, while Maggie was always both feet in, heart served up on a silver platter with a little note that said *While I'm yours, I'm one hundred percent yours.* And by accepting her gift of love, the other person also accepted the fact that it would end when Maggie said it did. No changing her mind. No second chances. No regrets.

If she'd trusted me—both with her secrets and with how I was handling my kissing season after everything with Isaac went to shit—things might be different now.

"She turned into someone I can't trust anymore. Someone I don't know. Talking about it won't change the outcome." And it won't erase all the accidents Isaac has endured or my guilt for defying the season's rules to begin with.

"Not true." Juliet lays her hand on my forearm, wrapping

her fingers around my wrist. "I know a thing or two about keeping secrets. The longer you keep them to yourself because you're scared of what someone else might think about you, the more they eat you up inside. But when you finally tell someone, it strips the secrets of their power and they become nothing more than words."

I so wish that was true, but some secrets when told continue to add to the body count. "Words are anything but harmless."

"I didn't say they couldn't hurt. Some words, the really important ones, will rip you to shreds. But I promise you, words are much less painful than guilt and loneliness."

As tempting as it sounds to unload all my emotional baggage onto someone else for a little while, I'll have to pick it all back up when we're done because these aren't the kinds of problems a person can walk away from. Freeing my arm from her grip, I say, "One amateur therapy session isn't going to fix everything that's wrong with me."

"Not with that attitude it won't."

"Please can we just talk about something else? Preferably something with a happier ending."

Juliet taps a finger on her lips as she thinks. After a moment, she says, "Would it be weird if the four of us dated each other? Not all at the same time obviously, but me and Maggie and you and Tobin?" She keeps her eyes on the table, but she smiles, hopeful.

"Weird? Probably. Going to happen? No."

Her smile melts away. "You don't think I have a shot with Maggie as anything but a friend?"

My sister's life has been so full of joy since Juliet moved next door, it's hard to remember a time when I've seen her happier. "Juliet, I think you could be Maggie's everything. I just don't know if she's ready to admit that. She's never been the long-term-relationship type before. But then again, she and I aren't exactly the closest anymore, and she could have crossed that line weeks ago and I wouldn't know, so I seriously doubt you have anything to worry about when it comes to how my sister feels about you."

"Really?" Her voice brightens with hope again.

For a second, I get swept up in her happiness, and I laugh. "Really."

"Okay, so now that I'm in the clear, does this mean you don't have feelings for my brother?"

That would make life so much easier. But I'm not that lucky. I have so many feelings where Tobin is concerned I've had to start stuffing them by the fistful into my pockets because there's no more room in my body to keep them contained.

My hope for fixing the curse is barely more than fumes now. Lilly Chastain hasn't called yet. I stop myself from pulling out my phone and checking right here. I'll give her another few days in case she's more of a letter writer than a phone talker, but if she doesn't respond, I'm all out of ideas for changing Isaac's luck and mine.

And any future with Tobin is dead before it even has a chance.

When I stay quiet, Juliet fills the silence. "If you're going to break his heart, can I at least get a little warning? He might not see it coming in his current state of infatuation, but if I've got a view, then maybe I can keep it from being totally devastating."

"Better his heart gets broken than his leg or his ribs or his head." She reaches for my arm again and squeezes. "Oh, don't look at me that way."

Juliet raises an eyebrow in challenge. She doesn't let me go. "What?" she says. "You're lying to yourself if you think what you're doing is protecting him instead of yourself."

"Is it so wrong to want to protect myself too?"

"It is if you ignore someone who would make you happy. I mean, the season is supposed to lead you to true love, right? Maybe that's what you have to do to set things right. Open yourself up to love again. None of this running away bull. That's clearly not helping."

Whether it's helping or not, it's the only option I have. I promised Seth I wouldn't kiss anyone else. So far, he's kept up his end. I can't be the reason this cease-fire fails. I meet her eyes, silently begging her to understand. "There's a difference between keeping a safe distance and ignoring."

"Safe distance for whom? Tobin or you?"

"Both," I say. "Once the season ends and the magic leaves me, I won't be a threat anymore." And maybe by then I'll know if what we feel for each other is real because until then, I can't trust him not to use my heart the way Isaac did.

I've been calling Lilly Chastain once a day since I got her number. She never answers. But I try calling anyway. One of these times she has to pick up, right? If she was dead, the number would be disconnected. All I can think is that she's either seen enough news segments on how scammers like to target the elderly and she's screening her calls, or she's got a significantly more active social life than I do. Not that it would take much.

When someone actually picks up today, I nearly drop my phone in shock.

"Oh, hi. I'm looking for Lilly Chastain," I stammer.

"This is her daughter, Delilah. Can I help you with something?"

"Yes. I was hoping to talk with her about my grandmother. They were friends when they were younger." It's not a complete lie. If what Mrs. Chastain said is true, Nana and Lilly were extremely close for one summer.

"I'm sorry, that's not going to be possible. My mother isn't in any shape to talk to you or anyone she doesn't know."

I curl my hands into fists to keep them from shaking. *Lilly's still cursed.* The thought pulses in my head as wild as my heartbeat. Was whatever kissing Nana or her sister did to her strong enough to follow Lilly her entire life? For my sake—for Isaac's—I have to hope not.

"Is she...is she okay?" Unlike my hands, I can't keep the tremors out of my voice.

"She has dementia. We're trying to manage it as best we can, but she gets confused easily, and she forgets where she is or who people are sometimes. Adding strangers into the mix causes her undue stress."

"I don't want to make things worse, but I *really* need to talk with her," I say. "Do you know if she remembers things that happened when she was a teenager? Remembers people? If I could just speak to her for a few minutes or have you ask her some questions for me, I would really appreciate it."

"Her memory is unpredictable. One day she can tell me exactly what she ate for breakfast on her very first day of school, and other days she doesn't remember what she ate that day. I hate to tell you no, but I just don't think it's a good idea to make her focus on things from so long ago when she thinks I'm *her* mother some days."

"I understand, I do. It's just I think she knows something about my grandmother, about my family, that could literally save someone's life. Anything she can tell me could help. Could you at least ask her about my grandmother, Ada Holloway, and see if she remembers her and the summer they spent together in Talus, North Carolina? I wouldn't ask if it wasn't really important."

She sighs over the phone, like she knows I won't give up so easily. "My mother's talked about Talus before. I think she spent a summer there with some family when she was young. She talks about that summer sometimes when her memories are blurring. None if what she says makes sense, though."

"What does she say?" The Holloway magic wouldn't make sense to someone who doesn't know it exists. But maybe to Lilly, it's all fresh in her mind.

"I honestly can't remember. I only remember thinking her imagination was running wild. Even if I did ask her about that time in her life, I'm not sure it would help you."

It can't hurt. But I'm not going to get anywhere with Delilah. I need to find a way to talk to Lilly directly. I take a breath to swallow down the urge to tell her about the Holloway magic and what I think happened to her mother. She'd think I was as addled as Lilly and never let me anywhere near her. "If she has any good days where you think it might be okay to talk to her, will you call me just in case?"

"We'll see how she does, okay? I check in on her most days for a few minutes at least. On her good days, I try to give her as much freedom as she wants, but if she brings up anything related to Talus, I'll try to make sense of what she's saying and let you know."

After giving her my phone number, I say, "Thank you. So much."

I may not have all the answers yet, but I know more now than I did yesterday. Like the fact that on Lilly's good days, she's left to her own devices.

If there's a way to fix a Holloway curse, Lilly Chastain is the key to finding it. Her daughter may not think she's in any condition to talk to me, but I can't just sit here and ignore what I've found out.

The need to tell someone runs through me like an electric current. I'm a live wire, sparking, ready to light up the whole world.

I settle for telling one person: Laurel. She's the only one who believed my theory of the missing Book of Luck pages. The only one who helped me look for others who had been cursed. She deserves to know her faith in me was not misplaced. Even if she's avoiding me these days. Laurel doesn't answer my texts so I wait until she's almost done with work to go tell her in person.

I make my way downstairs and out into the darkness. The

late-summer flowers blooming in the boxes under the front windows effuse a honey-like scent as I pass. Iggy has abandoned his post, and I make it to the street and the relative comfort of the darker road unnoticed.

Winding my way to the heart of downtown on autopilot, I avoid the main roads in favor of backstreets, cutting paths through neighbors' yards and dense patches of woods where only the moonlight reaches. Occasionally, a sound mars the sleepiness of the town—an exhale here, the rustle of fabric there.

"You might as well show yourself," I call out, more to prove to myself that my mind is just messing with me than because I think there's anyone actually tailing me. When I glance back over my shoulder, all I find is darkness. A smile tugs at my mouth like I've won.

Then a few feet ahead, a shadow peels away from a tree.

My atrophied heart makes a sudden and miraculous recovery, each frantic beat a new explosion of pain as the shadow solidifies into Tobin.

"So this is what you do when you sneak out at night," he says.

I smother the lingering panic, extinguishing the life force it's giving to my heart. I have no need for either where Tobin's concerned. Walking past him without so much as a pause, I say, "No, you're hallucinating this. Really, I'm setting the town on fire one building at a time, but I've tricked your brain into believing I'm doing something as mundane as going for a midnight stroll. Glad to know the magic's working."

"Funny."

"I take it you're on stakeout duty again?" I ask. "Have you followed me before?" Isaac's dog still hasn't come home, and I've all but given up looking for him. Though if things go the way I hope with Lilly, maybe he'll miraculously turn up as proof that the curse is broken.

Tobin tilts his head and gives me a very slow smile. "Someone's got to stop you from turning this place into the Inferno."

If I respond to that, he will too. And then we'll be knee-deep in conversation, which flies in the face of my reinstituted strictly friends rule. We continue in silence.

After five minutes or so, I stop by a brick wall that's been painted with a mural of Firelight Falls. The glow from the streetlight ten feet away is just enough to make out the deep reds and oranges of the sun hitting the water, the phenomenon that gives the waterfall its name. Another half a block and I'll be at the movie theater where Laurel works. And whatever this is with Tobin ends.

"What did you really think I was doing?" It's a question. It's a dare. The words just slip out, quiet and unsure, before I can stop them because I think I need to know. So much for not talking to him.

"I don't know. I thought maybe you were out putting sugar in gas tanks or some other prank to get back at everyone you seem so pissed at." Tobin leans against the wall, the fingers of his right hand tapping out a rhythm on the brick.

"They all talk like I'm the devil incarnate, but I'm not. I don't want to hurt them. Most of the time I don't." A half laugh escapes. "But even then, wanting to and following through are very different things."

"So what are you doing? Really?"

"Tonight, I'm going to meet Laurel when she's done with work."

"And other nights?"

I look him dead in the eye, hoping he hears what I'm saying. "Ruining boys' summer bucket lists by refusing to kiss them."

"Maggie told you?"

"God, no. But if you think you're the only guy she's trying to get to kiss me, you're not as smart as you look."

"So you think I look smart? That's promising," he says.

I shake my head, refusing to fall for his act. It's too easy to let all the things I like about him make me forget what he's after. "You look like every other guy in town who thinks he can charm his way into a Holloway kiss."

"I don't care about the luck—you know that."

"I know that's what you say to my face, but I heard you

with Maggie. The luck is still a factor whether you think it is or not."

Tobin bites his lip, considering. "I mean, yeah it's there. And despite how you think I look, I'm not stupid enough to turn it down if it's offered."

"I guess it's too bad for you that I'm not offering."

part three

THE FAINT
LUSTER OF LUCK

28

IT's A THREE-AND-A-HALF-HOUR DRIVE to Lilly Chastain's house. Even if I could manage to talk my way into using our car for the day, Maggie would want to know what I needed it for. And then, being Maggie, she'd insist on coming with me. Things are still strained between us despite my slow thaw toward her. Besides, this isn't a conversation I want my sister there for.

If Lilly does know something about the season giving bad luck, she'll be more likely to tell her story to a Holloway girl who's trying to set things right, not one who had a successful season.

Despite how I left things with Tobin the other night, he's the first person I think of. If only he was a viable option. I try Laurel instead, but she falls through because her mom won't let her drive that far without an adult in the car. So if Tobin's serious about being friends with me, I'm hoping he'll overlook the fact that I won't kiss him and come with me since I don't want to go alone.

The used music store where he works is playing a song I recognize but can't quite place when I walk in the door. Tobin's humming along while he reorganizes the collection of vinyl stored in the custom-made wood shelves. Each of the twelve square cubbies are empty, and the stacks of records are piled around him on the floor.

"Did someone screw up your alphabetization?" I ask.

He looks up, lip rings caught between his teeth in concentration, then he grins. Like I'm exactly the person he was hoping would come interrupt his workday. My heart reacts first, revving into overdrive at the thought. And I almost turn around and walk right out without asking for his help. That long of a car ride might be more than my heart can resist.

Upholding my end of the agreement with Seth will only work if I can keep my relationship with Tobin squarely in the friend zone.

"Please tell me you're not one of those people," he says. "There are only two acceptable ways to categorize music. By how much you love the band or album, which is how I personally sort them, or by category, which works better when someone is trying to buy one."

I fake-gasp. "But then people have to go through everything

to even know what's there." Apparently, my mouth doesn't understand the line between friends and flirting.

"Yep. And they might stumble across something they weren't expecting to find while they're doing it." He motions to himself mixed in with all the music. "See? There is a method to my madness."

"Oh yeah. I definitely see the madness."

"Did you come in here to flirt with me despite your protests, or was there something else you wanted?"

"What are you doing tomorrow?" It's the last day of summer break, so if I can't get to Lilly by then, it'll have to wait until next weekend.

"Working until two." Tobin pulls a couple albums from one stack and fits them into the first cubby on the shelf. Then he turns his full attention to me. The thin stripe of eyeliner around his gray eyes makes them shimmer when he smiles at me. "Why? Are you asking me out?"

Oh, a date is definitely out of the question. "If that's how you want to think of driving me to Raleigh to meet some lady who knew my nana when she was a teenager, then sure."

"That sounds more like a chauffeur."

Tapping my fingers on the pile of records closest to me, I say, "I like to think of it as asking a friend for a favor."

"And I'm the friend you chose? Must be my lucky day. Even without a Holloway kiss."

I roll my eyes at his word choice. If Lilly Chastain has the answers I need, this might be one of the last times I have to worry about what I did to Isaac happening to anyone else. And maybe—there's that damn word again—maybe fixing Isaac will let me change the terms of the deal.

No, I can't think like that.

"Holloway kisses are why the bakery truck was vandalized, so you really should take our lack of kissing as a sign of gratitude."

"And Isaac? You kissed him because you *didn't* like him?"

I want to laugh and say something like, *Do I look like the kind of girl who kisses and tells?* But my mouth refuses to comply. "No. Things with Isaac are complicated. I liked him a lot at the start of the summer, but those feelings don't exist anymore."

"Did they exist a few weeks ago when you kissed him again?"

"That was an experiment of sorts."

Tobin rifles through more records, selecting another few that fit whatever criteria he's looking for. He doesn't glance at me when he says, "You're saying words in English, yet somehow I don't understand them."

"The only thing you need to know is that there's nothing going on between me and Isaac. There never really was." I need him to believe that. Badly. Somehow Tobin managed to sneak past my defenses with nothing more than a smile. I see it every time I close my eyes, like I've been looking at him every day of my life instead of a handful of times over the past month plus. And even though I barely know him, my body gets all tingly when I'm near him.

It's ridiculous, really, how I react to him.

Tobin grabs my hand and holds it up to the light to inspect the ink smears on my fingers, a remnant from the last bout of Isaac's bad luck I'd added to the Book of Luck—a broken arm from slipping on the freshly mopped floor at Pour House. His thumb traces a pattern on my palm, and my skin erupts in goose bumps. "You okay?" he asks.

"I'm fine. It's permanent marker."

He gives me this look that says he knows that I know he wasn't talking about the ink stains, but he lets it slide. "Let me guess, you were making bake sale signs to bring all the boys to the yard?"

"I think that's milkshakes. And they were actually *stay off the grass* signs."

"Is that, like, a test to see who's the most creative or resilient or determined or insert-adjective-here?"

Right. Because guys doing daredevilish things to get my attention is just what I want right now. "While that does sound entertaining, no. If I actually thought signs would keep people away, then my yard would be plastered with them." Though as long as Seth and his friends abide by their end of our deal, I shouldn't have to worry about them anymore. That just leaves Tobin I have to keep in check. "You would obey those signs, right?"

Tobin shakes his head, mock serious, his hair flopping down over his eyes. "Oh, c'mon. You and I both know those signs wouldn't apply to me. Or Juliet, in Maggie's case."

He's still holding my hand captive. He knows he's got me in this.

He didn't even have to try.

Is this what love feels like? A barely controllable urge to be near someone? To want to see them smile and know it's only for you?

"Oh, no," I say. "They would apply to you most of all." I steal my hand back and thumb through the stack of records closest to me without actually registering any of them. Breaking contact does nothing to dispel the feel of his skin on mine that lingers like he's left fingerprints directly on my soul.

Tobin flashes a grin, and I know that was the exact wrong thing to say to convince him I'm not interested. "Anyway," he says, "back to this favor. Why are you going to visit some old woman who knew your grandmother, like, fifty years ago?"

"My family records all of the luck that's been given, going back generations. I found Lilly's name in the book. Well, actually it wasn't in the book anymore, which means that it was on one of the pages that someone removed. And since no one in my family can tell me why certain portions of our family history have been excised, I'm hoping she can."

"You think she's not in the book anymore because she's cursed like Isaac?"

It makes me a total witch for wanting someone to be cursed, but I can't help it. Lilly is the only lead I have. "Maybe. I talked to her daughter last night who didn't know anything about the kissing season or the Holloway luck. She said Lilly has dementia, so I won't know anything for sure until I talk to her directly."

"And you want me to go with you because...?" Tobin says.

"Oh, I thought that part was obvious." It's my turn to grin at him. "You have a car."

He splays a hand on his chest, fingers thumping over his heart. "Damn. That's gonna leave a mark."

"If it helps any, you're also probably the only person I could stand to be around for that much time besides your sister and Laurel. But Juliet is already taken—best friend–wise. Not to mention she'd tell my sister what we're up to, and then Maggie would turn it into a thing, and I'm just not ready to deal with that."

Tobin pulls his phone from his back pocket and types just the letter *R* as a reminder on his calendar. "I'm going to pretend like you didn't say that I'm the runner-up best friend to the runner-up best friend. Meet me between our houses tomorrow afternoon at three. And bring snacks."

I fight the smile that's threatening to take over my face. He's still willing to help me, even after everything I've done. Maybe there's hope for me yet. "Between our houses?"

"As in the yard you claim I'm not allowed in. Guess we'll see which one of us is right."

29

THE STEREO'S ON so loud I have to practically shout directions at Tobin to get on the right interstate. He's made a road-trip playlist for the drive—full of songs he's positive I will not just like but love—and he sings along. His voice is smooth and pitch-perfect, making my skin erupt in goose bumps.

There's something familiar about it.

Like I already know the way it will dip low on certain songs or go the tiniest bit gravelly on others. Looking over at him, the pieces click into place. Tobin's musical ability, the fact that he'd rather sing along to every song he hears than dance, the anonymous online playlist I listen to on repeat. It's from him. It *is* him.

He should never talk again, I think. *Just sing.*

Tobin turns down the volume instead, and for half a second I think I must have said it out loud. But he gives me a sideways glance and readjusts his grip on the steering wheel. "Now that we're officially on the road, I have a confession to make."

Here it comes. He knows he's been caught with the play-list, and now he's going to ask me what I think of his music. And there's no way I can tell him it's not just good. It's amazing. Perfect. Not without admitting it's more than his music I feel that way about. Twisting in my seat, I press my back against the door and pull one leg up so I'm all but sitting on it. "Let me guess, you're going to try to turn this whole thing into a date?"

"No. But if you're open to that, I'm more than willing to play along." He waits a beat, and when I don't respond, he continues, "What I was going to say is that I told Jet. About Lilly and what you're hoping to get out of today."

"What the hell, Tobin?" I say, his musical wooing momentarily forgotten. "Why would you do that? You know she'll tell Maggie everything!"

"Someone needed to know where we are. Just in case. She swore she wouldn't say anything to anyone, not even your sister. And as long as we're home by curfew, our secret's safe."

"If we're not home by then, it's because I've killed you, dumped your body, and gone on the run."

His mouth twitches like he's holding back a smile. "Death threats are a little uncalled for in this situation, don't you think?"

"Not if you do something that puts this whole plan in jeopardy. I get that you and Juliet have some super-twin thing going on, and under different circumstances, I might find it effing adorable. But Maggie and I don't have that kind of relationship. Not anymore."

"But you did once?"

It takes me a moment to answer, but I tell him the truth. "Yeah. So close we were practically the same person. You wouldn't have known I was there if you'd met us last year." The space between Maggie and me is like a physical presence some days, pushing and expanding, driving us even further apart. Acknowledging it, like I am now, seems to give it strength. It presses so hard I have to wrap my arms around me to keep from splintering apart.

"I can guarantee I would have noticed you, even then." He takes his eyes off the road long enough to meet mine. "It's gotta be hard for you to not be friends with Maggie."

Damn near impossible now that she's fully embracing her feelings for Juliet—or at least coming close—but too much has happened for us just to go back to the way things were between us. I unfold myself and turn back straight in the seat. Tobin can keep his puppy dog eyes and his pity all to himself. I don't need either. Especially not today when I'm so close to putting everything behind me.

"Some days are easier than others," is all I say. Being

friends with Laurel had helped, though now that she's pulling back from our friendship, I'm realizing just how much she'd been holding me together emotionally.

"I can't imagine what would be bad enough to come between Jet and me."

"She'd just have to show you she's not the person you thought she was," I say. Though maybe I'm the one who hasn't been honest about who I am. I shake the thought away, not ready to dissect it and uncover the possible truth hiding inside.

Tobin drums his fingers on the steering wheel in the silence that follows. When I don't elaborate, he says, "That's all you're going to give me?"

"You're not exactly overflowing with information over there either."

"What do you want to know?"

Anything. Everything. I stop myself short before saying that out loud. But I allow myself to ask a question I've wondered since the day we met: "What does your tattoo say?"

Tobin hooks a finger in his collar and tugs it down so I get a better view. "Not all those who wander are lost."

"I knew after that hobbit comment that you were a Tolkien nerd."

"Not exactly. The quote was something my dad used to say. Kind of a reminder to follow your own path in life even if it doesn't make sense to others."

Something flares to life inside me. Like maybe I'm not lost. Maybe I just don't know what I'm looking for yet. I ignore the voice that says what I'm looking for is right here, waiting for me to see it. "Is music your path? Like your dad?"

"Not exactly like him, I hope. But music, yeah."

"The music you sent me, is that your band?" The question is out before I have time to really think about it or stop it. Something about Tobin makes my self-control disappear. And I can't decide if I mind or not.

Tobin adjusts the air conditioning vent so it blows right on his face. "No, it's all me. I recorded each instrument and the vocals separately and then mixed them on my computer. It's not as good as if I'd been in a studio, but it does what I need well enough."

"Having heard what you can do—even though I didn't know it was you—I'm pretty sure you don't have to worry about anyone thinking you pursuing music doesn't make sense."

"My mom is most definitely not on board. She's terrified I'll lose myself to it like my dad did." His voice dips with a mix of hurt and defiance. "But what she doesn't get is that the music is what *keeps* me sane."

I have to bite my tongue to keep from telling Tobin that his music has been keeping me sane too. "Is that why you post songs anonymously online? So she doesn't find out?"

"No. That was for you. I have a YouTube channel and what amounts to a professional portfolio on SoundCloud both under my name. If I'd used them, though, you would've seen it was me and never even hit Play. I really wanted you to listen. Win you over first so I could maybe convince you I was worth taking a chance on once you found out."

That stings because after everything Tobin's done for me, I owe him the truth. It's the least I can give. "My reluctance to date you has nothing to do with what kind of guy you are. Which, for the record, is the opposite of bad."

"Careful now. With talk like that, I might start to think you actually like me."

"You joke, but not many people would've given up their last day of summer vacation to drive me on what's possibly a wild-goose chase. It means a lot."

"But I'm still on the no-kiss list, aren't I?"

The stupid girl part of me goes all fluttery at the thought of his lips on mine. It takes me an eternity to find words that aren't *No* or *Not anymore* or *What are you waiting for*.

"Is that why you're doing this?" My voice is so quiet I'm not even sure he can hear me over the music and the noise of the engine. Because if his answer is yes, I don't want to know.

Tobin reaches over and squeezes my hand. "I'm here because you asked. That's it. Nothing more."

He says it so openly, I can't help but believe him. I smile, letting the unexpected hope buoy me up.

After a few hours, one coffee break, and multiple wrong turns thanks to our GPS giving us terrible directions, Tobin pulls up to the curb in front of a brick ranch-style house with classic white shutters, hung just at an angle, and overgrown boxwoods halfway up the windows. The yard is spotted with dozens of brown areas where the grass has died, like a neighborhood dog has been marking its territory here for years. It's not the home of someone who was kissed by a Holloway and granted good luck, that's for sure. There's an old Mercedes in the driveway, but no lights are on in the house.

I try the doorbell. It's quiet enough to hear the bell doesn't make a sound inside.

The storm door screams, though, when I open it up to knock on the main door. No wonder she didn't bother to fix the doorbell. The door itself is enough of a warning that she has company. Pushing up on my tiptoes, I peek through the half-moon window. A small, dark hallway leads into a wider, darker room at the back of the house. If Lilly's home, she's sitting in there in the pitch dark. Or possibly dead in the back room.

I knock again, grinding my knuckles into the wood as if that added bit of pressure will make her hear me.

Tobin comes up beside me. "Maybe she forgot you were coming? Or got the days mixed up?"

"Unless she's psychic, that would be impossible."

"Hold on. You mean we drove all this way and she's not even expecting you?"

"She never answered when I called. And I couldn't take the chance her daughter would say no."

"So you thought an ambush would make her more inclined to help?" Tobin says it with a laugh, like he finds my lack of social skills adorable. "She's an old lady who may or may not have been cursed by someone in your family. Don't you think a little warning would have been nice?"

"It's not like it matters at the moment, given she isn't home." I scowl at him to get him to stop that damn half smile. It doesn't work.

He swivels so his back is against the house and crosses his legs at the ankles. "So now what?"

"Now, we wait."

"For how long?"

I check the time on my phone. We need to leave in the next hour or so to get home before curfew. "Until she comes back."

"While I appreciate your commitment to the cause, we have no idea when that will be. We could go grab another coffee and maybe something to eat and then come back to continue our stakeout."

"How are you hungry? You ate three whoopie pies, like, an hour ago." He'd practically inhaled them one after another, not even a pause between for more than a breath. I shake my head and pat the side of the house as a reminder that why we're here is important. "And besides, we can't just leave. What if she comes home and we miss her?"

"No, you're right. Definitely better to camp out on her porch until the neighbors call the cops. Of course, getting arrested is going to be much harder to explain to our parents than why we're here in the first place."

"I've met your mom. Either way, she'll lock you up herself if she finds out you're half a state away with a girl whose lips may be cursed. She'd probably think getting arrested was the smartest thing you've done today."

"But you aren't cursed and you haven't kissed me..." He leaves the rest of the sentence hanging, up to my imagination.

I quip back, "Is this you volunteering? Even though you told me earlier you weren't doing this for a kiss?"

Tobin shrugs. "I do want to be the next guy you kiss, but not because I want the luck. I like you, Remy. And I think you like me too." His tongue flicks over the rings in his lower lip.

I've spent an obnoxious amount of time staring at those rings today. Wondering how it would feel to run my tongue over them. He catches me staring and dips his head closer to me. His eyes are on mine, asking me to tell him he's not wrong. To trust him. To trust myself with him.

And I want to.

I want to remove the barriers between us. The fear/doubt/air. I don't move away. Each breath burns with the effort to not close the gap. We sit like that—an inch, maybe two, separating us—and the desire to give in builds inside me until I can no longer remember why I'm resisting. All I can think about is kissing him.

Reaching out, I brush my fingers against his cheek, down his jaw. He says my name like it's a prayer, like I'm the only thing he's ever wanted.

I jerk away from Tobin before I've done something I can't take back. No matter how perfect his words sound, I can't let myself fall for them. "This was a bad idea. Why don't you get that being with me—kissing me—could hurt you? As much as you think you like me, it's not worth it. *I'm* not worth it. Trust me." All this one-on-one time is lulling me into forgetting I'm supposed to keep him far away from my heart. Well, no more.

He drags his hand through his hair and knots his fingers on the back of his head. Disappointment settles over him like a second skin. "Why can't you just admit that you feel something for me too? When we're together, you forget that you're supposed to be mad at the world and you actually enjoy being a part of it again. And despite all of your protests and certainty that you'll hurt me, I don't really think you believe it or you wouldn't keep spending time with me."

He's right, of course. I'd asked him to come along because I'd wanted an excuse to be close to him. And I do like him. Under different circumstances, I might tell him so, but I can't do anything about it until the season is over. Or until I find a way to break the curse.

"My heart isn't reliable. I listened to it with Isaac, and you know how that turned out. I won't let that happen to you." Or to me. Not again. I curl my fingers into my palms to keep from reaching out to him again. "Why don't you go pick up some coffee, and I'll stay here?"

"I'm not leaving you by yourself. Cops, remember?"

"I'll be fine. I just need a few minutes to myself, okay? And then when you get back, if Lilly hasn't returned, we'll go home."

Tobin extracts his keys from his pocket and spins the key ring on his finger so the keys all clatter together. "If I do this, will you stop treating me with kid gloves and go back to the way you were acting on the drive here? Because that's the Remy I like doing things for."

Tobin can't know he's the reason for that change in me. That his voice, his touch makes me forget all the other shit in my life and I'm just me—or as close to me as I get these days. If he did know, he'd make it his personal mission to bring that version of me back here full-time.

Dropping to the top porch step to sit, I give us both a little breathing room. "That Remy will be here waiting."

I pray he doesn't hear the lie in my voice.

"Okay, then." He jogs across the yard but turns back halfway to hand me a small, spiral notebook he pulls from his back pocket. "Write her a note so she knows you were here. I'll be back soon. Call me if you need anything. And if the cops show, run."

I probably only have fifteen minutes at most to get my emotions back in line. What was I thinking almost kissing Tobin? I would have ruined everything.

Hands shaking, I open his notebook to find a fresh sheet of paper to write my note to Lilly. I don't mean to read Tobin's notes, but the words *luck* and *magic* and *convince* jump out at me from one page. It's a whole list of words under the letter *R*. *R* for Remy. The same way he put the reminder for today on his phone.

He can say a hundred times that he's not interested in me for the luck, but he's lying. Even if he doesn't want me being a Holloway girl to matter, it does. This list proves it.

And I hate myself for being disappointed that he's just like all the other guys.

By the time Tobin returns, to-go coffees in hand, I've

written a note to Lilly with my address and phone number included. Sticking it between the two doors where she can't miss it, I paste on a smile for Tobin, pretending to be the girl he wants me to be.

It backfires almost immediately. His smile ignites like a fuse. He could set the world on fire with a smile like that. And he'd willingly burn with it, I think, if he thought that would make me happy.

When we get in the car, he leans in close and whispers, "You're wrong, you know. Being close to you is just about the best feeling in the world." His lips skim my ear, the slick brush of metal from his lip rings sending a shiver up my neck.

I hold my breath in, hold as still as possible so I don't turn just enough for our lips to finally touch. I shouldn't still want to kiss him. Not after finding the truth in his notebook. So, why can't I make myself move away from him? Why can't I tell him what I saw and put him out of my mind like all the rest of the guys? "I can't, Tobin."

He refuses to make it easy on me. He trails his fingers, calloused from years of playing the guitar, down my arm and along an exposed strip of skin where the seat belt has tugged the fabric of my shirt up. His quiet laugh sends a ripple of hot air flooding over my skin. "That's okay. Unlike those guys out at the falls, I'm not going to guilt you into kissing me." Tobin pulls back so his mouth is a safe distance from mine.

I meet his eyes long enough to see the sincerity there. And that scares me more than anything Seth and his friends could do to me.

30

I SPEND THE WHOLE ride home second-guessing every conversation with Tobin. Every time I believed him, like Isaac. Every time I wanted his words to be true.

It's not his fault, though. It's the kissing season and the power it holds over both of us. We never had a chance. I have to stop letting either one of us think differently.

When he pulls into his driveway, I'm grateful for the darkness outside so I can't see him smile at me and change my mind. "Sorry for wasting your time today."

"I wouldn't say it was a waste." His voice is soft, playful.

"We can't keep doing this, Tobin."

"What are you talking about?"

"I know I asked you to help me today, but that was a mistake. This," I motion between us, "isn't going anywhere. It can't. And pretending otherwise is just going to hurt us both."

Tobin shuts off the engine but makes no move to get out of the car. "Remy, you don't know that."

"I do know. I've done this once already this season, and I won't do it again." Shoving the door open, I leave him—and this conversation—behind. I get halfway across the yard separating our houses before he catches up to me.

"Isaac was an idiot if he didn't see what a good thing he had with you. Whatever he did to you to make you so scared of getting close to someone again, I won't do it."

I pivot toward the baking kitchen so my parents don't overhear us. Tobin follows me inside. I close the door behind us and flip on the lights. Yep, the dark of the car was definitely better because now I can see the *you're making a mistake* look he's giving me.

"It's not Isaac. It's me." I don't even look at him when I say it because he has this way of getting me to open up even when I'm determined not to. And I can't give him an opening. Not even a crack. Or he'll pry me right open like a pomegranate, juicy seeds ripe for the taking. And I cannot—will not—let him know how badly I wish what he's saying is true. "There's something wrong with me. This magic inside me, it's fucked up. I know you think you like me, but you don't know the real me. What you feel isn't real because the girl you feel it for isn't real. I need you to trust me on this."

"Trust goes both ways. You can't ask me to agree that it's

all in my head when you won't even give me a chance to prove you wrong."

I extract the marker that's tucked into a mason jar on the counter and pull the cap off with my teeth. Pressing the soft tip to the first knuckle of my right hand, I scratch out a thick *K-I-S-S* across four fingers. Then I add *K-I-L-L* to the left. Seems like we both need the constant reminder that I'm not free to follow my heart. That the magic has my future in a choke hold as long as Isaac stays cursed.

I hold my fists up in front of his face, knuckles turned out for him to read.

He taps each knuckle in turn. "Is this that game where you pick three guys and decide which one you want to kiss, kill, or marry? And if so, does that mean *marry* is already taken so you've relegated me to one of these options? Or am I *marry*?"

"This isn't a joke."

"Then what is it? Because you spend so much time telling me why we can't be more than friends that you can't even see how right we are for each other."

My heart fights for life again. Fights for a life with Tobin. I take a few steps back to put space between us. Without a guarantee that the magic isn't behind his feelings and he won't end up hurt if I kiss him, I can't give my heart what it wants. "I'm not good for you. At least not right now." Not until I'm me again. Whoever that is now.

"I think I should get to be a judge of that too."

"People are surprisingly bad at judging things like that for themselves."

Tobin nods at my hands now fisted at my sides. "Ever think that maybe you *also* fall into that category?"

I relax my hands and hide them in my back pockets. "Trust me, this is the one decision I'm sure of. I can't start anything with you now. Not until I'm free of the Holloway magic and it can no longer hurt us. When there's no threat of luck hanging over us and we're both sure being together is something we want."

"I *am* sure. But if you don't want to kiss me or don't feel the same way I do, then just have the guts to say it. Don't blame it on magic or whatever you're doing now because that's just fucking insulting."

It's what I have to do to keep us both safe. "And this right here is why I don't want a relationship. With you. With anyone. You come across all swoony and caring most of the time, but the second I say I don't want to kiss you or that I want to wait to be sure it's real and not just you using me for what you can get from me, you lose your shit."

"Are we even having the same conversation here?" Tobin grips the back of his neck and blows out a hard breath through parted lips. "I'm trying to tell you that I like you. And I'd very much like to date you, and, yeah, kiss you at some point. But my feelings have nothing to do with wanting something from you other than you liking me back."

"So, I'm just supposed to believe you?" I'd followed my heart once already during the kissing season, and it cost me everything. I don't have it in me to do that again.

Not even for Tobin.

"Remy, if you think I'm the kind of guy who would use you like that, who would treat both our hearts like they mean nothing to either of us, I don't even know what I'm doing here."

"I saw your notes about me. The ones in your notebook about convincing me to kiss you and giving you luck. So don't tell me it doesn't factor into your feelings for me. You might not want it to, but it does."

"Not in the way you're making it out to be. It's a part of who you are, so of course it matters. But it's not *why* I like you. We could be the real thing, and you're willing to throw it away without even giving it a chance."

"It's not real," I say. "It can't be real during the season."

After everything I've done, I don't deserve real. That's why the Holloway magic steals everything good from me. It knows I'm not worthy. But that truth doesn't stop the void in my chest from threatening to swallow me whole when Tobin turns his back on me and leaves me standing there alone.

———————

I've been waiting on the steps to the baking kitchen for more than an hour since Tobin left. Maggie and Juliet snuck out, too, at some point tonight while Tobin and I were on our road trip, and they aren't back yet, though I'm hoping her night is going better than mine.

I tell myself not to care. That Maggie's business is Maggie's and has nothing to do with me. But in the back of my head, I hear Juliet telling me that my sister's heart isn't whole without me in it. So it's up to me to set things right between us.

And maybe I just miss my sister.

A few minutes later, they cut through the Curcios' backyard where the streetlight's beam can't really reach them. They're nothing more than a shadow at first. A whisper in the dark. Arms linked together at the elbow, they move in tandem, their steps growing shorter and more sluggish the closer they get to the space between our houses. To the moment when they have to go their separate ways and be apart for a while.

Stopping just that side of the divide, they hold on to each other. No lips meeting, just arms and hearts twining together.

I look away, giving them the privacy they thought they'd had a moment too late.

There's something a little bit humbling about watching someone you love fall in love themselves. Everything else dims in comparison to their hearts burning so bright and hot. It's almost—*almost*—enough to make you forget that they've ever hurt you. And then when you do finally remember it somehow doesn't hurt quite as much as it did before.

Maggie stays in the yard until Juliet slips in the back door of her house.

"Have you kissed her yet?" I ask. *Do you know you're in love with her?*

Maggie startles at my voice coming out of the dark. The security light Dad installed above the door of the bakery kitchen clicks on, flooding the backyard with light. Her hands fly up, whether to shield her eyes from the brightness or to press against her chest to try and calm her racing heart I'm not sure. "What?" she asks, her voice shaking.

"Juliet. Have you two kissed yet?"

She moves out of the light and after a few seconds it goes out. The soft *swish, swish* of her shoes on the grass is the only indication that's she's still close by. I don't follow her. We're not there yet. Back to the place where we're able share our secrets and trust the other would keep them safe. But we can get there. I think/hope/want that we can.

"She'd be a good choice. I mean, if you were thinking about it."

"Why's that?" Maggie asks. "Because you think you can't date Tobin if Juliet and I are together?" Juliet must have filled her in on our coffee chat. It's too dark to see the expression on

Maggie's face, but from the gritty sound of her voice I assume she's glaring at me.

"No," I say. "Because she's smart, full of energy and life, and she's gorgeous. Oh, right, and she's clearly into you, let's not forget that one. Which means there's a really good chance that you could fall in love with each other. And you both deserve that. To be happy."

It's quiet enough that I can hear Maggie's whispered response: "So do you." She says it as she walks away.

I allow myself one quick glance at Tobin's dark window before abandoning my spot and following her inside.

31

WHEN MY ALARM GOES off Wednesday morning to get me up for the first day of school, I practically fall out of bed in my haste. After spending most of the night replaying my fight with Tobin—and how I might have just made the biggest mistake of my life—anything that will force it out of my head for a few hours is officially going to be my new favorite thing.

But what do I get for allowing a little hope to sneak in?

A big, fat kick in the face from the universe in the form of a new song link in my email.

Tobin sent it from the anonymous email again, but this time the SoundCloud link takes me to his profile. The most recent song he uploaded is titled "Lucky Girl." I know immediately that it's for me.

Tobin wrote me a song.

Nothing short of an actual apocalypse could stop me from listening to it. Even then I'd probably still risk it.

I start the song, and chill bumps race across my skin from the first note. Then Tobin's voice hits me, and I'm desperately trying to keep it together as he sings:

> You call it luck, but I call it fate
> The magic that led me to you that day
> All I want is to convince you to stay
> But the galaxies of your heart are too far away

My heart starts to crack as I realize the words I saw in his notebook were brainstorming for song lyrics. And now he's given me exactly what I'd said I'd wanted all along: space/ time/disinterest. There's no way I'm letting the Holloway magic take this from me too. Even if I can't be with Tobin yet, I have to let him know that's what I want. That *he's* what I want.

Before I can even knock on the Curcios' front door, Juliet swings it open. "You said you'd give me fair warning."

"What?" I ask.

"Tobin. You were supposed to tell me before you went and crushed his heart." She steps outside and closes the door behind her with a bang, shutting me out of the house like I have no right to be here.

I move back to make room for her on the tiny porch, losing my balance when my heel slips off the edge of the step. She catches my arm and pulls me back up. "I'm sorry."

But she goes all mama bear on me, crossing her arms over her chest and emitting this little growl of frustration. "I know you're sorry. But you can't go rejecting a guy one day and then come over here the next, begging for his attention."

Music starts up from deep within the Curcios' house, the Royal Blood song on my playlist from Tobin driven by a raging guitar and heartache, telling him to run from the monster before it's too late.

"That's not what I'm doing," I say. But it is, even if I don't mean it that way. Flexing my fingers around my phone, my pulse throbs as the blood rushes back into my fingers. "And I didn't reject him. I just asked him to wait until the season's over so my magic can't hurt him. I didn't think I could trust how we feel about each other. I thought the magic would ruin that, too, so I pushed him away before that could happen. But I didn't mean to push him this far."

She narrows her eyes and studies me until the silence between us verges on awkward. "Then I hope you have a plan to fix this."

I'm zero for, like, a million when it comes to fixing things. But I haven't given up on curing Isaac, and I won't give up on Tobin either. "Currently, my plan involves coming over here to find out why he didn't tell me about the song he wrote when I accused him of only wanting the luck, and then, well, I haven't gotten past that."

"You're really terrible at relationships, you know that, right?" Juliet says. But she allows a small smile and loops her arm through mine.

"I haven't had have a lot of practice lately."

"Clearly. If you did, you'd know my brother is one of the good ones. And you wouldn't even think about doubting him. Not for a second."

But I'd doubted him a lot. I'd done everything I could to keep him out. Yet somehow Tobin had found a way in despite me and my cursed heart. "What if he doesn't forgive me?" I don't realize how badly I want him to until the words are out. Not just *want* him to but *need* him to.

"You've got magic on your side. He might be pissed, but until the season is over, you've still got the advantage."

Oh yeah. Lucky me. The magic *is* what's keeping me from giving in to my feelings for him.

As long as Isaac is cursed, so am I. At least metaphorically. And I have to stand by what I'd said to Tobin about waiting no matter how much I regret it.

I untangle my arm from hers and force a laugh. "That doesn't really seem fair."

"Nothing about the season is fair." Her voice lacks the

razors and barbs of anyone else saying the same thing, but coming from her the words cut deeper. "Except for the few people who end up with good luck. It's pretty fair to them. Everyone else kinda gets shafted."

"I know," I say.

Hesitating, Juliet looks over my shoulder toward my house. "Does Maggie know how you feel about him?"

"Not unless she's able to read minds now. Why?"

"It's nothing."

Her *nothing* sounds a lot like my usual *I'm fine*. A cry for help masquerading as a polite blow off. And friends—real friends, anyway—care enough to call you out on it. "No, what?" I say.

She chews on her lip a moment before answering. "Did you know those guys in the climbing class were right about Maggie? She did temporarily swear off kissing."

I shake my head. Maggie might be more cautious after what I said about her relationship habits, but there's no way she would give up love completely. "Maggie wouldn't do that. She loves falling in love too much."

"She also loves you, Remy. So if you were going down, she was going down with you."

"She can't give up kissing you because of me!"

"Give up? God, I hope not," Juliet says, her voice shaking with mock horror. "But ask me to wait until you came to your senses, she most definitely did."

That's just…I don't know. Stupid? Ridiculous? Revealing? Incredibly ironic since this summer instead of kissing Tobin like Maggie and Juliet must have thought I would, I'd pushed him further away. Sister of the Year award right here. "I can't kiss anyone else during the season. I made a deal. Maggie shouldn't have to put her life on hold because of me."

"It's about more than kissing, though. You see that, right? What happened between you two, you need to fix that too. Maybe things can't go back to the way they were. You're both different people now. *Separate* people. But you deserve the chance to find out what you can be to each other. Who knows, it could be even better now."

Looking up toward Tobin's window, I scrape my foot on the porch. There's no guarantee I can fix things—ever—with Tobin, but at least I can help Maggie get her happy ending.

Maggie sits crossed legged on her bed, tapping out a message on her phone. I hesitate in the doorway. It's been so long since I've crossed that threshold, and I don't know if Juliet's right about Maggie and me being able to start fresh. But nothing will ever change if I don't try.

I push inside, my nerves exploding like fireworks in my belly, and say, "You don't have to wait anymore."

"Wait on what?" Maggie asks.

"Kissing Juliet." I edge onto the end of her bed, and she drops her phone between us, giving me her full attention. "She said you've been waiting until I was okay again, but that's just stupid, Mags. You want to kiss her, so you shouldn't put it off anymore." Not because of me.

Folding her knees into her chest, she offers me more room. It's also an invitation to have a real conversation. "That's only part of the reason."

"What's the rest, then?"

"What you said to me during our fight really hurt and—"

I cut her off before this derails into an argument. "I know. And I'm sorry. I was scared and pissed at myself for what happened to Isaac. And I took it out on you."

"No, you were right. I think it hurt so much to hear you say it because it was the truth and I knew it, even if I didn't want to admit it."

"Did kissing Laurel mean something?" It's not the question I want to ask, but I don't know how to ask the other one. And I don't know if she knows how to answer it yet.

"I liked her, Remy. As much as I liked any of the guys I kissed. More than most." The confession comes out at a whisper. Though I can hear the smile wrapped around it. "I ignored it at first because I liked boys, always had. My hormones were just in hyperdrive because of the season, and it was making me see something in Laurel that wasn't there. But then one day we were all hanging out, and I couldn't stop sneaking glances at her and I kept finding reasons to be near her. And then I stopped caring why and started wondering *what if?*"

"But if you liked her so much, why did you let what I said stop you from being with her?"

"Mostly, I was scared. Because she was a girl. Because I didn't know what that made me. I'd always been so sure about who I was, and Laurel made me question it for the first time. It was easier to tell myself that it was just the magic playing tricks on my heart than to face the fact that I might not know myself at all. And then everything happened with you and Isaac, and I told myself it was safer to ignore what I was feeling. That it was fleeting, like all the others."

"You didn't think you could tell me that sooner instead of letting me believe you'd turned your back on me and everything we were taught to believe about love?"

"I wish I could have. I hated that you pushed me away because of it. But I couldn't even admit it to myself, Rem."

"What about Laurel? Were your feelings for her real?"

"I'm sorry I hurt her. And that I screwed up our friendship. But, no, I don't think they were. She deserves to be with someone who really loves her, and that's not me."

Laurel does deserve that. And so does Maggie. "Because now there's Juliet?" I ask.

Maggie's smile breaks across her face. It's sweeter than

every cake I've ever made put together. "Yes. Now there's Juliet. I'm dying to go kiss her, and I don't have a clue what it means."

"Why does it have to mean anything other than you're falling in love?"

The way Maggie continues to smile is answer enough.

And more than ever, I want that for myself too.

32

TOBIN LOOKS LIKE HE'S been taking lessons from me on how to avoid people. In the couple classes we share, he slips in just under the bell and is out of his seat the second class ends. During class, he avoids looking in my direction, so I can't even catch his eye and see how deep his anger at me goes.

During lunch, he's not sitting with Juliet and Maggie, who are all smiles with their hands fused together. And when I try to stop him after last period before he heads to his shift at the music store, he ignores my calling his name in the parking lot. At least when he's at work, Tobin will be cornered. I might not be able to make him talk to me, but hopefully I can make him listen to my apology.

Before I can make it there, Dad texts and asks me to stop by Bold Rock. Says he has a message for me. Cryptic much?

"Hey, kiddo," Dad says when I poke my head into his office. "How was school?"

"Too soon to tell." Though to be honest, I was too distracted by Tobin to pay much attention to my teachers today. "How's work?"

"Starting to calm down now that most of the summer tourists have gone."

"Finally, the invasion has ended." I raise my hands in a *hallelujah* motion, and he laughs.

"At least until the leaf peepers show up in a couple months."

"So, you said you have a message for me? I'm guessing since you wanted to do it in person it's not one either of us wants to hear?"

He stands and runs a hand over my hair, cautious, protective. "It's not bad, I don't think. Just odd."

"Odd how?"

"Your mom called and said Mrs. Chastain needs you to come up to the Lookout this afternoon."

"Oh. Okay," I say. It's been three days since I left my note at Lilly's. So far no response. I'm nervous that if Mrs. Chastain wants to see me in person, it can't be good news. Maybe Lilly is dead. And my last hope for saving Isaac and me along with her. *Please don't do this to me, universe. Don't take this away from me when I'm so close now.* Willing myself to stay positive, I ask, "Did she say why?"

"Something about someone named Lilly. It sounded like she was there to see you, but your mom wasn't sure about that."

"Wait. She's in Talus?" I toss my bag onto the desk and fish around for my keys like my life depends on it. "Can I borrow the Jeep?"

Dad cocks his head and gives me his concerned-parent look. The one that crinkles his eyes and causes the lines around his mouth to deepen. "Hold on a minute. Who is she? Why is she here to see you?"

"She's Mrs. Chastain's cousin-in-law, I guess. And I think she's like Isaac. Or she was and someone fixed her."

"Remy, we've talked about—"

"No, don't say Isaac's bad luck wasn't my fault." I stop in front of him when he blocks the doorway with his arm, not backing down. "If that was true, Lilly wouldn't have come all this way to see me."

"But why *is* she here? How do you even know her?"

"I found her name in the Book of Luck." That's mostly true anyway. I'd found at least part of it. "And Mrs. Chastain helped me get in touch with her to talk about a summer she spent here with Nana and Aunt Edith."

"Does your mom know about this? Maybe she should go with you if it's Holloway business."

I need to do this alone. The last thing I need is another

skeptic telling me the curse is all in my head when it's answers I need. And Lilly has them.

I smile as wide as I can because it's what he needs to see to back off. That I'm okay. That I'm in control of my emotions, not the other way around anymore. "We're just going to talk, Dad. See if Lilly can help me. There's nothing Mom can do. But I promise to fill her in as soon as I get home. You, too, if you want."

"I just need to know that you're all right." He drops his arm but doesn't move from the doorway yet.

"Got it. And I am. I promise. So can I—" I jerk my thumb toward the door in the international gesture for scram.

Shaking his head, he says, "Go on. But be careful, okay?"

"I will." I pop a kiss on his cheek and, keys already in hand, run for the door. "Thanks."

"I hope she's able to help you," he calls after me.

But I'm so far past hope that if this fails, there will be nothing left of me.

Maggie would like this woman. That's all I can think as I walk toward Lilly, who's smiling at me with Barbie-pink lips. The color would look garish on anyone else, but she's accessorized to soften the effect. Double-looped pearls dripping from her neck. Navy shirt dress, cinched at the waist. White canvas lace-ups, not a scuff mark to be seen.

We dispense with the greetings in quick fashion, and I sit across from her at the table where she's already set up with two cups for tea and what remains of her afternoon cake. Lilly explains that when she found my note, Delilah was forced to tell her I'd been trying to reach her, and Lilly insisted they come to Talus to see me in person at once.

"I take it from your note that you are in a bit of a predicament," she says.

"More than a bit," I say.

"I'm sorry to hear that. Though, I have to admit I was happy for a reason to come back to Talus after all these years."

"I'm surprised you're here at all. Delilah made it sound like you weren't this, well, together."

"My daughter, bless her heart, likes to worry about me 'in my old age' as she says. I have my fair share of bad days with my memory, to be sure. My mind's not gone yet."

She winks at me. I attempt to smile in return.

"Well, I'm grateful that you came. I don't know how to ask this, so I'm just going to do it." Unable to meet her eyes, I direct the question to my teacup. My entire future rests on her answer. No pressure, right? "Did you kiss my grandmother or her sister that summer you were here?"

She settles back in her chair, a soft laugh escaping. "That was the root of my problems. You see, I kissed Edith when Ava was the one I should have kissed. I didn't know at the time that was against the rules, or I might have done things differently."

"They didn't tell you the rules?" Nana made sure Maggie and I knew the rules from the time we were old enough to understand what the kissing season was—and that we had to be upfront with anyone we thought we might kiss—so that there were no misunderstandings. I guess this was why.

"I knew I could get luck from kissing Edith; she explained that right at the start. I liked them both. It was impossible not to. They were beautiful and smart and so full of life, not unlike you and your sister, from what I hear. Ada, I fell the hardest for her. I would have given anything to have her reciprocate my feelings, but it was Edith who'd wanted to kiss me. Edith who'd blushed so deeply the freckles on her cheeks had looked like spots on a ladybug.

"So, I let her. She was the first girl I'd ever kissed. I won't say it was disappointing because that makes it seem like it was Edith's fault, which it wasn't, but there was no heat. No warm tingle in my belly like when I was close to Ada. I was sure that was because I had kissed the wrong sister, so later that very night, I confessed my feelings to Ada, though I kept my kiss with her sister to myself. Unfortunately, I realized too late that kissing Edith when my heart already belonged to Ada was a magical no-no."

The situation's similar enough to mine that I can't help but see Isaac lying broken at the bottom of the falls with the start of his bad luck. I gulp my still-steaming tea to chase away the chill that's racing over my skin. "What happened?"

Lilly jerks a bony shoulder up, like we're talking about her last trip to the grocery store and not her kissing a Holloway girl and winding up cursed. "A bee stung me and put a quick end to any romantic thoughts when my throat closed up. The sisters were by my bed that first day in the hospital, holding my hands and whispering to each other when they thought I was asleep about how the Holloway luck should have kept me safe. Then they realized I'd kissed Edith when I was already in love with Ada, and they left. I never saw either of them again."

"They left you cursed?"

How could they do that? Just walk away knowing their magic was the cause of her pain? At least I've owned up to my mistakes and am trying to help Isaac. I can't believe my nana wouldn't have done the same. If Lilly thinks I can set things right for her, she's in for a major disappointment. But then that's what I'm stuck with, too, so at least she's in good company.

"'Unlucky' is what I called it." She blows on her tea. Then she takes a tentative sip, lips parted enough for only a drop or two to slide through at once.

"Cursed" or "unlucky," it's still the same result. All because of a Holloway girl. "I can't believe they didn't try to undo it before you left. Even if they didn't know how to fix it, they should have at least tried."

"I'm not sure any of us knew it was bigger than just the bee sting at first. One bad thing happening wasn't enough to make a correlation. But as time went on and my luck kept getting worse, I started to suspect it had something to do with the kiss." Lilly fidgets with one strand of pearls. Her nail polish is a richer shade of her lipstick. When she catches herself, she lets her hand drop back to the table. "I wrote them each a letter apologizing for my behavior and asking for their forgiveness. I didn't deserve it or expect it, but I asked anyway. And being the kind of girls they were, they wrote back promising to find a way to reverse my bad luck."

They'd known the rules and the consequences for breaking them. Same as I had. Though neither Nana nor Aunt Edith had purposely broken a thing, and I had. I can only hope that it might not matter if their attempts at reversing Lilly's luck were a success. "Did they?" I ask. There are a dozen other questions vying in my head, but that's the only one that matters. That's the one that can change everything.

"It took almost three years, but, yes, they did. I've been right as rain ever since," Lilly says.

Three years of bad luck. Yet here she is all this time later, free from it. "Do you know how they did it? If you never saw them again, it obviously wasn't something they needed you for."

"I don't know all of the things they tried. Only the one that finally worked." Lilly lifts her silver-colored purse from the chair next to her and extracts a folded piece of paper from an inside pocket. She opens it out, her fingers gripping just the corners. It's yellowed from exposure to light, and the ink has faded into a muted gray. But the name across the top is unmistakable.

Edith Holloway

Her original page from the Book of Luck contains Lilly's name as the third entry. I blink at it several times, trying to match it up in my head with the scratchy impression I made from the book. I hadn't even realized her page had been missing. "She sent this to you? Was there any explanation with it? Or something you had to do with it?" *Did everyone else Edith kissed lose their luck when it got removed?*

If they had, that's not a part of our family history I'm aware of. But the luck and the book are tied, so I need to know.

Lilly's face softens into half a dozen wrinkles, and she leans forward and pats my hand. "Whatever happened to you and whoever you kissed, it will be okay."

"No, it won't. Not if you don't know what I'm supposed to do." My voice is practically nonexistent, and I'm not sure she even hears me.

"You just have to remove the page. Taking the page from the book severs the bad luck, or so Edith told me in her last letter. I'd rather not share that letter with you, as it has some personal details in it, but I've shared everything pertinent about why she sent me her page."

There it is. The answer I've been so desperate to find. My breath trembles as I process what it means. "So I rip out my page, and it ends just like that?"

"Just like that," she says.

I have no way of knowing if, along with Isaac's bad luck, all of my Holloway magic will disappear when I break my bond with the book. But if I want to make things right, some things may have to be sacrificed.

Flipping through the pages of the Book of Luck, I find Edith's page. I hadn't noticed it was missing because it wasn't. She must have started a new one after removing her original page so the other people she kissed still got their luck.

Then I continue on to mine: half a dozen accounts of Isaac's bad luck. This could have ended after the accident if I hadn't added Isaac's name. If I hadn't detailed every bad thing that happened to him since. As long as his name is on my page, he's bound to the magic—and the bad luck we created.

His curse ends today.

I pinch the corner of the page and pull. The sound of paper fibers shredding stops me cold. This book, it's everything to my family. I can't steal one of its pages, even if it is my own, without my Mom's blessing. The Book of Luck may have been passed on to Maggie and me, but it was hers first. And she deserves to know what I'm doing to it.

The tear is small, not even an inch. I smooth the paper back in place as if it will magically mend itself until I'm ready to do this for real. I can only hope that since Nana never mentioned it, removing a page from the book doesn't have disastrous consequences and that it won't strip me of my magic. Either way, it's a risk I have to take.

Shutting the book, I carry it down to the kitchen where Mom's working on dinner.

I sit on one of the stools at the island across from her workspace, the book nestled in my lap. "I need to make some physical adjustments to the Book of Luck. But since it's not technically mine, I wanted to tell you before I did it."

Mom continues to stir the mixture of milk and shredded cheddar that's the base of a chicken potpie filling. Her eyes flick to me, her steady circles never faltering. "What exactly does that entail? And why do I get the feeling I'm not going to want to agree?"

"I have to take my page out of the book."

I wait for her to protest. She doesn't disappoint.

"Remy, your bond to the season's magic is through your page. You can't just take that promise back. And besides, you don't know that's why those other pages are missing."

"Actually, I do. That phone call from Mrs. Chastain? It was so I could go up there and meet with her husband's cousin who kissed Aunt Edith when she was really in love with Nana. That's why Nana was always so insistent that we know the rules and make sure everyone we want to kiss knows them too. She didn't want anyone else to get cursed."

"I don't see how permanently altering the book will help with that," Mom says.

"The bad luck is linked to the book. As long as Isaac's name is on my page, bad luck will follow him. I need to take it out." I lift the book from my lap and show her Isaac's list. I never added Gideon's name to my page after our kiss, so his accident during class was just that. An accident. But Isaac's bad luck is on me. "I need to make this right, Mom."

"I know you do, lovey. But let's think about this before we do anything irreversible, okay?"

"What's there to think about? Doing this will fix what I did to him. And it's just one page. It's not like I'm asking to burn the whole book or anything."

"That's good because that would be an automatic no." She takes the pot off the gas burner and, thinking better of leaving me and the book near an open flame, she twists the knob to cut the gas. With as important as this is, her answer should have been an automatic yes. No cautionary discussion needed.

I tighten my grip on the book. The tear on my page grows a millimeter longer. "C'mon, Mom. Aunt Edith removed her original page, and your mom must have agreed with her. Plus, I thought you wanted me to move past what's happened. The only way that's going to happen is if Isaac is back to normal."

"What if it doesn't work?"

"It will."

"How are you so sure?" she asks, her eyes finding the tear I've already made.

And I know I have her.

"Because it has to," I say.

Relenting, she kisses the side of my head. "Go ahead, then."

Then, with one palm pressed to the back of Maggie's page to keep it firmly rooted in the book, I rip my page free. For a moment, the blackness in my chest feels like gold, lighting me up from the inside out.

33

LATE THAT NIGHT, I wait until Maggie's done in the bathroom, then I knock on the wall between our rooms. Nothing. I try again, louder this time so there could be no mistaking what the sound is. She appears in my bedroom doorway within seconds.

"Everything okay?" she asks.

"Yeah." I throw back my covers, inviting her to climb in. "I just...wanted to talk."

She crawls over me and takes her usual spot against the wall. We settle in together, our bodies curving by memory to fit. Now that she's here, my courage goes AWOL. I've frozen her out for months. What right do I have to ask her about kissing Juliet?

"Have you changed your mind about kissing Tobin?" she asks. "I know he's mad at you right now, but that's just proof that he likes you for you, not the luck."

I don't know why. I haven't given him any reasons to think

I'd be good girlfriend material. But everything in me begs for it to be true. If I hadn't been distracted by Lilly's visit, I would have gone to apologize to him already. "In case everything with Isaac isn't enough proof, this thing with Tobin is making it very apparent that I'm not good at this whole kissing-season thing."

"The only thing that's apparent is that you're still trying to control what happens during the season. You only see what you think you want, and you ignore all the possibilities out there."

I tilt my head to see her better in the dark. "But what's so wrong with knowing what I want?" Or knowing *who* I want? "I'm not like you, Maggie. I don't need a dozen possibilities when one of them has already run off with my heart." Which Tobin has managed to do despite all my efforts to the contrary.

Maggie tucks her arm under the pillow. "Believe it or not, I'm starting to understand what that feels like." She leans back against the wall and closes her eyes.

I think of Tobin and the song he wrote for me. He's hurt that I didn't want to be with him yet, but Juliet's right. I have the season's magic on my side. I can still win him over if I try hard enough.

"Do you think he'll forgive me for pushing him away this whole time? Because I think I want to kiss him once I know for sure that removing my page from the Book of Luck actually ended Isaac's curse." As long as the curse is gone—and there's no risk of me hurting Tobin if I kiss him—I'm in the clear.

"Wait. I'm sorry. You did *what* to the book?" Her eyes are wide open now, lasering a hole right through me.

"I removed my page with all my notes on Isaac's bad luck. Don't worry, Mom knows."

"But you still have Holloway magic, right? Taking out your page didn't change that?"

I have to believe the magic wouldn't abandon me when I'm finally making things right. "No, it's just supposed to negate the bad luck that's recorded there. Fingers crossed that's true."

"Are you okay?"

I force a smile because I know that's what she needs. I guess maybe I need it too. "I'm fine." Things are still rotten with Tobin, but there's nothing either of us can do about that right now. After a minute, I ask Maggie one of the questions I've been scared to know the answer to in case I was wrong about her. "Do you regret not pursuing a relationship with Laurel after your kiss?"

"No. Being attracted to Laurel, wanting to kiss her was so unexpected, Remy. It was all too new and too much on top of the season. I wasn't ready for a relationship. I've apologized to her, and I told her I hope we can be friends again when she's ready." She sighs. Her warm breath smells like honeysuckle. "What I do regret is that I didn't tell you what was going on with me sooner. And that I made you feel like love was this infallible thing you had to find at any cost, when in reality the idea of love scares the shit out of me."

The surprising thing about the truth is that after all this time of being cooped up and ignored, it wants to be known. I close my eyes and let the words tumble out in response to her confession. "What happened with Isaac and me wasn't your fault. You didn't say anything about love that I didn't already believe. I'd just wanted everything the season had promised so badly, and I'd wanted Isaac to be the one I would have it with. And Isaac almost died because I kissed him knowing he might still be in love with Hannah and thinking a kiss would make him love me instead. At least now I found a way to fix that mistake."

"By taking out your page," Maggie says. "What if there are more repercussions? What if it affects your magic permanently?"

"It didn't for Aunt Edith, right?" Plus, I've already risked my heart and survived. I can survive losing my magic too—I think. I blink at her in the dark. I don't have to see her face to know she's frowning at me. "Taking my page out of the book is nothing compared to what Isaac's been through. I think he's paid for his part in all this enough already."

"You have too, Rem. You shouldn't have to give up your place in the book when you were following your heart."

"It's already done. Now I just have to hope it worked. Maybe then Isaac and I can both put this behind us and move on."

She grabs my hand, squeezing hard enough to turn her knuckles white. "If it works, do you think you and I will be okay too?"

"We're mostly there already."

But that doesn't mean things will ever go back to the way they were before. We're not the same people anymore. Not the same sisters. There are spaces between us now. Maggie and Remy. And I don't know if those gaps can ever be closed. The difference is now I don't know if they need to.

Maggie might need to wait until Laurel's ready to be friends again, but as the newly independent Remy, my friendship with Laurel isn't contingent on Maggie being a part of it. Now I just have to make sure Laurel knows that. Though I wouldn't blame her if she says she needs space from me as well as my sister. My life has been so intertwined with Maggie's it's going to take us all time to adjust to this new arrangement. Still, I have to try.

I scroll through the photos on my phone until I find the meme I'm looking for: *Friendship is all about finding others who are into the same amount of not talking that you are.* I send it to her.

Within seconds, she sends back one that says *Friendship Goals: You. Me. A basket of cheese fries*, and I know we're going to be just fine.

Maggie pops her head in my bedroom doorway on Thursday morning before school, her fingers curling around the jamb to keep her from coming all the way inside. "You might want to look outside."

I gather my hair, still wet from my shower, into a ponytail and secure it with a rubber band. Does Seth know I plan to go back on my word and kiss Tobin now that I've ended the curse? "Let me guess. Pitchforks? No, probably more creative than that. They're building a pyre in the Curcios' firepit so they can burn me at the stake?"

"Just look," she says and swings out of sight.

I wait until her footsteps in the hallway fade, then draw the window curtain aside. There in the backyard, sitting in a camping chair he must've brought with him, is Isaac. Lying at his feet is a golden retriever, the dog's leash wrapped tight in one hand. The prodigal dog returns. Based on the way he's glued to Isaac's leg, I don't think he's taking off again anytime soon. Isaac looks up and sees me watching him and lifts his other arm—covered in a cast from his knuckles to his elbow—into the air to wave. His face twists in pain.

I step away from the window, letting the curtain fall back into place, blocking him from view. If removing his name—and by extension mine—from the Book of Luck ended the curse, that should be the last bad luck caused by our kiss.

We should both be free. Though I'm still not sure of the repercussions.

Will the magic fade from my veins? Am I still guaranteed true love?

There's a *thwack* outside the window, like something hit the side of the house. A metallic squeaking follows. I pull the curtains back again and look down. Isaac has leaned a ladder against the house and is attempting to climb it, one-handed. I shove the window up and poke my head outside.

"Isaac, stop. What are you doing?"

He pauses, hooking his cast around one of the rungs for balance when he looks up. "Trying to get you to talk to me. Since you didn't come out when you saw me, I improvised. I need to tell you I'm—"

"It is seriously unsafe for you to be climbing up here with a cast on."

"It's only fractured." But he deflates, the hopeful optimism leaking out of him. "Do you want me to leave?"

I grip the top of the ladder to hold it steady. It won't help if he slips or loses his balance, but it's better than doing nothing. "I want you to be careful, Isaac."

"That's why I'm here." He shoots a glance over at Tobin's house, and the ladder shudders with the shift in weight. He stops his ascent there though he's still a few feet from reaching the top. "I wanted to tell you that me getting hurt after kissing you wasn't your fault."

"Isaac, don't."

"I've been blaming you this whole time. Letting everyone else blame you too. But I knew you liked me and used your feelings to get you to kiss me that night. Hannah said if I got the Holloway luck she'd stop breaking up with me because then she'd know she'd never find anyone better than me. And I loved her, Remy. I know that's insane, but I was so stupidly in love with her I was willing to do anything to keep her from leaving me again. I think that's why my luck's been so rotten. Because I didn't take my share of the blame, and I knowingly broke your rules."

Even suspecting he hadn't been straight with me about his feelings, it still hurts to have it confirmed. "It's not you. Now, please go back down. I did something that should have set everything right, and I'd rather not jinx it by having you on this ladder any longer."

"Not until you promise to come out here and talk to me. I want to apologize for real, Remy. And I want to know what it cost you to help me because I know curses don't just go away on their own, and you shouldn't have had to pay for it by yourself."

He's suffered so much already, but he's still worried about what I had to give up. I almost feel bad that he won't get the luck he had hoped for when he first kissed me. So, I agree. Then I wait until he's back on the ground—with no new injuries—before I head down.

When I reach him, I sit on the ground next to his chair, pulling my knees up to my chest.

Isaac doesn't say anything at first, just stares at the ground as if the words he can't seem to find will appear there if he waits long enough. He leans forward in the chair, the back legs lifting off the ground. His hands hover near mine where they're clasped around my knees, but he doesn't touch me. A dozen signatures are scrawled over his cast along with inside jokes and bright purple hearts and a message I can't bring myself to disagree with: FUCK THE KISSING SEASON.

Finally, he says, "So, you really found a way to fix me?"

"I had to sever the link to the magic. I've been trying since your accident, but nothing worked until the other day. You should be okay now." We both should.

"I am sorry, Remy. For using you and for not coming clean when everyone made your life hell."

Those words might have stitched up the hole in my chest a few months ago. Now, the scar tissue is too thick, and it leaves a slight tingling sensation. I press my knees harder against my heart to ease the feeling. "I'm sorry too."

There are no other words. The universe has used them all up and left me empty handed, with nothing else to offer him. But at least we're free.

34

IT TAKES A FEW days of scheming with Maggie and Juliet to come up with a way to convince Tobin I care. He's still ignoring me, but I've caught him standing in the yard, like first day he'd moved here, staring at me through the baking kitchen's windows. Each time, I've waved at him, and each time he's turned and given up with trying to approach me. But I don't want to take the chance that he sees me smiling at him and thinks I'm mocking him with it when, really, I'm just so stupidly giddy that he can't stay away even when he wants to that I can't help wanting to break out in a grin.

Maggie and Juliet don't dare roll their eyes at me because they can't keep their eyes—or hands—off each other. Apparently, Maggie being all in was all it took for Juliet to tell her mom she should be happy Juliet found someone who makes *her* happy. And, after a long-overdue mother-daughter chat, Mrs. Curcio agreed.

I've never seen my sister so happy. It's so clichéd to say she glows, but damn if she's not making a really strong case that she can replace the sun. I can't stop hoping that by the end of this she'll be able to say the same thing about me, but I've needed a plan. And it's taken a while to come up with one I think might succeed.

"I think today is going to be a good day," I tell my parents as they finish up breakfast. We're all up before the sun on a Saturday, so they must've already known something was up.

Dad halts his coffee cup halfway to his mouth. The steam curls off and disappears. "What's up?"

Maggie props her chin on my shoulder from behind. "Oh, nothing. Remy's just going to set a trap and hope she catches the boy of her dreams."

I dig my elbow into her ribs, but she doesn't move.

"And by 'trap,' I assume you mean something legal?" Mom asks, her voice tinged with laughter.

"And nonhazardous?" Dad adds. He sets the mug on the table, his coffee untouched.

"Yes, to both," I say. "I have a plan." Unfortunately, that plan revolves around trusting my heart and Tobin's.

"It's actually not a bad one." Maggie pulls back and joins my parents at the island.

"You're only saying that because you and Juliet helped me come up with it."

My parents look back and forth between Maggie and me and smile.

Mom focuses on me. "This is a nice change."

"It is." Dad pulls me into a bear hug and plants a kiss on top of my head. "But try not to lose yourself again, okay?"

I squeeze him extra hard. "I'll do my best."

Juliet comes over and helps us bag up the last of the whoopie pies. Over the past two nights after school, I've baked somewhere in the range of one hundred and fifty. All for Tobin. And I've enlisted Maggie and Juliet to help me carry out random drop-offs throughout the day. Juliet's already left a double chocolate whoopie pie on his bedside table, an espresso crunch on the sink in the bathroom, and a salted caramel on the dashboard of his car. All in individual cellophane bags. All with the word *sorry* written in black marker on the washi tape sealing the bags shut.

If my plan works, Tobin will be finding whoopie pies all day long. And hopefully by the end, he'll at least give me the chance to apologize in person and talk him into giving me a second chance.

Or, a first chance, if we're being technical.

Maggie wants this to work out as much as I do. She thinks if it doesn't I'll go back to being the Remy I've been all summer and she'll lose me all over again. But I'm done letting other people shape who I am. From now on I'm just going to be me and hope it's enough.

Hefting a tote bag onto my shoulder, I leave the kitchen to a chorus of *Good luck!*s from my sister and Juliet. I toss another two whoopie-pie apologies up onto the roof outside Tobin's window since it seems to be his preferred hangout spot. Or it was until a few nights ago. If he's avoiding the roof because he's avoiding me, I might have to send Juliet out to rescue the whoopie pies so they don't get hauled off by some curious animal.

As I walk, I staple bags to electric poles he'll pass on his way to work. Then I tape them to stop signs and street signs and leave them on the sidewalk, one whoopie pie every few feet, leading from the parking lot behind to music shop to the front door. Inside, I slip them into record bins and ask Tobin's boss to let me sneak a few into the break room.

Even if Tobin doesn't pick up a single one, he won't be able to ignore them.

Paige and Audrey are scooping up one of the whoopie pies from the sidewalk when I get back out front. I haven't spoken to either of them since the confrontation at the falls, and the anger from that day rushes back, storm clouds ruining a sunny day.

"Put that back," I say.

Dropping the package, Paige backs away from it. And me.

Audrey bends down and flips over the whoopie pie so the message is visible again.

"We weren't going to take it. Any of them," Paige says. She doesn't meet my eye. "We just wanted to see if they all said the same thing."

I open the tote bag of remaining whoopie pies as proof. "They do."

They both nod, like that's that. Like they don't even remember we used to be friends. I turn to leave, but Paige calls me back.

She says, "Isaac finally came clean about what happened between you two. He said the bad luck wasn't your fault."

"If anything, everyone should be apologizing to *you*," Audrey adds.

Neither she nor Paige do apologize, though. Not out loud anyway. But maybe them talking to me is an olive branch. All I have to do it take it.

I'm not ready to forgive and forget, to tell them about Tobin and this ridiculous plan to show him I was wrong. But if I want him to give me a second chance, shouldn't I do the same for my friends?

I wait an awkward amount of time, then say, "This isn't about Isaac."

"Oh." Audrey's cheeks pink up, and she looks to Paige to save her.

Obliging, Paige says, "Do you want some help? I mean, you don't have to tell us who it's for or anything, but if you want to give us some whoopie pies, we can put them around town for you."

"Yeah, sure," I say.

It doesn't fix everything between us, but it's a start.

The rest of the day I feel light enough to float away. I wrap my feet around chair legs while I get caught up on homework and curl my hands into the grass as I lie in the side yard, waiting for Tobin to come home from work. When I want to be left alone, I can't get rid of him. But now that I feel like me for the first time in forever, he's not around to celebrate with.

I fall asleep in the sun and wake up to a bruising sky and stars winking to life. I smile to myself. To the universe. Even if things don't work out with Tobin—though I'm not ready to give up on that front yet—I'm happy. Actually happy.

Pushing my luck, I look at Tobin's window. A light shines from inside, silhouetting a familiar figure up on the roof.

"Tobin!" I call as I get to my feet.

No response.

"I was waiting for you."

Still nothing.

Stopping under his window, my smile wavers. He's up

there and he won't say anything. But I'm not giving up. Not until he tells me to. Even then, I might not listen. Turnabout is fair play. "Why didn't you wake me up?"

"I wasn't sure if I was ready to talk to you yet." He says it without looking at me, twisting an empty cellophane bag between his fingers.

And just like that, I plummet back to the earth. The weightlessness that's kept me afloat all day seeps right out with my next breath. "Oh." My apologies weren't enough. I turn, gravity weighing my feet down.

"Remy, wait." It comes out as pure frustration, not a single encouraging note to his tone, but even that's better than him letting me walk away.

I spin back around.

"What exactly are you sorry for?" he asks.

"If you want the annotated list, we might be here all night."

Tobin cracks a smile. "Bullet points will work."

"Do you think you could come down here so I can say this to your face?" So I can get close enough for a kiss.

"Step back." He crouches as best he can on a slanted roof to jump to the ground.

"Tobin, don't."

"I've done it before. How do you think I always sneak out when I follow you on your late-night walks?"

"Can you please just go inside and use the stairs like a normal person? Just to be safe." There's no longer a risk from the Holloway magic, but I've been living in fear of it for so long, it'll take some time to forget.

He disappears back through the window, and for a second I worry he's not going to even come down. Then the front door *whooshes* open, and he's jumping the three porch steps. He lands a foot away from me.

"Okay. I'm listening," he says.

This is it. My chance to put my heart on the line and wait for him to catch it. I hold up one finger and begin my list. "I'm sorry for not seriously accepting your offer of friendship. For not telling you how much I love the playlist you made me. And not realizing the notes I found on our road trip weren't proof that your feelings for me were fake. But mostly for not telling you that I like you back and would very much like to date you and kiss you at some point. Like maybe right now."

Tobin holds his palm out to mine, wrapping his fingers around the ones I'd used to make my apology points. "Then what are you waiting for?"

I close the distance and press my lips to his. Everything I've been trying not to feel for him rushes to the surface. Every place our bodies connect—lips/chests/hips—aches with the need to be closer. The kiss builds slowly, our lips colliding with just enough pressure to coax our mouths open, to let us discover each other in a whole new way.

And in that moment with the season's magic put to the test, I believe in it with my whole heart. No doubt. No second-guessing. No room for anything but Tobin and me and the possibility that this kiss could be the start of everything.

"I thought this was too dangerous," he says against my mouth.

"It might be." I settle my hand on the back of his neck, pulling him in again. "But I can't ignore who I am."

"And who is that?"

"A Holloway girl."

And then he's kissing me again. Or I'm kissing him. It's hard to tell who initiated it. All I know is that I never want it to stop.

35

I MIGHT BE THE first person in all of history to die from smiling too much. But it wouldn't be the worst way to go, though knocking off now that I've kissed Tobin would be more than a little inconvenient.

Not listening to his playlist while I contemplate what to do with my page from the Book of Luck would probably buy me some more time. I can't make myself turn it off, though.

The kitchen door swings open, and I pull my face tight to keep from looking like a psychopath, just sitting here surrounded by reminders of Isaac's bad luck, grinning.

"Okay," Maggie says, as she skips inside. "I keep waiting for you to bring this up, but you haven't yet, so I figured it was up to me."

That could mean a million different things coming from Maggie.

She unwinds the straps holding the leather cover of the Book of Luck closed and fans the pages to find hers. The paper refuses to lie flat thanks to the ragged edge where my page used to fall after it. She turns the page to a blank one. "Tobin's name belongs in the book."

He's more than earned his place in it by fetching my heart from the brink of nonexistence. And with my original page now torn out, I could start over. Clean slate.

"I know. I was thinking I might start a new page. Not just so I can add Tobin and record his good luck later on but so future Holloway girls know one mistake isn't the end."

"So much yes," Maggie says.

"Really? You don't think it's tempting fate or something?"

"Not at all. You're a Holloway girl. You deserve to have your name and your legacy in there along with all the others. Right next to mine like we're meant to be. MaggieAndRemy."

The lack of spaces between our names is impossible to miss.

My heart flinches, sending a sharp pang reverberating through my chest. "I don't know if we can go back to being MaggieAndRemy. Not the way we were anyway. We've both changed so much in the last year."

"I know. But you're talking to me in full sentences— without biting my head off, I might add—and you're finally with Tobin, so I figure you're getting closer to being you again."

"What if this is me now? I don't think I'll ever go back to the girl I was before." And I'm not sure I would want to. That Remy wasn't really me. She was Maggie Light. Same great taste, fewer calories. You know, if calories stand for personality.

Maggie turns and walks past me without a word. It's a benign enough rejection that it should gloss right over me without so much as a scratch. But after all that's happened and how much better things have been, it arrows right into my chest, threatening to puncture my little bubble of happiness.

But instead of leaving, she stops behind me. "Then I'll get to know the new you and love her too. You've just got to give me a chance." Then she sweeps my hair back from my face, her fingers automatically sectioning it into three chunks and starts to braid.

"Okay," I say because she's my sister, and I don't want to fight anymore.

Because maybe love can be that simple.

Moving on might mean letting go of the past. Sometimes what you're leaving behind is a feeling or a state of mind. And sometimes it's a physical thing, which once discarded allows you to breathe for the first time in years.

When Maggie's done with my braid, I detour to the Curcios'

backyard instead of going into the house. Tobin's lighter sits on the rim of the firepit; charred sticks and half-burned crumbles of newspaper are piled inside. Crouching next to it, I flick the lighter button again and again, my thumb clumsy and slow, until it sparks. I hold my torn-out page over the pit and touch the flame to one corner. The paper catches/curls/burns. I drop it into the firepit before the flames reach my fingers. Bits of ash flake off and blow back onto my legs, sticking to my skin. They smear into streaks of gray, like the powdery scales from a moth's wings, when I wipe them away.

I look back at the pit and can no longer tell the difference between the dregs of the last bonfire Tobin and Juliet had and what's left of my page—or of the girl I've been for the past few months.

For now, I'm just Remy. A Holloway girl who might have snagged a little bit of luck for herself.

Epilogue

EIGHTY-SIX HOURS AND COUNTING. That's how long it's been since I kissed Tobin, and not a single person in town has uttered the word *cursed*. It's like the word has been culled from the English language. If that's all I'd gotten out of the season, it would have been enough.

But at eighty-six hours and counting, Tobin still hasn't lost interest in me. And judging by the frequency/intensity/epicness of our make-out sessions he's not about to anytime soon.

We meet in the grass between our houses when no one is watching us but the curved slice of moon and a smattering of stars. He threads his fingers with mine and leads me across our front yards. As we pass out of the glow from the streetlight into the shadows beyond by the peeling birch trees, he twists our linked arms behind my back, spinning me around to face him. I tilt my head back to kiss him without hesitation, the heat building slowly, his lips moving against mine with just enough pressure to coax my mouth open. Burying my free hand in his hair, I drag him against me. His teeth scrape over my bottom lip before capturing my mouth again.

I arch my back to try and get closer. Always closer. Never close enough.

His hot fingers skim underneath my jacket and shirt, across the dimples in my lower back, and settle on my hips. The never-ending kiss morphs into a series of shorter ones that have us both desperate for air by the time we finally release each other.

"I've been wanting to do that all night," he says.

"Same here."

"Our sisters have the right idea, running off together as soon as the sun's up. This waiting-until-dark thing is absolute torture."

"I don't think spending our lunch break in the chemistry lab counts as waiting. And anyway, I thought you had something you wanted to show me tonight, hence the late-night sneaking out," I say.

"Maybe I just wanted to kiss you good night." He leans in to nuzzle my neck, tracing my pulse point with his tongue. I shift, guiding his lips back to mine before he drives me mad.

Pulling away a moment later, I somehow manage to keep a straight face. "Good night, then."

He clasps my hand again, but it's his rumbling laugh that tethers me to spot. "No, wait. I do have a surprise for you."

"You didn't tell me it was a surprise."

He just starts walking, keeping to the edge of the road, though no one's ever out this late. "Well, I was going to let you find it on your own, but I kinda want to see your reaction firsthand."

"Why's that?"

"Because now that I know what a real Remy smile looks like, I'm on a mission to make it happen as often as possible."

My cheeks hurt from trying to keep my smile in check. I turn my face into his shoulder until I'm sure I have it under control. "Just be careful with that whole supply-and-demand thing. I would hate for its value to drop because it was no longer considered rare."

"You could smile constantly for the next seventy years and it would still be a rare and beautiful thing."

My willpower throws its hands up in surrender at that. My heart follows seconds later. I'm too busy trying to stuff my vital organs back inside my chest cavity to notice anything on the rest of our ten-minute walk.

As we approach Thistle Street, he releases my hand. Then he shuffles behind me, covering my eyes with his hands. I stop short, and he plows into me. His chin knocks into the back of my head. He lets out a *whuff* of breath against my neck. Possibly, it's a laugh.

"What are you doing?" I ask and try to pry his fingers away.

Not letting my attempts derail him, Tobin readjusts his hold. "Surprise, remember?"

"Right."

He nudges me forward. I sigh, but I move with him because this is a sweet, possibly romantic gesture, and I'm done being the girl who doesn't believe in those anymore.

His hands drop away a few moments later, and I blink against the sudden light. In the window display at the record store, dozens of pages of sheet music hang from fishing line at varying heights. Lyrics stretch across the pages, written in all caps half a page tall. A song come to life.

> *When I get lost in the dark unknown*
> *Your heart is a light leading me home*

I'm mesmerized. By the words. By the intention behind them. It's the most beautiful thing anyone's every said—well, written—to me. I catch Tobin's gaze reflected in the window. His teeth tug on his lip rings as he waits for my reaction.

When I turn to face him, the smile I unleash on him radiates a tingling sensation all the way to my toes. "Is this what you were wanting to see?"

"Yep," he says, dipping his mouth toward mine again. "That's it exactly."

Remy's Musical Education Playlist

1. "Breaking" by Anberlin
2. "All Who Remain" by Beware of Darkness
3. "Black Honey" by Thrice
4. "Follow You" by Bring Me The Horizon
5. "Uncharted Territory" by Tobin Curcio
6. "Do I Wanna Know?" by Arctic Monkeys
7. "Bloodfeather" by Highly Suspect
8. "Little Monster" by Royal Blood
9. "Stardust" by Tobin Curcio
10. "Breath" by Breaking Benjamin
11. "I Don't Need You" by Asking Alexandria
12. "The Opposite of Gone" by Tobin Curcio
13. "Letters from the Sky" by Civil Twilight
14. "Heavy" by Linkin Park
15. "I Am" by Hands Like Houses

16. "Down with the Fallen" by Starset
17. "In My Bones" by Tobin Curcio
18. "Every Time You Leave" by I Prevail
19. "Got Me Going" by Ra
20. "Periscope" by Papa Roach

Acknowledgments

This book tried to break me on multiple occasions since I started writing it in 2015. It's been a long (and sometimes tough) road to get here, to a book that's finally on shelves and in reader's hands. And it would not have been possible without a whole mess of lovely people.

I will be forever grateful to my agent, Jenny Bent, for seeing something special in this book and knowing exactly what it needed when I was this close to believing it was broken beyond repair. Massive thanks to you and the whole team at The Bent Agency for helping me grow as a writer and always being in my corner.

My amazing editor, Annie Berger, and the Sourcebooks Fire team are a dream. Your enthusiasm and vision for this book is so much more than I could have ever hoped for. Thank you to everyone involved, including: Kay Birkner, Catherine

Onder, Annie Berger, Jenny Lopez, Cassie Gutman, Kelsey Fenske, April Wills, Brittany Vibbert, Nicole Hower, Kelly Lawler, Sarah Cardillo, Michelle Mayhall, Stephanie Rocha, Holli Roach, Tina Wilson, Deve McLemore, Jessica Zulli, Tina George, Beth Oleniczak, Madison Nankervis, Rebecca Atkinson, Ashlyn Keil, and Jess Elliott. (Please forgive me if I missed anyone; it was not intentional!) And thank you Ana Hard for the gorgeous cover illustration.

All the hearts to my critique partners: Jessica Fonseca, Zoë Harris, and Courtney Howell. You ladies have kept me going over the years when I didn't think I could face another revision or another hope dashed. I would be lost without you three. Hugs and gratitude to my writing friends from Nova's Djerassi YA Alumni workshop and the Saluda, NC Wordsmith Workshop who read early pages of *The Holloway Girls* when I had no clue what it would end up being, especially, Nova Ren Suma, Rebekah Faubion, Marie Cruz, Jess Capelle, Shelli Cornelison, Carrie Brown-Wolf, Beth Revis, and Cristin Terrill; as well as to the fabulous Laura Ruby and Anne Ursu, and the writers in our Writing the Unreal workshop at Highlights Foundation for helping me see past the first version of this story to what it could be. Other early readers who deserve major kudos for their invaluable input include Kelly Harms, Marci Lyn Curtis, Christina June, Hayley Chewin, and Stacee Evans. Thank you, Roselle Lim and Megan McGee for being extraordinary writers and friends. You've all made this book better, and I cannot thank you enough.

Tall Poppy Writers (past and present!), your generosity and support make my heart full every day. #22Debuts, the talent in this group is astounding, and I am so lucky to be a part of it. Pitch Wars (mentors and mentees and hopefuls alike), the shared excitement, camaraderie, and commiseration over the years makes the hard days easier and the good days that much sweeter.

This story would not be what it is without the music of the bands mentioned within these pages, especially Breaking Benjamin, Starset, Bring Me The Horizon, I Prevail, Papa Roach, The Amity Affliction, and AFI. I wrote so much of this book to their songs on repeat, and I can only hope a little of their brilliance rubbed off on the story.

To my family and friends, who are my fiercest (and loudest) cheerleaders, thank you from the bottom of my heart. Your love and support have kept me motivated and determined to keep following my dreams. I love you all more than you'll ever know.

And always, thank you to Mark for living with these characters as long as I have. With this book, more than any other, I needed your calm presence and unshakable belief in me. Here's to many more wee drams and adventures together.

To everyone who reads this book: thank you, thank you, thank you.

About the Author

© Belinda Keller

Susan Bishop Crispell earned a BFA in creative writing from the University of North Carolina at Wilmington. Born and raised in the mountains of Tennessee, she now lives twenty minutes from the beach in North Carolina with her husband and their two cats. She is very fond of baked goods and is always on the lookout for hints of magic in the real world. Visit her online at susanbishopcrispell.com.